QUESTIONS

Thurman disarmed the pistoleros and tied their hands behind their backs.

"You know who I am. I'm the man he sent you to kill. What're your names?" They didn't answer him right off. He took out his jackknife, opened it, knocked off the short one's sombrero, snatched a fistful of hair, and sliced it off.

"Your right ear's next. You know your name now?"

"Andre—Andre Petrillo."

"Ramon Sanchez."

"Glad to meet'cha. But for your children's sake, we better never meet again. Now I need your boots."

He jerked off their boots and gun belts. Then he saddled their horses, tied their boots on the horns, and stuffed their guns and knives in the saddlebags.

He started to lead their horses off and stopped. "Oh, tell Señor Corrales that if he's concerned about it, I won't ever be back to his place."

"He will get you, hombre."

"Then he better not send you two. I know your faces. So wear the funeral suits that you want to be buried in if you try me again."

Titles by Dusty Richards

THE HORSE CREEK INCIDENT
MONTANA REVENGE
THE SUNDOWN CHASER

The
Sundown
Chaser

DUSTY RICHARDS

BERKLEY BOOKS, NEW YORK

THE BERKLEY PUBLISHING GROUP
Published by the Penguin Group
Penguin Group (USA) Inc.
375 Hudson Street, New York, New York 10014, USA
Penguin Group (Canada), 90 Eglinton Avenue East, Suite 700, Toronto, Ontario M4P 2Y3, Canada
(a division of Pearson Penguin Canada Inc.)
Penguin Books Ltd., 80 Strand, London WC2R 0RL, England
Penguin Group Ireland, 25 St. Stephen's Green, Dublin 2, Ireland (a division of Penguin Books Ltd.)
Penguin Group (Australia), 250 Camberwell Road, Camberwell, Victoria 3124, Australia
(a division of Pearson Australia Group Pty. Ltd.)
Penguin Books India Pvt. Ltd., 11 Community Centre, Panchsheel Park, New Delhi—110 017, India
Penguin Group (NZ), 67 Apollo Drive, Rosedale, North Shore 0632, New Zealand
(a division of Pearson New Zealand Ltd.)
Penguin Books (South Africa) (Pty.) Ltd., 24 Sturdee Avenue, Rosebank, Johannesburg 2196,
South Africa

Penguin Books Ltd., Registered Offices: 80 Strand, London WC2R 0RL, England

This is a work of fiction. Names, characters, places, and incidents either are the product of the author's imagination or are used fictitiously, and any resemblance to actual persons, living or dead, business establishments, events, or locales is entirely coincidental. The publisher does not have any control over and does not assume any responsibility for author or third-party websites or their content.

THE SUNDOWN CHASER

A Berkley Book / published by arrangement with the author

PRINTING HISTORY
Berkley edition / April 2009

Copyright© 2009 by Dusty Richards.
Cover illustration by Ben Perini.
Cover design by Steve Ferlauto.

ISBN: 978-0-425-22696-4

BERKLEY®
Berkley Books are published by The Berkley Publishing Group,
a division of Penguin Group (USA) Inc.,
375 Hudson Street, New York, New York 10014.
BERKLEY® is a registered trademark of Penguin Group (USA) Inc.
The "B" design is a trademark of Penguin Group (USA) Inc.

PRINTED IN THE UNITED STATES OF AMERICA

10   9   8   7   6   5   4   3   2   1

I am dedicating this book to Jim Bob and Dottie Tinsley. Jim Bob's in that big pasture in the sky making camp, and I figure the coffee will be on when we get there. In his book *He Was Singin' This Song: A Collection of Forty-Eight Traditional Songs of the American Cowboy, with Words, Music, Pictures, and Stories*, he left a wonderful record of the old cowboy songs and the real history of the cattle business. One song, "The Texas Cowboy," is so fitting for the 1880s in the Big Sky country.

> *Oh, I'm a Texas cowboy and far away from home.*
> *If I get back to Texas I never more will roam.*
> *Montana is too cold for me and the winters are too long,*
> *Because before the roundups do begin, your money is all*
>   *gone.*

I can still recall Jim Bob and his wonderful wife Dottie polkaing around the floor at so many past Western Writers of America conventions. What a treat they were.

Check my website for more information:
www.dustyrichards.com

PROLOGUE

Through the lens of his field glasses, Thurman Baker studied the boiling dust far down in the south but coming in pretty hot pursuit. Whether they were men from Corrales's hacienda or *federales,* him and the boys would need to make tracks to reach the Rio Grande. Thurman planned to make a stand there. He stuffed the glasses in his saddlebags and remounted the circling sorrel. When he looked up, his bunch was already a quarter mile north of him. He set spurs to the gelding to catch them.

In a short while, he was riding in a cloud of dust in the drag, stirrup to stirrup with Tomas. The eighteen-year-old Hispanic was swinging his coiled reata and shouting at the tail-end horses to hurry.

"Are they coming for us?" Tomas shouted.

"Yes, and they're making lots of dust doing it."

"I will hurry then." Tomas grinned big from behind a mask of dirt and spurred his sweaty buckskin at the laggers. The herd bolted ahead in the swirling grit and confusion.

Ramon and Contra, who kept them bunched on each side, began to make ky-yipping calls that sounded like Comanche war cries.

The horses galloped hard over the rise. Then, stiff-legged, they went sliding down the steep sandy slope. Tall gnarled cottonwoods loomed ahead. Beyond those trees lay the Rio Grande and the U.S. of A., known as Texas. If the pursuers were *federales,* they'd more than likely rein up at the water's edge. But if those cloud makers back there were Corrales's hacienda men, then Thurman and his boys would need to make a tough stand. The border would never stop them.

His three vaqueros were crack shots. They each carried a new .44/40 Winchester. But to be across what the Mexicans called the Rio Bravo and have Texas dirt at last under his horse's hooves would make him feel a helluva lot better.

At the river's edge, he shouted at his two point men, their horses already knee deep in the water, one on each side, to keep the horses headed toward the north shoreline. "Bunch the herd over that first rise and then ride back. If they want us, they can come get us. We'll make our stand on the north bank."

"*Sí,* Señor Baker." Their shouts and waves as they herded errant horses back into the bunch, along with their wild, carefree attitude toward the whole situation, amused him. He'd known men who would have frozen in their tracks knowing the law or a posse was on their back trail. Not these men. It all went with horse stealing. The whole thing was one fun-filled adventure for them.

A short while later, the four men lined up belly-down on the ground atop the sandy rise above the river, stationed ten feet part. Each man's well-oiled rifle and pistol were ready with an open box of fresh cartridges close by. They waited for their pursuers' arrival.

"Don't get too anxious," Thurman said, lying on the hot sand in the middle. "They have to get halfway across before you shoot them. We don't want no international problems."

The boys laughed and joked in Spanish about his remark.

When the first rider filed over the ridge, a smile crossed Thurman's dry lips. In their olive-green uniforms, they rode with military precision. The *federales* soon came to a halt at the base of the slope, a hundred yards back from the Rio Grande. They formed a line to the right, and then a noncom with a white flag raced to the river and skidded to a hard stop at the water's edge.

"My *comandante* says that you are not welcome ever again in Mexico, Señor Baker."

Thurman rose to his feet and pushed the straw sombrero back on his shoulders. The rawhide string caught at his throat. "Give that son of bitch my best, soldier. And thanks for the warning."

Then he saluted him, and Thurman's men snickered.

He watched the noncom ride back and speak to his officer. As he expected, the unit did an about-face, filed out, and went back over the ridge. When the last soldier disappeared, the boys rose with a cheer, gathered their rifles, pistols, and cartridges, and started for their horses.

"That was Captain Ortega," Ramon said. His dark eyes narrowed with hatred. "He hung my brother, Manuel. That son of a *coyota* bitch."

"What for?"

Ramon grinned. "For being in bed with his wife when he came home."

They all laughed, clapping each other on the shoulder and raising clouds of dust as they waded in the loose sand for their mounts.

Thurman looked back one more time to be satisfied, and then he followed his boys. "A man I know up in the hill country is going to be real proud of these ponies. Yes, siree. I'm real proud of you boys, too. But I'm even prouder that not one of us is getting our necks stretched."

They all agreed.

Ramon handed Tomas his rifle to hold, and ran for his horse. With both hands on the top of its butt, he vaulted in the saddle. The cheers and catcalls followed his leap aboard.

"Make my escape easier." Ramon reined his horse around, caught his rifle, and left out to ring in some of the strays.

By late evening of the third day, Thurman's outfit approached the 7 Bar headquarters. Thurman sat the sorrel on a small rise and looked over the green scene. Spread out like an oasis in the dull, spiny brush country of south Texas, tall gnarled cottonwoods huddled over the *cienega* that covered a hundred acres or more up and down the wide draw. He nodded with approval to his boys, and then he loped ahead to open the gate of the lot for them.

The horses were soon headed into a large rail-fenced trap where Old Man Hanson's ranch hands had put out hay in small piles for the herd.

"Thurman Baker!" The salt-and-pepper-bearded Burt Hanson came out of the door of his adobe jacal, hobbling on a crutch, and blinked in disbelief at the sight of the horses filing into the pen. He looked Thurman up and down. "Why, in all that leather clothing and sombrero, you could pass for a damn Messican. I'm not used to seeing you out of a business suit."

"I needed this identity where I've been."

"I bet that's so." The old man put the crutch under his arm and was ready to move on. "I want a closer look at them fancy scudders."

The two men stood at the fence and Hanson admired the herd for a while. Then he turned back to speak. "By Gawd, you done got the best set of horses yet. Some *ha-see-enda* guy is sure pissing in his pants over them rascals being taken. You got a good market for 'em?"

"Yes. I don't like to risk my neck unless it's worthwhile."

"Aw, I knew that. You're a good man, Thurman Baker, and I'm always glad when you come by to see me. By Gawd, you didn't miss the time you said you'd be back here by much."

"We're close to my schedule."

Hanson nodded.

Thurman watched his head-tossing ponies arguing with each other over the hay in the fiery light of sundown. The bloody glare glistened on their sleek hides. They were the best he'd ever brought from south of the border. These barb geldings represented some of the finest animals in their breed. A bloodline that went back to when the Moors conquered Spain. Before that, their ancestors were the desert horses of the Bedouins.

"How much do I owe ya for tonight?" Thurman asked.

"I'd not charge you, but we'd get in a damn big argument about that. Five bucks is enough for the hay and feeding them boys."

Thurman nodded at the man in overalls. Hanson was the picture of a damned dirt farmer, and would always be one. They'd bury him in bib overalls. He'd lived close to the border for decades, and still considered anything with skin browner than his own less than a human being. Not even the big roundups he held each year gathering thousands of cattle bearing his brand, nor even his awesome sales in Kansas of stout three-year-old longhorn steers would ever change him—he'd still be a damn dirt farmer, dress like one, act like one, and would never sit on his haunches and speak Spanish to boys like the three that worked for Thurman. He was best described as a square peg who'd never fit into any round holes in his lifetime. Over the years, he'd invested every dime of his cattle sales proceeds into buying all the sections of Texas brush around him. Hanson's holdings were larger than most counties.

His woman, Sadie, smoked a corncob pipe, gummed her food, and sounded like a screech owl. "Invite him in. Invite him in. We don't get many white folks come by to see us anymore."

"Hold your horses, woman. We're coming." Hanson dropped his chin and looked at the ground. "Why don't you just buy me out? Me and her, we ain't got no kids to leave this to. I'd make you a real good deal on this ranch."

"Hell, Hanson, I couldn't buy this place if I had three bunches of good horses to sell." He handed over the currency for the hay and feed.

"You think on it. I'll give you a year." Hanson shoved the folding money into his chest pocket. "I want someone to hold this ranch together. I'd sell it to you and then we'd move back to Arkansas—too damn dry here. You could send me enough money each year to live on till me and Sadie died as the price for it. I'll even give you a year to think on it."

"I'd do that, all right, on one condition. I had two sons once. They'd be long grown by now. If I could find one or both of them in that amount of time, I'll be back here. I'm over fifty. My back gets sore on the long days when I ride.

One or both of them boys should have thirty years left in him to ramrod this place for me."

"Where're they at?"

"If knowed that, I'd ride there and get them." He pulled on Hanson's sleeve to stop him before they reached the house. "I made a bad mistake in my life once. I quit a good woman for another that wasn't so good. I left my wife with a small ranch and enough for her and three kids to get by with." He nodded grimly and continued. "You guessed it. When my money ran out, that floozy left me for a tinhorn."

Hanson cut him a frown of disbelief. "You never went back—"

"Your food's a-spoiling!" Sadie screeched from the lighted doorway.

"Hold your horses, woman, it won't rot that fast." Hanson turned back to him. "Well?"

"I closed *that* gate when I left 'em."

With a serious look on his weathered face, Hanson nodded. "Then, you go see if you can find them boys. You've got a year."

They shook on it.

That night, Thurman sat on his bedroll and looked at the array of stars that pinpricked the night sky. He pulled on the last of his whiskey and considered Hanson's thousands of deeded acres in this tough brush country that could be his own. The old man's 7 Bar brand was burned on thousands of cattle—no telling how many. It all could be Thurman's and his sons'—if he could find them. Damn, they were Bakers, they had to be out there somewhere. They were tough as pine knots and it ran in their Scots-Irish bloodlines to survive. He tossed aside the empty bottle and lay down to sleep. If they were alive, he'd find them.

* * *

Three days later at the big Three C Ranch headquarters, Martin Coleman looked over "his" horses filing in. The forty-year-old rancher tried to hold a poker face, but the corners of his blue eyes glinted at the sight of the three- and four-year-olds. Thurman and his buyer stood on the middle rail of Three C Ranch's main corral fencing, and used their knees for balance.

"Those surely aren't Mexican horses." Coleman glanced over at Thurman with a look of doubt.

"You said you wanted the best horses I could find. Don't ask lots more."

"Fifty bucks a head?"

"That won't even cut the gray hair I got getting 'em here."

Coleman shoved his felt hat back on his head and blinked at Thurman. "What do you have to have for 'em?"

"A hundred and a half apiece."

"Hell, man, you can buy bangtails all over." He stepped down off the fence.

Thurman eased himself to the ground, then spoke with a tinge of shortness in his crisp words. "I didn't bring you cull mustangs. That's not what you ordered."

Coleman shook his head. "I can't use them at that much money."

"Fine. I'll pay you for the feed tonight and ride on."

"Ease off a little, hoss. You and I have done business before."

Eyeing the broad-shouldered rancher, Thurman took a deep breath. This would be his last run out of Mexico with stolen horses. He aimed to make it that—his last. Down there, they had an X marked between his shoulder blades for some old Mauser rifle. If Coleman expected to pay anything less, Thurman planned to haul his tired butt out of there in the morning for San Antonio.

"Them boys of yours know the chuck routine here," said Coleman. "Chelsea'll feed 'em. Let's go to the house and find us some whiskey and talk this over."

Thurman glanced back at the corral. A couple of the ranch hands were forking hay. If Coleman thought whiskey was going to lower his price, he'd better save it for the next sucker.

An hour after supper, they sat on the leather chairs that circled around the native-stone cold fireplace in the open-beam living room, and sipped Coleman's good Kentucky whiskey. Thurman's spur-clad, run-over boots were stretched out and crossed in front of him on the tile floor. He wondered how many steers this large rambling house had cost Coleman to build. Someday, he'd have one of his own this big.

"How long have you been below the border?" Coleman asked. "Hell, the way you're dressed, I thought you was a vaquero when you rode up in that outfit."

"Too long. I now want to speak Spanish all the time."

"That's too long."

"What's the word coming down from up north?"

"They've closed Kansas forever to cattle drives."

"Honyockers caused that," Thurman said, thinking about all the homesteaders that he'd had to avoid the last trip north with a herd.

"Yeah, and the railroads are charging rates too high to haul cattle, and now they've got barb wire blocking the way as well."

Thurman pulled his boots back to the chair and moved out to its edge. "Your food and whiskey's been very good. I'm dead serious about the price on them ponies. If I owe you for your hospitality, let me pay you. Me and them boys are heading out at sunup."

Coleman rose and went to stand in front of the dark

hearth. "Why, I'd be a damn fool to pay that much for those untried horses."

"You want to try them. Fine. The price is the same."

"You and I have traded before, Thurman. Why are you being so damn stubborn?"

Thurman nodded in understanding. "'Cause this is my last ride down there and those are the best ponies that's ever been brought out of Mexico."

"Aw, hell, they may be a little fancy, but not that fancy."

"The price stands."

"You'll have trouble selling that many anywhere you go."

"I don't care if I sell them one at a time—my price holds. What do I owe you for feed and care?"

"Not one damn thin dime."

"Thank you. I can find my way out." He set his glass down and moved toward the tall front doors. He paused before opening one of them. "You're losing a chance to own the best."

"Can't pay that much for them."

Thurman nodded and stepped out in the night. By sunup, he and his boys'd be on the road to San Antonio.

In the predawn, Thurman, his crew, and the horses were ready to move. He took the last swallow out of the whiskey bottle he carried in his saddlebags and studied the outline of the fancy house on the hill. *Your loss, Coleman.* "Let's ride, boys."

Close to noon, he checked the sun time and noticed a rider coming from the south. The man looked familiar and Thurman reined up. It was Andy Debbs, Coleman's segundo. Sliding his pony to a stop, Andy grinned big. "Boss man said for me to get you to come back."

"He ready to do business?"

Andy chuckled. "Most surprised man I ever saw. He said, hell, Thurman's really serious about this trade. Go get him and them bangtails back here. I need them horses and I guess he knows it, too."

Thurman stood in the stirrups, whistled hard to get his boys' attention, then made a waving sign over his head to turn them around. "We're going back. We've sold the horses, boys."

They gave a cheer.

A week later, he was putting $16,800 in a canvas bag as a Texas banker across the desk was talking about investing that money with his bank. Coleman shook his head the entire time, obviously amused at how Thurman wasn't listening to any of it.

They left the First National Bank of Texas and went out of the lobby into the lacey shaded San Antonio Square. Thurman shook Coleman's hand, thanked him, and then started off down Crockett Street.

"Where in the hell're you going?" Coleman shouted after him.

"I've got to settle up," he said over his shoulder.

He found the boys squatted in the shade by the ruins of the Alamo where he'd said he'd meet them. Their good hacienda horses were standing hipshot at the rack across the dirt street in front of Bekoo's Livery. He set the canvas satchel down and squatted on his boot heels.

"You boys can keep those ponies." He motioned to the ones they'd selected out of the herd.

"I'm paying you two hundred apiece. One year from now if you need work, I plan to own and be living at Hanson's 7 Bar. If I am, you can have work."

A flash of their snow-white teeth and nods signaled

they'd be there. He paid them, slowly counting out twenties. "We made a good run. But that's my last. I aim to be a rancher from here on. Going to find my boys and then buy Hanson out."

"Where are your boys at?" Ramon asked.

"Be gawdamned if I know, but I'm going to find 'em."

They nodded solemnly.

"Watch your back, Señor. Miguel Corrales will send his best pistoleros to kill you over this," Ramon said, shifting his weight to his other foot, stuffing the money in his pants pocket. "He will want revenge."

"I always watch my back. But I'll be more careful from here on. *Gracias, mis amigos.*"

They nodded.

"Raise some hell for me," he said, getting up, and they laughed.

Ten minutes later, with his dusty sombrero in hand, he spoke to the man behind the desk in the outer room of Charles T. Watson's law office.

The man ushered him in to see Charles T.

"Good day, sir, may I help you?" the man with gray sideburns said, unhooking his reading glasses as he stood up.

"My name's Baker. I need you to make out a will for me."

"Fine, Mr. Baker, have a seat, Yule, get a pad and we will get Mr. Baker's will written for him," he said to the man from the outer office.

"What do you wish to bequeath?" Watson asked Thurman, showing him the oak captain's chair and taking his own seat.

"Fifteen thousand dollars."

"Hmm, a sizable sum. Where's it at?"

"Here." He raised the bag. "I am going to store it in a bank safe deposit box and bring you back a key. Banks go busted, lockboxes don't. If I die, I want my wife to have it. Jennifer Baker, General Delivery, Mason, Texas."

Watson frowned at him. "You and your wife are—?"

"Yes, we're separated and have been for over fifteen years. That's no problem. If she isn't alive, then my three children will get it."

"Certainly. Where are they at?"

"I don't know right now. I'm going to try to find them—at least my two sons."

"I understand. Yule will have the will drawn up and you can sign it. Anything else I may help you with?"

"No. I'll have a key made for you, too."

"Yule can go along with you for the firm and sign for it."

"Good." With that matter settled, Thurman had a few more things to be taken care of. He had to pick up his new Boss of the Plains Stetson hat at the store, and the boot man was supposed to have his new boots made before sundown. The Jewish tailor would have his new suit ready, and he'd at last be out of his leather vaquero clothing. Then he could be on his way.

He shook the lawyer's hand, signed the will, paid him the fee, and accompanied by the slender young man, went across to the Farnsworth Bank and rented a deposit box. He stowed the canvas bag inside, put the key in his pocket, and gave another to the young man to take to the lawyer.

There used to be a sometime outlaw up in the hill country in Mason County who for a few bucks might know where the boys were at and not care at all about Thurman's reasons for asking. He was a man Thurman could question and get answers from who would keep his mouth shut. If that individual was still alive, Thurman would find him on his two-bit outfit south of the town of Mason.

* * *

Two days later, Thurman dismounted at a jacal in the hill country and hissed the barking curs away. An unshaven man with lots of white bristles came to the doorway putting up his galluses.

"Harkin?"

"Do I know you, mister?" The man tried to focus his eyes against the glare.

"You did years ago. That ain't important today. Fact is, you can forget I was even here today. I need some information and I'll pay for it. Where are the Bakers? Her and the kids?"

The man blinked and pointed a finger at him. "Gawdamn, why, you're Thurman Baker. Why, I ain't seed you in years."

"Where's she at?"

"Didn't you know? Why, she died five years ago."

"I didn't know." Thurman nodded. "Where are the boys?"

"One of 'em I *heared* was dead and the other's in Montana the last that I knew."

"Which one's dead?"

"Travis, I think. That girl of *you's* Rosie is married and lives down on the San Saba somewheres."

"You know her married name?"

Harkin shook his head.

"Think, man, where in Montana is Herschel at?"

"Hell, I could scratch my head all day and not even know where that is. I ain't heard or I plumb forgot."

Thurman handed him two silver dollars. "Keep your mouth shut about this."

"Hell, I ain't seed you in fifteen years." He kept gazing at the shiny coins in his dirty palm. "No, siree. I won't tell a damn soul."

"Good."

Thurman rode north from there aiming to catch a train in Fort Worth. However, by mid-morning the next day, it became obvious that he was being trailed. Twice he'd stopped and with his field glasses caught sight of the two riders. Their Chihuahua sombreros gave them away. Pistoleros. It was no coincidence they were back there—the boys had warned him. Corrales would want to extract his revenge over losing those horses.

Who were those two hired guns? He slipped the glasses in his saddlebag. The new boots were still tight on his toes when he remounted. Especially the right one. The boot man had promised him they'd stretch.

All day he rode north, and then when he figured the prairie grass mat would not give the pistoleros many tracks to follow, he swung east and pulled back. He waited in a draw among the post oaks, and at last watched them ride on north. Good enough. He patted his horse on the neck—he had plans for those two.

Hours later, a coyote's mournful howl cut the night. Thurman had squatted long enough listening to their Spanish as they cursed each other over where that gringo had gone while feeding wood to a blazing campfire. He drew his .44 and eased his way in from behind them.

"Grab some stars or die."

"Huh?" But they rose slowly with their hands in the air.

He disarmed them, then tied their hands behind their backs and seated them on the ground as they asked him who he was and what he wanted with them.

"Ha, you know who I am. I'm the man he sent you to kill. What're your names?" They didn't answer him right off. When they weren't quick to reply, he took out his large jackknife, opened it, knocked off the short one's sombrero, snatched a fistful of his hair, and then sliced it off.

He let the chopped hair fall like snow on the man's face. "Your right ear's next. You know your name now?"

"Andre—Andre Petrillo."

"Ramon Sanchez."

"Glad to meet'cha. But for your children's sake, we better never meet again. Now I need your boots."

They protested, but he ignored them. Without any care, he jerked off their boots and gun belts. Then he saddled their horses, tied their boots on the horns, and stuffed their guns and knives in the saddlebags.

"What will happen to us?" Ramon complained.

"I don't care if the damn coyotes eat ya. You come after me again, I'll kill you the next time and not ask any questions."

He started to lead their horses off and stopped. "Oh, tell Señor Corrales when you see him next time, if he's concerned about it, I won't ever be back to his place."

"He will get you, hombre."

"Like I said, he better not send you two. I know your faces. So wear the funeral suits that you want to be buried in if you try me again."

Ignoring their loud threats, he went for his horse in the draw and rode off to the north leading their mounts. The next day, he sold their outfits to some hard cases he met on the road. At first, they looked suspiciously at the two horses' brands.

"That Mexican owns the brand ain't going to bother you. He's far across the Rio Grande," Thurman said, and soon pocketed the forty dollars he got for the horses and the tack. He booted his horse northward, deciding he wasn't a train rider anyway. Besides, where the hell in Montana would he get off?

He grinned to himself. Those hard cases back there would talk for a long time about the big buy they made on the trail. He short-loped the red horse, grateful that he, too, had one of the fine Corrales barbs to ride.

ONE

YELLOWSTONE County Sheriff Herschel Baker stood in his slicker with three other men looking at the corpse lying facedown beside the road. With rain dripping off the brim of his hat, he studied the dark circles in the dead man's back from two bullet holes.

"Anyone of you seen him before?" Herschel asked.

"I think he did some day work for Toby Grant," Bill Michaels, the rancher, said.

"I've seen him at the dance a few times," said Louis Shultz, a short cattle buyer who had ridden into Billings earlier that wet May morning and reported finding the dead man.

"They called him Wally," Perk, Michaels's ranch hand, added.

"Who called him Wally, do you remember?" Herschel asked.

"Hatch and that bunch."

"Anyone that you know want him dead?"

They shook their sodden hats in reply.

"Well, boys, someone damn sure must have wanted him dead. Let's load him over my saddle and I'll take his body in for the coroner. Keep an ear to things. Someone might slip up and say something. He damn sure didn't expire from natural causes."

"I'll ride back to Billings with you," Shultz said as they put the corpse across Herschel's saddle.

As he rode with the body in his lap, Herschel considered what he knew about the man's demise. The five-foot-two cattle buyer Shultz had discovered the body earlier that morning. No sign of the dead man's horse, and the rain had beaten out any readable tracks. Michaels and his hired man Perk were headed for town to report the same discovery when they met Herschel and Shultz heading out to the scene of the crime.

Wet outside the rubber slicker and chilled to the bone under it, Herschel studied the gray sky that looked like a ruffled goose's belly. Thunder in the distance growled like an awakened bear who'd been hibernating in a cave. More storms were coming their way. A man should never complain about rain in Montana. But at times like this, it was no convenience for a lawman investigating a murder.

What time did the rain start up there? The dead man wore no slicker. It might mean he was shot before the rain began. Two many questions needed answers. Herschel booted the roan horse Cob around a large mud hole that had been made by a heavy wagon wallowing in it.

The downpour turned the road sloppy, and his big roan gelding sunk into it with its double load. The dead man, shot twice in the back, didn't even wear a gun. Or else the killers had robbed him and taken it. They called him Wally, Perk had said.

Herschel would have to ride up to the Soda Springs schoolhouse on Saturday night and check with those folks about the dead man. Besides, he needed to shake some hands—that was an elected official's obligation. As well as showing some interest in that part of the county. He'd get Mrs. Randolph to stay with his three stepdaughters so his wife, Marsha, could come along. She'd enjoy that. She'd campaigned up there before for him when he was laid up by those two who were hired to teach him a lesson and burn him out. He and Marsha could take a bedroll and a batch-cooking outfit, and camp out after the dance.

With the rain streaming off his hat brim, he felt kind of warmed by the notion of having some time alone with her. With a lightning flash, he remembered those long lonely nights when he'd ridden herd on nervous Texas longhorns driving them to Kansas, first as a drover, then as the trail boss, and his final drive to Montana. If anything bothered or startled them, they'd jump up and run off in a maddening stampede. Such panic often took many a cowboy's life. It made his stomach curdle to think about the number of crude crosses he'd planted on the plains marking some boy's death. The crosses soon faded or were knocked over, and no accurate record was ever kept of unmarked graves their mothers could never decorate or even find. *We planted him a mile north of the Cimarron—east of the trail.*

To Herschel, those days were in his past. Montana wasn't Texas. Winters in Montana made the ones he recalled from Texas seem like light frosts. But he still appreciated the big country of the north. He'd found himself a respectable place in the community being sheriff, and as long as he solved most of the crimes, he'd probably have a job enforcing the law.

This particular murder might be a hard one to solve, but usually the smartest criminal tripped up, spoke out of turn, bragged to the wrong person, or left obvious clues. So far, there was no glaring evidence that Herschel could see. He huddled in his saddle under his slicker as the wet wind increased.

"You got any cattle to sell?" Shultz asked, riding beside him.

"We have some two-year-old steers that'll have lots of size by this fall." Herschel thought about the stock they could sell off his wife's ranch at the end of the season.

"I like threes better. What'll they weigh?"

Herschel turned his shoulder to the crosswind to save his hat. "By fall, seven-eight hundred pounds. They're big twos."

"Can I go look at them?"

"Won't hurt. They're down on Marsha's home place. They've got lots of shorthorn blood in them. Many are out of the second cross away from longhorns."

Shultz nodded. Cattle buyers were like poker players, they never acted excited. But those Midwest farmers liked to feed out those British crosses much more than they did the old longhorns from Mexico.

The two men rode on a long ways in silence, fighting the wind and the driving rain. When they reached Ramsey's funeral home on Main Street, Herschel stepped down and shouldered the corpse. He waved away Shultz's offer to help him and sent him to open the door.

At last inside the building under the heavy load, he removed his wet hat and put it on a tree rack. A young man rushed in and looked shocked at him carrying the dead man.

"Let me take him, Sheriff Baker."

"No, you lead the way. I'll need a coroner's report on his death, so we need to lay him out back there."

"Who is he? The dead man, I mean."

"Wally something. All we know now is his first name."

"What happened to him?" Leading the way back, the youth twisted around to look at Herschel and Shultz.

"He got in the way of a couple of bullets, I suspect," Herschel said, and put the corpse on the tin-topped table. Grateful to have the load off his shoulder, he stepped back and looked at the man's pale face under the lamplight. He still didn't recognize him.

"I don't recall ever seeing him."

Shultz nodded. "I've seen him at a few dances up there."

Herschel spoke to the boy. "We're going to put our horses up and find some hot food. I'll be in my office later if you need anything. I've checked him, but I want anything you find on him for evidence. No matter how small or insignificant it may seem."

"We can do that, sir."

"You don't need to show us out," Herschel said to the youth "We know the way."

"I'll handle notifying the coroner, too."

"Good."

They left the funeral home with its strong chemical smells and rode down the muddy street to Pascal's Livery. They left their animals' care to a hostler and beat the wooden boardwalk back to the Real Food Café. When they got inside the door, Maude hollered to them, busy with her midday crowd and her arms full of dirty dishes.

"The table in the back is reserved for the big shots." Her words drew some laughter from the folks eating lunch. Herschel shook his head and smiled at the onlookers. "She must be blind."

Their wet hats and slickers were hung on the crowded coat rack, and the warmth of the room soon began to saturate Herschel's damp clothing. The smell of cooking food filled the air as he and Shultz settled in the chairs at the special table with the sign that said it was reserved for politicians, ambassadors, generals, and high dignitaries.

"Which one are you?" Herschel asked the cattle buyer.

"I'm with you." Shultz laughed.

"Roast beef, taters, gravy, and carrots are on the menu today," Maude said, standing over them with two coffee mugs and a large pot.

"Coffee smells great. We're on for the plate luncheon special," Herschel said.

"I need cream in mine," Shultz said as she filled his cup.

"Next round—no, grab some off that table. Thanks, food's coming." She was gone in a swirl of her skirts, re-filling cups and collecting for meals in the busy place.

"Well, you ain't said much about this dead guy." Stirring his coffee, Shultz looked at Herschel curiously.

"I don't even know his name, let alone who'd drygulch him in the rain."

Shultz laughed. "I just wondered how your mind worked on such things."

"Seen ya brought in a dead man, Sheriff. Who was he?" a man called Arnold asked. Arnold was a farmer who lived over east, and was no doubt in town for parts or supplies on this rainy day.

"All I know is Wally somebody. Shultz found him on the road early this morning coming down from Soda Springs. I think he did day work for some ranchers around that area."

"Wally, huh?"

"You know any Wally?"

Arnold lowered his voice. "No, but yesterday two tough-looking men each leading two horses apiece crossed by my place. They was avoiding the road and heading north. One of them was leading a bald-faced sorrel horse you could spot a mile away."

"Know the men?"

Arnold shook his head. "But them horses didn't belong to that bunch, I'd bet a dollar."

"I'm not betting, but I appreciate your watching out for me."

Arnold beamed. "Thanks."

"Get any word on where they're at, let me know."

"Oh, I will, Sheriff. See you."

"That how you learn things?" Shultz asked him, looking over the heaping platter of food that Maude had just delivered.

Herschel nodded, ready to eat. "I can't be everywhere. Chances are those horses were stolen in Nebraska and are headed for Canada. I probably won't ever get an opportunity to question those two. But if I do, I'll know who they are."

Busy cutting his beef, Shultz agreed.

Maude's husband, Buster Cory, came from the kitchen in his stained apron to greet them. He was an old pard of Herschel, who smiled at the man's stiff approach.

Shultz knew him and nodded.

Herschel filled Buster in on the murder victim as the old man sat on a chair and tried to roll a smoke in his gnarled fingers. At last, the cylinder was licked shut; he struck a match under the table to light it. Soon, little puffs of smoke came out from between his sun-scarred white lips. "Wally, huh? Could be Carter. There's a Wallis Carter useta work for the 66 outfit."

"This man's slender-built, about five-eight. Hadn't shaved in a while, but no beard or mustache. Black hair, looked a little Injun. High cheekbones."

Shultz nodded. "Just like I saw him. No hat either when we found him."

"I never saw one on the ground," Herschel admitted.

"That ain't Carter. He was a big man, red-faced all the time."

"Keep you ears open. He was shot in the back and un-armed."

"That rules out suicide." Buster slapped his knee and laughed. Then he drew hard on the cigarette and exhaled with a cough. "Better get back there. She's piling them dishes in there for me to wash. I'll listen and if I hear anything I'll let you know."

"See you," both men said.

Buster went off in his rambling small steps toward the rear.

"He's failing, ain't he?" Shultz asked quietly.

"Yes, some, but he's still a great guy."

"Wonder what we'll do when we're that old," Shultz said, shaking his head. "You've got a wife to look after you. I ain't got anyone."

Herschel looked across at him and chuckled at the man's plight. "Maybe you should find one."

"Maybe I ought to."

They both laughed.

Herschel went back to the jail after their meal. Shultz said he wanted to look at those steers as soon as Herschel had time to show them to him. After soaking his boots good in the mud while crossing the streets twice to get to his office, Herschel stomped his feet several times before going into the county building.

Inside, he took the stairs to the second floor by twos.

"Anything happened since I left?" he asked his new desk man, Darby Mueller.

"No." The young man looked flushed. "Was he dead?"

"Yes, and his name may be Wally. Shot in the back. It probably happened sometime overnight, or someone else would have reported his body. He wasn't wearing a slicker either.

"The young man, his name's Adam Cline, at the funeral parlor is getting all his personal things gathered for us. No horse, no gun. I think he may have been robbed. Maybe someone knows him and can furnish us some ideas. We'll have to see."

"A Mr. Accord was by and wished to speak to you."

Herschel frowned at his man. "He local? I've never heard of him."

"New to me, too. But he wouldn't give me a hint about the nature of what he wanted."

Herschel thanked him as he went on into his large office and stirred up the fireplace ashes to drive the chill out. His predecessor had chosen the office. It was nice, but too large and expansive for an ordinary sheriff. Oh, well. He placed some split firewood on the blazing coals and went to his desk to look at his paperwork, the part of the job he hated the most. It might be May, but the weather seemed more like March to him as he looked out at the water splashing on the windowpanes.

"Sheriff! Sheriff Baker!" Someone was calling him from out in the hallway. "They're robbing Ted Taylor's store."

Oh, my God. He rushed to the door and saw the red-faced youngster out of breath.

"Who is?"

The boy shook his head. His breath was whistling in and out of his throat as he gasped for air. "Don't know. They've got flour sack masks."

Herschel took a shotgun off the rack, grasped a handful of brass cartridges out of the drawer to jam in his vest pocket, and nodded to his new assistant, who also had taken a scattergun off the rack. "We don't shoot unless we're positive that we won't harm anyone. We can always run them down, but we can't bring back dead citizens."

"Yes—sir."

Herschel rumbled down the stairs, cramming cartridges in the chambers before he reached the bottom and hit the street. With both barrels loaded, without his slicker, he rushed out into the cold rain toward Main Street in case the robbers came in his direction. He could hear the thunder of hooves and the pop of shots headed toward him as he ran for the intersection.

"Get out of the way!" someone shouted. Then more shots. By then, he was near the corner and faced a masked man racing by on horseback with a smoking pistol. Putting the stock to his shoulder, Herschel took aim and squeezed the trigger, and some of the shot must have struck the horse for it went to bucking. When Herschel rounded the corner, he could see the other two masked riders galloping away.

"Don't shoot," he said to restrain Darby. "Someone may get hurt."

He rushed over to the robber who'd been thrown off his horse and was lying in the mud. Alive, but hit hard. Bent over, Herschel jerked off the mask—the man was a stranger. Herschel told the crowd rushing to the fallen man to take him to Doc's and not to get any idea about lynching him or he'd see they were tried for murder.

"Aw. Jest let him lie there and die then," someone said.

"I said take him to Doc's. That's an order, mister, and if you want to see the inside of a jail cell for a month, keep it up."

"Aye, we're taking him," the man said in surrender, and shook his head in dismay.

"See that they do," Herschel said to Darby. "I'm checking on the store."

Soaked to the skin, rain streaming down his face, Herschel hurried the block to Taylor's store. "Stand aside!" he told the curious people who'd rushed out on the boardwalk to see what had happened.

Inside, he saw Ted Taylor seated on the floor and his wife, Martha, kneeling beside him.

"You all right?" he asked the man in his forties who was on his butt and holding his head.

"They pistol-whipped him," Martha said, straightening up in her stiff white apron.

"I see that. Did they get much money?" Herschel squatted down beside the storekeeper, who shook his head.

"A couple hundred dollars. I had the safe locked, thank God."

Herschel wasn't so sure—it might have cost him his life. "I have one of them if he lives to talk. But I think the ones with your money ran the other way when I shot him. Too dangerous for us to shoot at them in the street, folks and all out there."

Taylor nodded.

"You see any faces?"

"No, they were all masked."

Herschel rose and looked at the concerned, curious crowd filling the store. "Anyone else see anything that identified them?"

No one answered him. He shook from the wet cold as he thanked the the crowd. A woman ran over with a blanket from the store's stock and put it on his shoulders as he shivered. He closed his eyes for a minute—grateful for her kindness. "Thanks."

"Sheriff Baker, take a slicker as well if you're going out," Martha said. "You'll catch you a death of cold." She rushed to get him one. "Here, bring them back any time."

He thanked the ladies and, using the blanket for warmth, he put the slicker over the top of it and started bare-headed for Doc's. A man murdered and now a robbery—he was really having his share of problems for a rainy Tuesday morning. Being sheriff had suddenly taken a turn for the worse.

TWO

Fort Worth's stockyard district was a tough place, populated by equally hard people: gamblers, prostitutes, wanted-poster criminals, con men, drovers on a wild spree, pickpockets, commission men, order buyers, and riffraff. Over the past fifteen years, Thurman had lived on that edge of this same society. He put the gelding up at the Wallace Livery. Before he left the stable, which stank of horse piss, and walked out in the daylight, he checked the rounds in the .44. Satisfied, he replaced it in the belt holster under his coat and went into the glaring sunshine to look over the street, crowded with drays, carts, riders, and a buggy with fringe around the edges and a spanking team driven by an impatient well-dressed driver who threatened with his buggy whip anyone who blocked the street. Seated in the back was a rich-looking man wearing a top hat, with a woman under a dark veil close beside him. His wife or his mistress, no way to tell.

A wide-hipped woman with stringy gray hair in her face, dressed in a soiled brown shapeless shift, charged out on the boardwalk and slung a bucket of slop water at the hipshot horses tied at the hitch rack. She paused to put her thick forearm on a post and buried her face in it for a few seconds. Then she straightened her broad shoulders and laughed aloud.

Her blue eyes met Thurman's gaze as he approached her. "Ain't no rest for the damn wicked, is there, mister?"

"I don't guess there is, ma'am."

"There ain't." With a shrug, she flounced back inside.

She probably was right.

On the next corner, a con man tried to sell him a watch. Thurman shook his head. "I ain't got anywhere I need to be on time. I'd never use it."

"Ah, mister, it would be a mark of distinction to carry this lovely watch. You'd impress others—"

Thurman left him on the corner and headed for the Lucky Deuce directly across the street. There were chairs and tables on the boardwalk, and the building's front corner was cut off so the front doors faced the intersection diagonally across from it.

A few men nursed hangovers in the outside chairs. Thurman pushed his way through the batwing doors. The dark interior stank of cigar smoke, sour beer, and a hint of cheap perfume. Some hussy halfway down the long, polished bar, resting her elbow on the edge, raised her eyebrows at the sight of him.

A mild shake of his head, and she looked away with a scowl as if bored by his refusal. A smoky yellow ring of light hung over the table in the back that interested him more. The legendary twenty-four-hour poker game that never stopped. He appraised the players at a distance.

A short barmaid, no older than sixteen, bumped her hip against his leg. "Need a drink, mister?"

He looked down into her brown eyes and smiled. "Not yet, sister, maybe later."

"Suit yourself," she said, and sashayed off with her tray of dirty glasses and a towel on her arm.

"We've got an open seat," said a bulldog-faced, bareheaded man with a cigar stuck in the corner of his mouth and holding up his fanned-out cards toward the light to see his hand better. "Sit down. You can lose your money quick as I've been doing." He tossed in his cards. "I'll fold."

He turned when Thurman sat down, and stuck out his hand. "My name's Mick, stranger."

"Baker's mine." He nodded to the other five and took the captain's chair. The legs scraped on the floor as he moved in. In such chairs with their arms, if you ever needed to draw a gun, you had to rise up to get it out. That was the reason some gamblers wore shoulder holsters and others carried derringers up their sleeves or pigstickers in their boot tops.

But in the thousand or so games of chance Thurman had been in, he had seen few such altercations. Such incidents were more likely to occur sitting cross-legged on some trading blanket under a mesquite bush playing with some worn-out cards against a couple of Injun whiskey traders out on the Llano Estacado.

"Ten-buck raise is the limit," Mick said. "Five-card, but only a three-card draw."

Thurman understood. There was a gambler who wore a silk vest under a tailored coat across from him who mumbled his name was Crawford. Frenchie was a Cajun on his right. The other side of Mick was a drover named McNard, with snow on his sideburns, his head topped by a weathered gray hat that drooped in the front, and a bilious handlebar mustache.

The last man in the circle was clean-shaven with sharp facial features. Andrews was his name. Thirty years old or so, he reminded Thurman of a mountain lion. He seemed tense, and looked ready to claw your eyes out at the first threat toward his person.

"Where you come from?" Frenchie asked as he showed three eights and raked in the pot.

"South," Thurman said, putting enough money out on the table to show he was serious.

"South of town?"

"A ways."

"Oh, good, south of town is a good place." Frenchie shuffled the cards. "Ante two dollars."

"I saw you in Dodge City two years ago," Crawford said to him, sitting up with his hands on his lapels.

Thurman nodded. "I was there ramrodding a herd for the Calvin brothers at that time."

"Gents, Mr. Baker is no one to mess with. Trust me. That day I saw him, two cowboys decided he'd done something they didn't like. When they approached him, they went for their guns." Crawford picked up his new hand and arranged the cards in a fan.

"Finish the damn story," Frenchie said with a look of impatience.

"Anyway, they both died in the dust with their boots on. Lucky for Mr. Baker, he had just arrived in town and had not had time to check his gun in. Dodge had a gun law."

"That was lucky," Frenchie said.

"Marshal Earp accused me of planning it that way, too," Thurman said, looking at his soft hand—all number cards, none matched. "Actually, a few minutes later and I would have checked my gun in at the Wild Horse Saloon." He folded.

By mid-afternoon, he felt he'd learned all that they knew about everything from the latest arrival at Millie May's whorehouse—a fiery new redhead that had amused someone—to the price of cattle on the Fort Worth market. None of them had heard of a Herschel Baker.

Ahead perhaps a hundred dollars, he excused himself. Down in the stockyards, he squatted on his haunches beside the tall wooden plank fencing and shared a pint of his whiskey with some loafing Mexican cowboys. He asked them if they knew a Herschel Baker.

"No, Señor, I never hear of him," an older hand said, and handed him back the bottle, wiping his mouth on the back of his hand.

"We are having a fandango tonight," the one-eyed hand said. His blank white eye looked sightlessly around. "You can come, uh, hombres?"

"*Sí*. Join us."

Thurman took a swallow from the bottle and sent it back around again. "Naw, I'm heading out in the morning early, boys. I need to find him."

"Who is he, Señor?"

"My son who I haven't seen in fifteen years."

"Good luck in finding him, amigo," the older one said, and tossed the empty pint aside with a clink.

Thurman thanked them and moved on. In questioning several bartenders and stockyard men, he found that some of them remembered Herschel but didn't know where he'd gone, though they'd heard rumors of him heading toward Montana. He looked off to the north. Montana was a long ways up there. He'd better hitch his belt up and ride that way.

The second evening after leaving Fort Worth, he reached Doan's Store on the Red River. It was little more than a reminder of the old days when, by this time of year, there would be herds in the tens of thousands lined up to ford the treacherous Red. In the store, he bought what he needed for supper. A hunk of summer sausage, a loaf of fresh-baked sourdough bread, and a can of peaches. Seated in a rocking chair on the store porch, with his jackknife he punched a hole in the top of the can and washed down his sandwich with the sweet juice.

Uninvited, an older cowboy joined him like a man wanting company from another wearing a high-crowned hat. Seated on a crate beside Thurman, he looked like a man who wanted to talk. Thurman offered him a sandwich.

He shook his head mildly. "You know, I've been up that trail over a dozen times."

Thurman nodded. "Baxter Springs?"

"Baxter Springs, Abilene, Newton, Wichita, Dodge, and some others—hell, I even went to Sedalia, Missouri— once."

"Them were the days," Thurman said between bites. "Ever know a man named Herschel Baker?"

The man squeezed his unshaven chin and looked across the snag-dotted Red River. "Name sounds familiar. Did he have any other tag?"

Thurman shrugged. "I don't know."

"There was a horse-wrangling kid I recall—Travis Baker."

"Yes. That could be his brother. They tell me he's dead."

The old man looked disappointed. "That's a damn shame. He sure was gutsy for a kid back then. The outfit we was with—I'll recall the boss man's name later—had a big stout bay horse in the cavvy that had been cut after he was too old. The puncher that drawed him in his string got throwed every time he climbed on him. Travis, he got disgusted that the puncher couldn't ride him.

"We was laid up for a day or so up on the Canadian to repair the chuck wagon, and Travis had another cowboy saddle a horse that wasn't afraid of that proud cut bastard and snubbed him up close. Travis got in the saddle and told the other ranny to pitch the lead to him. They went off like a cyclone. Spinning and bucking. Man, it was a real sight.

"That Travis rode that devil till his nose ran blood and he finally stood plumb still, dripping in sweat. And after that, a kid could have rode him to gather milk cows. Yes, sir, that Travis was a real hand with horses, but I never knowed no Herschel. What's them boys to you anyway?"

Spearing a peach half out of the can with his jackknife, Thurman paused. "They're my sons."

The old man looked away. "Sorry I can't help you." Then all of a sudden, he must have felt like he didn't belong there. He cleared his throat, said, "Sorry about you losing your boy," and left.

Even well chewed, the slippery peaches proved hard for Thurman to swallow.

Before he took the ferry across the river, he bought three pints of whiskey to stow in his saddlebags, along with some jerky, dry cheese, and crackers in case he got stuck out there somewhere. Riding the sorrel horse up the well-worn road on the far side to the top of the steep north bank, he passed a sign.

Warning: The Indian Territory is a dry territory. Anyone selling or transporting alcoholic beverages, beer, or spirits in these lands will be prosecuted in the federal court at Fort Smith, Arkansas.

Issac C. Parker, Federal District Judge

He nodded at the message. A notice that he'd read many times after crossing the Red headed north with cattle herds. *Too bad, Your Honor, I'm on a quest and I need a few spirits to get me though this.* Maybe he'd need a whole lot, but there would be sources in the Nation. Corn, sugar, and a still were all it took. There was no shortage of wooden barrels, copper coils, and bootleggers to make their own in the territory.

He knew a man who lived with a Choctaw woman up the road a ways. He planned to look Fred Hayes up if he could find him. That first evening, outside a small store, he ate a meal cooked on a campfire by a young Indian woman. She called it beef stew and served it to him from a large Dutch oven in a turtle-shell bowl.

He sat on the ground and after he took the first sip from his spoon, he nodded his approval to her. It was good. The rich meaty flavor was delicious. The woman brought over a coffeepot to fill his tin cup. She was in her twenties, and when she grinned at him, he noticed that she'd lost two top teeth. She was a little thick at the waist, and he wondered if she was with child. He extended his cup for her, and she poured the boiling brown liquid into it.

Before she spoke, she checked to be sure no one heard her. "You a Parker man?"

"No, why?"

"You dress like one." She motioned to his clothing.

"I'm a cow buyer headed north."

"You better stay here tonight, mister," she said in a low voice.

He looked up at her hard. "You got a good reason?"

She checked around, then nodded at him. "Bad place. That outlaw Chickenhead may try to rob you."

He frowned at her. "Who's he?"

"Bad outlaw. Murder, rob, even rape women."

"Can't Parker's deputies catch him?"

She shook her head, standing above him with the pot. "They try. He is like smoke."

"He ever bother you?"

She didn't answer him at first. Then she nodded and went off to serve some of the others that were gathering to eat. There was some laughter, and she joined in at the various groups. Her laughter was like a silver bell and stood out. Some of her customers were Indian boys in their teens. There were couples, and even a few 'breeds that kept to themselves.

The coffee was so hot it burned his upper lip. He blew on it, set it aside, and went back to his stew. She returned with a small kettle and a gourd dipper to refill his bowl. "It is good luck to eat out of turtle shell."

"Good food, too." He wanted to say it wasn't such good luck for the turtle, but he didn't.

"You can sleep at my place tonight," she said in a whisper as she ladled more in. "You would be safe there."

"You have no man?"

"He died."

"How will I find your place?"

"Ride north, take the creek road left. Turn left at the broken-down wagon bed. Take that lane to my cabin."

"No one will bother me for doing that?"

Looking serious, she shook her head. "No one."

"I'll do that if you say so."

With the warm shell in his hand, he began eating the stew. Was her offer a trap? Or an actual goodwill gesture? Was she lonesome? She'd sounded sincere. He watched her move about in her willowy way feeding the others and refilling cups. His instincts told him she was all right, and he relied on them a lot. The chatter of guttural Indian words mixed with broken English filled his ears.

When he finished, he returned the bowl and paid her two bits. She thanked him and looked concerned.

"You have a way home?" he asked under his breath.

"Oh, yes. But I have to work here for a while. Make yourself comfortable there. You can find candles when you get inside."

"Thank you. If I am asleep, I'll see you in the morning."

She nodded, and then looked hard at the quarter in her palm. "I owe you change."

He shook his head.

She smiled, pleased at his generosity.

He left riding north, then turned on the creek road. In the last hour of daylight, he watered his horse in the small stream, and when he was through, rode on west. Sure enough, he found a broken-down wagon bed and a little-used lane. He sent the sorrel up the grassy ruts through the post oaks to a cabin as the sun dropped lower. When the gelding was unsaddled and put in the pen, he fed the horse some corn in a log feed trough.

An excited stock dog fresh from swimming somewhere joined him, wagging its tail until he paused to pet the black and white collie. With the saddle on his shoulder, he went toward the house.

The drawstring opened the door, and the dark interior carried wisps of cooking odors and some fragrance like flowers. He stepped over the threshold and struck a match. A stub candle in a shiny sardine can on the table told him lots about her neat ways. With the wick lit, he could see the stone fireplace, a rocking chair, a camelback trunk, and homemade patch quilts on the bed. He set the saddle down with the horn to the side so no one would fall over it, and then he shut the door. He put his hat on the wall peg and turned to inspect the rest of her cabin. There was a dry sink, cupboards made of crates, and a canvas water pail with a gourd dipper. All very neat.

He located a pint in his saddlebags and took a drink, popped in the cork, and stowed it away. The small supply had to last him. Seated in the rocker, he soon dozed off. The dog's whining outside awoke him. He eased the Colt out and put it in his lap—just in case.

"You found it," she said, out of breath as she opened the door and stepped over the threshold.

"You must have walked home," he said, holstering his gun.

"I always walk home. But I take a shortcut."

She drew out a ladder-back chair. Seated before him, she straightened her dress. "You must think I am brazen for inviting you here."

He shook his head. "I thought you had a reason."

"I see things sometimes."

"Like fortune-telling?"

"Yes, it scares some people. Does it scare you?"

"No. What did you see?"

"I saw you in harm's way."

"From who?"

"I thought it might be Charlie Chickenhead who was after you."

"And?"

"I know you are a man looking for something—something very important to you." She rubbed her palms on top of her dress and seemed anxious.

"Will I find it?"

She shook her head in disappointment. "It is far, far away. I don't know the answer. I am sorry. I only see some things. Others escape me."

"I understand. My name is Thurman Baker."

"Mine's Mary Horsekiller."

"I appreciate your concern for me, Mary."

Her eyes like dark coal peered at him as if she could see through him. "You have no family?"

"Right. That's who I am looking for."

She jumped up and went to the cupboard. With a small furry pouch on a leather thong in her hands, she returned and motioned for him to lean forward. Standing on her toes, she strung it over his head and around his neck.

"It has some magic in it. Wear it. It is the most powerful medicine I have for you."

"Thank you. My heart goes to you for your generous ways. In the morning, you know, I must ride on."

"Then we will sleep."

"Yes. I have a bedroll."

"No, you must share my bed. The floor is cold and dirt."

"As you wish."

"I wish that." She bent over and blew out the candle.

The room became engulfed in deep darkness. *Far, far away.* Those were her words. But she did not know where. He closed his eyes, standing in the room's blackness. Was it in Montana?

THREE

T HE side room in Doc's office smelled of alcohol and iodine. Lying under the white sheet drawn up to his black-whiskered face, the wounded outlaw looked ghostly pale.

"My name's Herschel Baker. I'm the sheriff of Yellowstone County. Doc says you'll survive. I think this bed is better than the one in my jail right now for your recovery. But it comes with rules. Try to escape, you'll end up in irons in my jail no matter how bad off you are. Harm anyone here, the same applies."

The man nodded stiffly, staring at the tin-squared ceiling.

"I can tell you that folks were ready to lynch you out there in that street if you didn't know that—so if you try to escape, I can't be responsible for your life when the posse finds you, and they will."

"What else, law dog?" the man asked in a rusty voice.

"What's your name?"

"John Smith."

Herschel closed his eyes as if in pain and dried his right palm on the side of his canvas pants. "I could jerk you up and shake the fire out of you. Mister, I expect straight answers—start giving them to me."

"Kermit, Kermit Taunton."

"How long have you been in this county?"

"Week, maybe more."

"You come looking to rob someone?"

"What did it look like?"

"I asked you."

Taunton closed his eyes. "Yeah, there ain't no work in this country. We decided to rob the damn store."

"Who's we?" Herschel straddled a chair backward and rested his arms on top of it.

"The others."

"I want their names."

"I ain't no snitch."

"Taunton, you better think about your position here. You've got a real bed and clean linens. The county jail has an iron bed and a couple of stinking blankets."

"All right. All right. Slide Jennings and Euford Malloy."

"Where did you boys stay while you planned the robbery?"

"I can't tell you that—"

"Why not?"

"He'd kill me."

"Who?"

Taunton took a deep breath. "Anton Pleago."

No surprise. Pleago lived on the edge of the law. Herschel nodded and rose. "Don't get any idea that you're well enough to travel and take off."

"I savvy," Taunton said.

A half hour later, Herschel was back in his office with

his deputies Darby, Art Spencer, and Phil Stevens. He told them what he'd learned from Taunton.

"What about Anton?" Art asked.

"You know he's been a pain in my backside for over a year. He's as slick at rustling as any man alive, or you boys would have caught him. We know he eats beef and don't own a calf."

"We know that. What do we do now?" Art asked.

Herschel set his lips tight for a moment before he spoke. "I think I'm going to ride up there and give him an eviction notice. And I'm going tell him if he wants to stay around for the trial, then he'll be tried as an accessory. That's three to five years."

Art, who was a burly ex-teamster in his late thirties, laughed. "I'm going along. When are we going up there?"

"Daylight in the morning. Meet at my place.

"Phil," Herschel said to his former desk clerk, who'd recently turned twenty-two, "you check on Taunton. He's got it too good over there to mess up, but you never can tell. Since we don't have any tracks of where those other two went, I want a detailed description of the others from him to telegraph out. He gives you any trouble, tell him you've got the authority to move him across the street to a steel cot."

"Yes, sir."

"Shultz and I are going down to my wife's old ranch for a few hours this afternoon and I'm going to show him some good steers."

An hour later, Herschel met the cattle buyer at the livery. They short-loped down to Horse Creek and found Mae Pharr, the hired man's wife, at the house. She came to the door, a plain-looking gal holding her head like she didn't feel good.

"Oh, it's you, Sheriff. Sonny is out checking cows today. Didn't say which way he was going."

Herschel nodded. "Tell him to fix that fence up there. Cattle will be getting in the hay meadow."

"I know. He mentioned it the other day."

"He better see about the mower and get it ready. In a few weeks, it will be haying time."

"I'll do it, sir. I been too sick this spring to help him much."

"He needs my help, send word or drop by when you're in Billings."

She nodded, and they rode on east. Herschel didn't like the look of things around the home place. The ranch wasn't being kept up like he wanted. He'd better check on the Pharrs more often. Sonny Pharr was getting good pay to keep that place up.

"You sounded upset back there," Shultz said.

"He's not been earning his pay. I'll keep a better eye on him from here on. He came up here, he was the best hand I figured I could hire. Today, that place looked trashy, and the fence needed fixing."

"My daddy said if hired hands were worth a damn, they'd own their own place."

"Your dad knew hired help."

They found several bunches of fat two-year-old steers. Many looked like pure shorthorns. Big stout roans and reds, they eyed the two riders suspiciously, then went back to grazing.

"I do think they'll make big enough steers this fall. Man, they are nice," Shultz said.

Riding past one group, Herschel noticed one of the steers. On his right side, like a cloudy letter in the red roan hair, was a large white S. Herschel pointed it out to the buyer, who agreed it was unusual.

All the way home, Shultz wanted to talk price, but Herschel let it ride. They'd talk again later in the season. That night, he told Marsha that he had to look in more often on their hired man.

"You think he's not working out?"

"We'll see. I wasn't too happy at what I saw today. We better get some sleep. I can handle it."

Early the next morning, Herschel sat at the breakfast table with his three stepdaughters and his smiling wife.

"The strawberries are blooming," Kate, the oldest, said.

"Yes, and we have to weed them today, too, before you three ride the pony," Marsha announced.

The news drew some sour faces from the three girls.

"I thought Art might come early for breakfast," Marsha said, going for more coffee.

"Not since he got his own wife." Herschel chuckled. "He ain't near as footloose as he was before."

"She's nice."

"Oh, yes. But she can cook, too."

"Will this man Anton put up a fight over you evicting him?"

"I don't really care what he does besides leaving the county." Herschel stood up over his chair. "I'm ready to make ice cream with fresh strawberries, aren't you, girls?"

"Yaay!"

He smiled. "Then you all get the weeds out of them for me."

"We will, Daddy."

He leaned over and kissed his wife on the cheek. "I should be back by supper time. Art's outside, I hear him."

"You all have a nice day," he said to the girls. "It looks wonderful outside today. Won't be long and we can plant some other things. Mr. Stauffer has the garden plowed and with all this rain, why, I bet our corn will grow higher than Cob's back."

They shouted good-bye and he put on his hat and vest, and carried his gun belt in his hand, strapping it on going out the door. Marsha followed him to the porch, and she spoke softly after him. "Be careful. We need you."

He looked back and nodded with a wink. Earlier, he'd saddled and brought Cob around front. The tall roan stood hitched at the rack. With a cordial word to Art, he gathered the reins with a hold on the saddle horn. In an instant, he knew when his leg swung over the big gelding's rump that the horse was ready to buck. He checked him, getting his right foot set in the stirrup.

His move was enough for Cob. The powerful gelding took it as an advantage and tried to bury his head between his knees. Ready for him, Herschel hauled up on the reins and gouged him in the sides with his spurs at the same time. Cob's halfhearted hops ended with stiff landings on all four legs, but he never really got as high as he wanted to.

With Herschel threatening him all the time, Cob finally settled down, and began a swinging walk he could keep up all day.

"I sure thought you were going flying this morning," Art said, amused.

"Naw, I ain't got wings."

"I love that horse," Art said. "But he'd sure throw me about every time I tried to ride him if I owned him."

"I got Cob with some young horses I had bought when I was on that place down on Horse Creek and breaking horses for living. He was a long two-year-old then and, man, he was a handful. When I got him dusted off, several folks wanted to buy him and they tried him. He wiped them out and they brought him back, so I finally decided I'd keep him. Never regretted it for a day."

"He don't buck every time?"

"That's right. Those are the good days. But he seldom bucks more than once except when you resaddle him. That's why I don't unsaddle him in the daytime."

Art laughed. "Helluva tough horse."

Herschel agreed.

They rode till mid-morning, and then found the lane that led to Anton Pleago's place. Some shaggy-coated Indian ponies nickered at their horses from a stomped-out haystack ring. They were winter-thin, and with them was a gray-faced Jersey cow that was bawling. A man could have used her hips for a hat rack.

A skinny white sow came running over, grunting like the two men might feed her. Then some black Indian dogs set in to barking as if awakened by the pig. They were the slinking kind that no one ever fed—they found their own meals. The crude log cabin and sheds were set in a grove of stunted pines. Smoke came out the tin chimney pipe. But no one was in sight.

Herschel reached back and adjusted his Colt. *Hell only knows how this will go.*

FOUR

Thurman saddled the sorrel before the sun came up. With the cinch tight, he turned at the sound of soft footsteps and dropped the stirrup. With the reins in his hand, he faced Mary Horsekiller in the half-light.

"I will make some food and coffee," she said, standing before him wrapped in a blanket. "Sorry I did not hear you get up."

"Only if you let me pay you."

"Pay me?"

"Yes, pay you for the food."

"Come." She tugged on his sleeve. "We can talk about it while I make us some food."

"And I will pay you."

"So you will pay me." She shrugged and pulled the blanket tight. She was obviously not dressed underneath it.

They went back to the house.

Once inside, she said, "Excuse me, I must put my clothes on."

"Sure, I won't look."

She laughed and shook her head in dismay. "Where will you go from here?"

"There's a man I once knew, Fred Hayes, who lives with a Choctaw woman north of here."

"Smart man."

"You know him?" He turned and frowned at her.

She finished buttoning up her dress. Wiggling down the bottom half, she pushed her breasts out and smiled big at him. "No. I mean he is smart for having an Indian wife."

He dropped his chin and shook his head amused. "Why?"

"They are easy to please. They have the power to make you well when you are sick."

"Oh, that's what you mean."

"I bet your friend would agree."

"No telling about him."

She began heating grease, and soon dropped dough off a spoon into the hot oil.

From his seat on the ladder-back chair, he half raised up to look at her cooking. "What is that?"

"Indian fry bread."

"It's different than doughnuts," he said.

"Yes."

Her fry bread proved to be delicious. But her coffee made from scorched barley was too bitter for him. Seeing the face he made at his first sip, she quickly shaved some tea from a bar and fixed him a cup of it. It wasn't half bad. They laughed through the meal and when he finished, he tried to remember the last time he'd laughed at a meal. What had made it so hilarious? He couldn't remember exactly what they'd laughed at. It was some kind of free spirit they'd shared.

In the end, he gave her money to buy some real coffee, and she walked him to the horse.

"What I told you about Chickenhead is not funny," she said, looking down at her bare toes. "He and his gang are bad men. Watch yourself until you are well out of these mountains and beyond the Canadian River."

"I will, and thanks for everything. I've got to find my son. I think I may have a wonderful chance for a second life. If I wasn't in such a hurry, I'd stay much longer."

She squared her shoulders. "I will be here."

"Don't turn down a good man's offer. I may never be able to ride this way again."

"Go," she said. "Before I cry . . ."

Mounted, he sent Red northward. Once he twisted in the saddle to look back, but she was gone. He turned around, disappointed she wasn't there so he could have had one last sight of her to remember.

At mid-morning, a thundershower began building in the hills to his left, and he decided to find a place to stop over and wait it out. Across the forest floor the mayapples, short, umbrella-like weeds, were ready for the rain. A deserted home place on the right seemed like it might offer some protection until the storm passed. He reined Red off the road through a field of head-high sprouts that had once been farmland. The shake-roof barn looked like the best choice. He dismounted and led Red inside.

Big drops soon struck the cedar shakes and thunder rolled down the valley. A drop or two made him move a few feet to a drier location, but even with a leaky roof, it wasn't as bad as being out in the heavy downpour. In a half hour, the storm moved on, the sun came out, and he re-mounted. Jogging Red, he headed for Dutch Creek. Fred had mentioned that location. Thurman might not be able to find him there, but he'd look some.

On the road, he met two men in long-tail canvas coats. One drove a wagon and a team of horses; the other rode a proud cut bay horse that kept acting like a nasty stud toward Red. Both men were in their thirties and wore mustaches, and he had no doubt they were the law. For a second, he remembered about the last bottle of whiskey in his saddlebags

"Good day," the one on the bay said, reining up like they wanted to talk. He was hard-eyed and his mouth made a small line over a sharp chin. "Afternoon, mister. That's a spanking fine horse you've got there."

"Same to you. He's a barb. His ancestors came from North Africa with the Moors to Spain."

"I seen some of them somewhere's before, ain't you, Hank?"

The friendlier of the two, who sat on the spring seat of the tarped-down wagon, nodded and grinned. "He's Deputy U.S. Marshal Levitt Morris and I'm Hank Youree from Fort Smith."

Thurman put his hand on the saddle horn cap. "Thurman Baker's my name. Guess you two're looking for Charlie Chickenhead?"

Morris reined up his bad-mannered horse and frowned hard at Thurman. "What do you know about him?"

"Folks been warning me about him since I crossed the Red River. Said that he was prowling around these parts avoiding you marshals."

"We'll get him," Morris said with a toss of his head toward the south. "There been any sighting of him back down there?"

"No actual ones that I heard about. Just lots of folks are afraid of him."

"Well, if he'd ever seen that fancy horse of yours, you'd known he was around. Hell, Hank, let's go back to Ditch Creek and spend the night. You headed there, Baker?"

"Is there a Dutch Creek around here?"

They shook their heads.

He smiled. "I guess that's what he meant. Ditch Creek. You know a Fred Hayes?"

"Yeah, a Texan married him a Choctaw woman so he could graze his damn cattle up here."

"He used to be a nice guy."

"He's all right," Morris said. "I fought you damn Rebs."

Thurman shook his head in disbelief. "Hell, that's been a long time ago."

"Not for me. I ain't forgiving or forgetting one damn thing about it either." He spit off the side of his stomping horse and wiped his mouth on the back of his glove. "So you know where you stand with me."

"Excuse me, General Phil Sheridan, I'm riding on. I wouldn't want that smoldering fire in your belly catching a blaze."

"Aw, hell, he had a bad time back then," Hank said. "Hold up. We'll make camp at Ditch Creek."

"Thanks, but just the same," Thurman said, riding past him, "I ain't staying where I ain't wanted."

"Aw, damn," Hank swore. "You and your Rebel complaining. . . ."

Thurman found a small crossroads store before dark. He bought a hunk of sausage cut off a new tube, a half loaf of freshly baked bread, and a can of peaches from the tall man in an apron behind the scarred counter. His purchases also included five pounds of corn for Red. After he paid the man, he asked, "You know a Fred Hayes?"

"He lives at Sullyville. Ten miles north and west of here."

Thurman thanked him. It was too late to ride over there. He'd find him in the morning. Outside in the dimming light, he led Red into an open meadow to let him graze there. He unsaddled and hobbled him.

With his back against a big oak, he studied the darkening outlines of the sugarloaf mountaintops covered in hardwoods and some pines. He cut the sausage into slices and, wadding up the warm bread, enjoyed the garlic-sourdough flavor of the sandwiches he made. He washed them down with the sweet juice of the peaches, and savored the sounds of the night's insects and frogs.

After supper, he found a place in the wiry grass to pour out some of the corn for Red. Soon, the gelding was chomping on the grain, and Thurman brought out his blanket and ground cloth. The canvas sheet could serve as a poncho, but he'd never thought about it earlier while dodging storms. He'd buy a new slicker first chance he got. Somewhere off in the distance, a hound dog was barking treed.

Wrapped up in the bedding and still dressed, he sat with his back to the tree. All this Chickenhead business had him on edge. If Mary had known anything. . . .

He woke with a start. Someone knelt in front of him. Then a small hand closed over his mouth. "Shush. Chickenhead and three men are close by," Mary said.

The six-gun in his fist—he nodded. A hundred feet away in the starlight, Red was nickering to another horse.

He could make out a figure using a blanket over him for cover and sneaking on his hands and knees toward his horse's silhouette. With his forearm, Thurman swept Mary aside and aimed down the barrel of his gun. At the red muzzle blast, with the acrid gun smoke in his nose and eyes, Thurman threw back the blanket and half rose. Two guns out of nowhere answered him, and he felt the mule-like kick of a bullet hit his left side. They were getting away with his horse.

Mary gasped. "Let them have him."

He aimed, but all he could see were outlines of horses. They'd cut loose Red's hobbles and were leaving the meadow with Red and probably Mary's horse, too. No chance to shoot them. The outlaws made yipping sounds while thundering away. He holstered the Colt and reached over to feel his left side. His hand came back sticky and dark. He'd been shot.

"You're wounded," she said. "Sit down."

"Listen—listen," he said, sinking to his butt on the ground. "There's money sewed in my boots and money sewed in my coat. It's—yours if I don't make it."

"Don't talk now." She put a wad of the blanket under his head. He felt dizzy and fought to not pass out. The pain in his side grew to a hot fire.

"You're not going to die. . . ."

What was that hissing sound? Damn—he drew up at the sharp pain in his left side. Where was he? Lying down on his back and looking up at the blue sky laced with large green leaves, he decided he was being carried on a travois over the road he'd come along on the day before. The end of the pole on the right side went over a rock and then dropped, jarring out an exploding shot of fire in his left side.

The travois stopped, and Mary came back and knelt beside him. "I am sorry. There was no wagon there."

"Where?" He couldn't clear his thoughts.

"Last night you shot one of Chickenhead's gang. Billy Dog. There was a fifty-dollar reward on him, the marshal said, and he gave me a receipt. Does your side hurt much?"

"I'll live."

"The doctor said it was good you had that whiskey. I used it to clean the wound."

"I could stand some whiskey now."

She shook her head. "I used all of it. I have some laudanum. Then you can sleep. It will be after dark before we get to my place." She ran off, and quickly brought back a spoon and bottle. "Here."

It tasted awful. He reached out and squeezed her hand. "I don't deserve your kindness."

"You rest. Get well. Marshals went to find your horse."

"Yes, yes, I'd . . . like him. . . ."

It was raining when they reached her cabin in the dark of night. She pulled him up off the travois, and he was not much help. Going toward the house, he looked at two long ears and thought *jackrabbit*. Obviously, she'd brought him there behind a mule.

"Your mule?" he asked with his right arm slung over her shoulder for support.

"Yours." She laughed in the rain. "It was all I could buy with your money."

He nodded, wanting to laugh, and then they half fell over the stoop getting inside the cabin doorway. He owned a mule. It hurt him to even chuckle. When they recovered their balance, she pushed him toward the bed.

Seated on the edge too dizzy to argue, he felt her pull off his boots and socks. She talked all the time about how he needed rest to recover—it was all like she was miles away—outlaw—reward—a mule—his mule brought him back there—he could see the head-tossing Red—his fine mane lifted by the wind—he had no time for this . . .

"Wake up. Wake up, you've been dreaming. Who's Tomas?"

He raised up in the bed looking for them—the three boys. A hot flash of pain in his side made him flinch. "One of my boys."

"Your son?"

"No, he worked for me."

"You were really dreaming."

There was daylight coming in the row of bottles that formed a window. With his fingers, he combed through his rumpled hair. "How long have I slept?"

"All night. Can you eat?"

"I think so. I wonder where he went."

"Who?"

"Chickenhead."

"The law went right after him, but they lost the trail."

"Maybe he's a spirit."

She shook her head vehemently. He could see the anger in her brown eyes. She knew he was not a ghost. No reason for him to pry. She'd said she'd felt Chickenhead's wrath.

"What did the doctor say about me?"

"A rib in your side stopped the bullet and then the bullet went out of you. He said the rib would heal."

"It's why I feel like I was kicked by that mule."

She nodded. "I am sorry. I needed to get you a place—"

"Hey, I'm not mad. You did so good. I had no one."

"I learned that morning at the store they were trailing you—I still owe a man for that horse they stole—"

"We can pay him. How much?" He squeezed his left elbow against his fiery side—the pain was sheer hell.

"Seven dollars."

He about laughed, but realized it would only add to his suffering. "It wasn't much of a horse?"

She shrugged and smiled. "It was a horse."

Thunder made him turn an ear. More rain coming. Tired, he lay back down, realizing he was soaked in his own sweat. "Take some money and when you go there, pay him."

He stared at the underside of the cedar shakes. Here and there in the room, water pinged into a tin can she'd set out to catch the drip.

"I have some chicken soup," she said, and came back with a turtle bowl of steaming broth.

"Oh, I don't know—"

"I know it hurts you to get up. But you must get your strength back."

He met her worried look. "You're thinking he'll come looking for me?"

"Both of us."

Both of us echoed through his mind. It felt like lightning running though his entire body as he sat up again with her help. With his back propped up with a pillow stuffed with straw, she sat on the edge of the bed and began to feed him from a spoon.

"Mary, it's none of my business, but why does he bother you?"

"I live alone. I have no gun." She straightened her back and delivered another spoon of the tasty soup to his lips. "I am a rabbit. He is a hawk. Do I need to say more?"

He swallowed the sip of her hot liquid and nodded. "There's a rifle over there. There is a small loaded .30-caliber pistol in my saddlebags—be very careful. It is loaded. So is my handgun."

As she lifted up another spoonful, she said, "My dog Blacky hates him. He usually warns me."

He remembered the friendly dog from the first night he'd stayed there before she came home. So it wouldn't only be him that Chickenhead sought, but her as well.

"You had a husband?" he asked softly.

"Yes. He died and so did my two children, three years ago. There was a plague on our land and many of my people died. I was very sick, but I lived."

"I'm sorry."

"You have a wife? A family?"

He shook his head. "I've been separated from her for fifteen years. I just learned that she died five years ago. My son Travis, they say, is dead. My daughter Rosie is married, lives down in Texas. I am looking for my oldest, Herschel. They say he's in Montana."

"Oh, that is so far away." She shook her head.

"I know, Mary. But I need him."

"What for?"

"To run a large ranch for me."

"How long since you have seen him?"

"Fifteen years."

Her eyes narrowed and she set the empty bowl in her lap. "Will he do that for you after all that time?"

"I never have prayed much in my life, but I've been praying about that."

FIVE

Dealing with hard-nosed men like Pleago, Herschel decided, was a pure waste of his time. The man would never heed his stern warning to leave the county. That was all right; he could rot in prison for being an accessory. Next time, he'd get no warning.

From Pleago's place, Herschel and Art rode east to look over the spot where they'd found Wally's body. They followed cow tracks over rolling ridges bristling with pines, and crossed the broad, grass- and sage-covered valleys with bubbling streams. The water was cloudy from the runoff of the day before.

"What're we looking for?" Art asked.

"Like the man said, we're looking for anything you can hang your hat on. I have a suspicion he was shot elsewhere and dumped on that road. Maybe even before the rain came in. No hat, no gun, and no money on him according to the boy at the funeral home. Being broke ain't no crime, but maybe whoever shot him robbed him as well."

They reached the Soda Springs Road, and Herschel told Art to spread out. "You take that side, I'll take this one. We'll ride through this sage and bunchgrass alongside the road. We may or may not find anything. Just look."

"How far do you reckon those store robbers got to?" Art asked as they reined their horses through the pungent low sage.

"Ain't no telling. I'm hoping I get word where they are after Phil sends out their description today by telegraph. They probably went through the Crow reservation and headed for Wyoming. There's plenty of places to hide and folks to hide them in the Big Horn Mountains and especially on south of there. Or they could have headed for northwest Nebraska. No law in that country either."

"I know you've been down there after some others."

"Be a great cow country. Grass belly deep on a good horse. But those homesteaders can't keep horses for all the thieves."

Art shook his head. "That would be a bad deal."

"You know a guy named Hatch that lives up here near the Soda Springs schoolhouse?"

"Hatch—hmm."

"Shultz or Perk, one of them, said that Wally was what Hatch and his bunch called him."

"Wait. Roscoe Hatch. He runs some cattle up here somewhere." Art twisted around to try and get his bearings. "I met him one time in a Miles City bar. Kind of a rough guy. He never bothered me, but he got into a couple of fist scraps over there when I was around. I'd call him a big bully."

"I wonder what his connection to Wally would have been."

"Can't answer that." Art reined up his bay and swung down. He looked off down a cow track that went east, then bent over and picked up an empty brass casing. "There's two here might be connected to something."

Herschel rode over and joined him. "What caliber?"

"A .38 Smith and Wesson." After Herschel turned them over in his palm, he followed Art's stare to the east. "What do you think?"

"Like you said, something to hang your hat on, right?"

Herschel nodded. "Wally's body was a quarter mile or so north of here. Suppose you brought the body over there, dumped it, and started back. Then you recalled firing two shots, and reloaded off the road."

"Of course in a million miles of Montana, finding two empty casings is like locating a needle in a haystack."

"You're right, but my gut feeling is we need to ride out on this cow trail. Maybe it will lead us nowhere, but we don't have anything either."

Art agreed.

Long past noon, they found themselves on a ridge looking down on a dark log cabin and some badly decayed pens. The place could have belonged to an early settler who ran off in the Sioux War some years before the Little Big Horn battle.

"There's horses down there," Art said.

"Trouble, too."

Art frowned at him. "How is that?"

"Arnold, he's a farmer over south and east of here, told me yesterday in the café that he saw two hard cases riding clear of the road in his country to avoid attention. One of the horses that they were leading was a bald-faced one."

"Holy Christmas. There's one down there, ain't there?"

"You can see him a mile away."

"Reckon who they are?"

"No telling. But I once tried to sell a horse to a drifter

who came by my place one time, and I felt certain he was on the run needing bad to swap a worn-out pony for a fresh one. All I had was a sweet bald-faced horse and a rough Roman-nosed bronc about half broke. He laughed at me. Said a lawman could see Baldy a mile away. He took the bronc and, man, he left my place making a show that folks would have given good money to watch his ride."

"And the sheriff just seen Baldy." They both laughed.

"Keep your wits about you, they may put up a big fight," Herschel said as they dropped down off the steep hillside on their horses.

"Anton's deal went easier this morning than I thought it would."

Herschel shook his head. "But that business ain't over either. It'll be harder than that to get him to move on. But I'll ship him to the pen if he don't move. We don't need that trash in this county."

"You're right."

Herschel reined up at the halfway mark where a point jutted out for their horses to rest. With care, he checked the five rounds in his .44—Art did likewise. Words weren't necessary between them. His partner wasn't missing any details or movement around the cabin, nor was he. Then, with a nod, he booted Cob on. It could be that their next move might alert the ones in the cabin.

There were few windows in those first cabins settlers built, but without much wind, sounds carried. The snort of the horses, the creak of leather, spurs jingling, even a horse testing a bit, made sounds that could jar a man living on the edge. Of course, these men might be innocent of anything but passing through. However, most folks took the main roads to get where they were going, not the back ways.

On the flat, Herschel looked at the bald-faced horse in

with the others when they rode past the pen. Good-looking horse. They rode on.

When they were twenty feet from the door, Herschel reined up Cob. "Hello the house," he called.

He could hear some quick conversation inside.

A tall man with a black beard cracked the door. "What the hell do you want?"

"My name's Herschel Baker. I'm the sheriff in these parts and I need to talk to both of you."

"What about?"

"Your horses."

"They're our damn horses." The man turned and hissed over his shoulder.

"There's two of them," Art said to Herschel.

"I guess you have a bill of sale for all of them," Herschel said to the bearded man. "Come on out here. I want to see the two of you in the daylight."

"What if we don't?"

"I'll roast you out."

"Hell, what'll we do?" The man at the door about closed it. "All right, we ain't got nothing to hide. We're coming out."

"Good. Don't try nothing. You won't survive it."

Whiskers came out with his hands held up, followed by a short redheaded kid—maybe older than he looked.

"Watch 'em," Herschel said to Art, and his deputy moved his horse so he was off to the side. Both men were unarmed, so Herschel signaled for them to put their hands down. When Art was in place, he dismounted.

"Now what'cha need?" the short one asked with a curl of his lip.

"Names for starters."

"I'm Doff Porter. He's Clyde Snyder."

"I counted six horses in the corral. Any of them stolen?"

"Hell, no. We bought them horses."

Herschel looked pained. "You have any brand inspection papers?"

"There ain't no brand inspector where we bought them."

"Montana law says you need one or a bill of sale."

"Where in the hell would we find one?" Porter asked. "We ain't seen anyone in days 'sides you two."

"You ride the side roads, there ain't much of anyone going to see you either except a ranch hand or two. Where did you boys come from anyway?"

"Miles City."

"That's easy to check on. I know the sheriff over there. Who did you buy them off of at Miles City?"

"Ah, we got them in the Dakotas."

Herschel narrowed his eyes, looking hard at them. "I think you came out of Nebraska with them ponies."

The two frowned at each other and then shook their heads.

"Dakota," Porter said.

"Art, go inside and look that cabin over."

"We ain't got nothing to hide. What do you want out of us anyway?" Porter asked, his voice at a higher pitch.

"I think we need to make a ride to Billings tonight. You boys and these horses can come along. We'll check around on your story and see if we can find the truth."

"Mister, I ain't a damn liar." Porter puffed up like a banty rooster.

Herschel nodded. "You better not be."

Art came out holding a hat and a slicker in his hands. "This belong to either of you?"

"Naw, it was here when we got here yesterday evening," Snyder said.

"Where exactly did you find it?" Art asked the pair.

"It was on the floor in a wad when we got here. We just throwed it aside," Porter said.

"This hat belong to either of you?" Art asked.

"No, we said it was here when we got here. We don't know whose it is."

"Herschel, you better take a gander at this slicker. It's got two bullet holes in the back and some blood on the inside."

Deep in thought, Herschel stepped over to the doorway and looked at the rubber slicker. Lots of dried blood.

Then Art handed him a well-worn, water-stained envelope that he'd taken from the side pocket. Herschel read where it had been forwarded several times to a Wallace Hamby. At last, it was sent to General Delivery, Billings, Montana.

Herschel nodded. That must be the dead man. He turned to the pair. "You know anything about this coat and hat?"

"I said it was here—"

"Get your things and saddle up. We're all going to Billings. Looks to me like there's more to this than those horses out there." He looked over at Art with a serious nod, knowing there were lots more questions that needed to be answered.

SIX

WITH his chest bound in Mary's bandages, as long as Thurman didn't use his left arm, he felt better. She'd been applying some of her herbs on the wounds, and she told him it was healing. After a sponge bath and her shaving him, he'd felt half alive and had stopped taking the laudanum. He worried about addiction. Too many soldiers injured in the war could never ever quit it. How long had he been resting there? A week.

Anxious to move on again, he sat on the stump and whittled. Her future worried him the most. Leaving her behind for that worthless Chickenhead to abuse again bothered him. He pulled too hard on the cedar stick in his left hand, and his side complained. The marshals had lost Chickenhead's trail, and there was no sign of Thurman's good red horse. That was a big loss with him facing such a long ride.

Mary came from the spring with a canvas pail full of water. "You look deep in thought."

She stood with the rope bale in both hands. "What's wrong?"

"I need to get on. They won't find Red, but—"

Her dark eyes looking concerned, she shook her head. "You can't ride a horse yet. That would hurt you too much."

"Exactly."

"What say I buy a buggy that's for sale and we hitch Ira to it and go to Fort Smith? You can get that reward and can find yourself a better horse there."

"How much will the buggy cost?"

"Harness and all, fifteen dollars."

He closed his eyes at the thought of being jostled around on a buggy seat all day, but that was an answer. Not a bad one either.

"That's plenty cheap enough. How far is Fort Smith by buggy?"

"Three-four days." She wrinkled her straight nose as if to say that was nothing.

"When you go to buy the buggy, buy some material for a new dress for you and the food supplies we'll need."

She acted affronted. "This dress is good enough."

He shook his head. "Not to go to Fort Smith with me."

She set the bucket down, stepped over, swept off his hat, and kissed him on the forehead. "Thank you, Thurman Baker. How far is Montana from Fort Smith?"

He half closed his left eye to stare at her for an answer. "You're wanting to go all the way up there?"

She looked around the area. "I don't see anyone else around here who's going to take care of you."

"Six weeks to three months by buggy, which is the way we will be going most of the time."

"Depending on how much your side can stand?"

"That, too. I can carry the water—" He started to get up.

She elbowed him aside. "I am the woman. I carry the water. Besides, I want you well enough to ride in that buggy tomorrow."

"We're leaving that soon?"

"I can make the dress while we are on the road. What else is to keep us here?"

He reached over with his right hand and petted Blacky, who had become his companion. "He better go, too."

"Fine. I have an aunt in Sullyville. Can she go, too?"

He chuckled and shook his head. "No. We only have a buggy if you can buy it."

"Money talks in these mountains. I'll ride Ira over there and get it."

"Here's a twenty-dollar bill."

She made a face. "That bill is too big to trade for a twelve-dollar buggy. He will think I am too rich. Besides, he won't have any change for it either."

"Keep the twenty for supplies. Let me see." He took all the change out of his pocket, found some pesos, a few singles, and a five-dollar bill. "Will he take that?"

"Sure, and he'll think he got all my money." She laughed and ran for the cabin. "I'll get ready." In a short while, she caught Ira and bellied up on him.

Thurman looked up at her as she tossed her thick braids over her shoulder. "You better buy some moccasins, too. There's lots of things to cut your feet where we're going."

"Can I buy some with beads on them?"

He frowned at her. "Why?"

"They cost more, but they are pretty."

He was so amused by her, his laughter made his side hurt. He eased off the stump to his feet, then went over and handed her another twenty. "Beads, whatever. Oh, yes, get a big tarp if he has one we can use for a fly."

"You mean like to make a tent?"

"Yes." It wouldn't hurt to have it along.

In a few hours, Mary returned with a woman beside her on the buggy seat. He got up to greet her, and nodded to the Indian woman she called Birdwoman.

"She makes pretty dresses," Mary explained, bounding out of the buggy and then shaking a thin wheel to show him. "It is a good buggy. I bought it and the harness for nine dollars. So I had money for the dress, moccasins, and for her to help me make it this afternoon."

"What can I do?"

"Nothing. Rest. You will get very tired going to Fort Smith." She left him, busy unbuttoning her dress and talking in guttural Cherokee to Birdwoman.

They had to be discussing how to make the dress, Thurman figured. He and Blacky better entertain themselves for a few hours outside. A gray fox squirrel in the hickory tree chattered at the dog. When the tree climber hit the ground, Blacky gave pursuit, but he was no match for the speedy squirrel.

Herschel took off the folded canvas cover, and opened the two wooden crates of food in the back of the rig. Plenty of canned peaches and tomatoes. Coffee, flour, sugar, baking powder, raisins, dried apples, bacon, lard—they'd eat well anyway on the way up there. He went around back and settled in a hammock. In a few minutes, he was asleep in the shade.

It was Ira's braying that woke Thurman with a start. Blacky joined in, barking. When Thurman sat up, his side caught and he rolled off the hammock onto his knees. The pain took his breath away, but he held the .44 in his fist. On his feet at last, he came around the corner and saw the two lawmen riding up the lane, Youree on the wagon, Morris on horseback.

Holstering the handgun, he leaned his good shoulder on the corner of the cabin to see what they wanted. The sharpness began to ease in his side.

"We ain't found your horse yet," Morris said. "But we're still looking."

Thurman nodded. "I reckon I'll never see him again."

"Man. We sure hated not finding him. You healing?" Youree asked, climbing down from the wagon heavily and pulling his pants out of his crotch.

"Slow. Sore as hell."

"I bet," Youree said. "But you're lucky. Not many have lived through a shoot-out with 'em. But they can't avoid the law forever."

"I bet Baker's been in worse scrapes than that," Morris said. "We need a drink of water."

"Them women are making a dress inside. The path to the spring is right up there."

"Yeah, we've used it before. See you got a buggy." Morris clapped a hand on a narrow iron-rimmed wheel and tested it.

"Yes, we're going to Fort Smith and collect that reward."

"I better warn you. They won't pay that in cash. They'll give you a warrant and you'll have to either keep it till the court gets money, which could be six months, or discount it to a merchant."

"You mean the federal government has no money?"

Youree shook his head. "They owe both of us money and expenses for the last two months."

"Good to know. How bad do they discount 'em?"

"Oh, fifteen bucks on a fifty-dollar reward like the one you've got coming," Morris said, and dismounted and started on the path through the post oaks.

"Thanks, that's good to know."

"I wish you'd shot all of them," Youree said, and then he followed Morris up the trail. "But they can't avoid us forever."

Holding a dress in front of her at the door and half hidden behind the wall, Mary asked in a low voice, "What do they want?"

He winked at her. "A drink of your springwater."

She nodded and disappeared again.

When the two lawmen returned, Morris took off his hat and wiped his forehead on his sleeve. "Getting hot. Well, we've got a wagonload of prisoners rounded up. So we're going back, too."

"What did they do?"

"You name it," Morris said. "We serve warrants issued by a federal grand jury. They range from pig stealing to murder and rape. Lots of whiskey makers." He shrugged. "But I've got to get my prisoners there alive for me to collect three dollars. Get a dollar a day to feed them and ten cents a mile for our own horses and wagon. Youree gets a dollar a day as my posse man, and I collect the fees for the arrests."

"Sounds like work."

"Yeah, and it ain't easy. We both had a fight on our hands night before last with this guy's wife and mother-in-law when we tried to arrest him for failure to appear on a warrant. Crazy damn squaws anyway."

Thurman nodded. "You looking some more for Chickenhead?"

"Can't. We've got fourteen prisoners and need to take them in."

"Reckon Chickenhead knows that?"

"What the hell do you mean by that, Reb?"

"I mean if someone doesn't stay after him, he can go on robbing, raping, and stealing what he wants."

"Listen, I risk my damn life about every day for three lousy dollars an arrest. If I get shot up, they won't pay my doctor bills either. Chickenhead'll be here when I get back. I'll get him."

"How many will he rob and rape in that time?"

"You shot one of his gang. Why don't you go find him?"

"I have things to do. Besides, it ain't my job."

"We'll get him." Morris mounted and nodded at Youree, who took his seat in the wagon, and they left.

Mary came out wearing her wash-worn dress to sit on the ground by him. "What did he say?"

"Nothing. I really don't think he wants to mess with Chickenhead."

She hugged her knees while seated on the grass and nodded. "If he ever shoots a marshal or robs a train, Parker will send the tough ones down here."

"That gets results?"

"Oh, yes. I hope you will like my new dress."

"I will. Why worry?"

"I want you to be proud of me. Should I take down my braids for Fort Smith?"

He rubbed his palms on his pants and laughed. "Why?"

"They will call you a squaw man. I could wear a bonnet?"

"You know any of those folks that will talk about us?" He chuckled at her concern.

"No."

"Then don't worry about what they say. I sure won't."

She jumped up and kissed him on the cheek. "I won't. Oh, that food and the tarp cost seven dollars . . ."

"We'll need it."

She nodded, but still looked uncertain. "What will they think of me in Montana?"

"That you are a nice-looking young lady and they'll be jealous that you are with me."

"Can I ask you one more thing?"

"What is that?"

"Do you really want me to go with you and meet your son?"

"Yes, Mary, I do. I am old enough to be your father. You're a pretty young woman. I'll be proud to have you with me."

"Good. Birdwoman and her family are going to live here until I ever come back."

"Sounds fine. You may grow tired of me."

She smiled and shook her head. Then she pushed off and rose to her feet. In front of him, she bent over and looked him in the eye. "I am excited about tomorrow and the next days."

"You ever been to Fort Smith?"

"Yes, but I was a blanket-ass Indian's wife then, with a baby, and people sneered at us."

"Hell, we're only going in there with a buggy and a mule this time."

"And you. I have your suit coat fixed and most of the bloodstains out of the shirt. If you will wear the coat, they won't see them."

"I'll be proud." He leaned over and looked at the house. "Is Birdwoman staying here all night?"

"No," Mary said, looking embarrassed. "I know you want to leave at sunrise. Right?"

"Let's do that." He felt anxious to get on the road again.

The next morning, with their bedding, his saddle, and some cookware tied down on top of the supplies, they left in the first light. She saved her new blue dress to wear until they got close to Fort Smith.

Ira acted spunky and a little spooked by the buggy chasing him. With Mary on the reins, he left the yard high-headed and struck the creek road in a jog trot. Blacky joined them, and went through the woods chasing cotton-tails, then showed up later with blood on his chin—breakfast. Then he fell in for a while beside a wheel, tongue lolling out, and tracked the buggy.

She rigged the scabbard so Thurman's Winchester was hung on the dashboard. With him on the left and her on the right, they took the bumps on the horsehair-padded bench seat, but she did a good job of guiding Ira around the worst bumps. The narrow iron rims were churning up dust as they moved along.

He smelled wood smoke, and they soon drove past a clearing in the forest. Several haggard men stood in chains forming a line getting breakfast. Thurman looked them over. They were Morris's prisoners. He waved at Youree, who was standing guard over them with a shotgun. Then they were gone and the hardwoods closed in on the narrow road.

Next, it opened to clearings and fields of new corn— small green shoots. Other fields, he decided, were planted in cotton. It was too small to tell. He closed his eyes. He hated farming. His life began on a dirt farm in Alabama and like Mary, when he went to town on Saturday, the boys that lived there called him names as though he was trash.

But he showed them. With his work-calloused hands as fists, he gave them black eyes, bloody noses, and sent them home crying. When he was married, he took his wife and went to Texas. Settled west of San Antonio and went to trading horses, mules, oxen, and cattle. He soon made enough money to buy a suit and looked respectable. After that, he never wore overalls again. He hired others, and let the boys do the chores and break the horses he brought in. But they never had any dealings with cotton, hoeing or picking it. Those boys were cowboys from the start. Knights on horseback, he always called them.

Mary elbowed him to awareness, and pointed ahead as she reined up Ira. "Do you see those men in the road up there?"

"Yes. Who are they?"

"Road agents. They are wearing masks."

He considered them. Four men with flour sacks over their faces sat their horses less than a quarter mile ahead of the wagon. Split-rail fences crowded both sides of the dirt ruts so the road agents could force the wagon to halt.

Bending forward with some pain, Thurman jerked the rifle out and told her to stay on the seat and hold the reins tight. He stepped off the buggy, chambering in a cartridge—not listening to her telling him to be careful. If they wanted to rob him, let them come get him.

"Make Blacky stay here and hold on to Ira when I shoot," he told her.

"Clear the road," he shouted, and the men laughed like they were amused. They sounded pretty drunk—damn them anyway.

He knelt on his right knee and used his left one for his elbow. With the .44/40 rifle steadied, he aimed through the buckthorn sights for the tallest black hat. When he shot, one of their high-crown hats went flying off. A horse exploded. He came bucking hard out of the group and quickly piled his rider off. The man's three partners whirled around and left on their own mounts in a cloud of dust.

"Bring the mule and rig," he said, and ran up to where the man bucked off lay on the ground groaning. The outlaw hugged his right leg as if it was broken.

Filled with fury, Thurman jerked off his mask. "Who in the hell are you?"

Before the moaning young Indian could answer him, Mary slid Ira to a stop beside Thurman, telling him, "He's Harvey Needles, one of Chickenhead's men."

Thurman heard the throaty sound, and whirled around in time to see the stiff-legged Blacky advancing wolflike on the boy. His lips curled back and growling, he was ready for the attack. Needles threw up his hands in wide-eyed fear.

"Here! Here, Blacky," Thurman said to the dog. "Get back there. He ain't worth chewing on. Now you go on."

He stamped his boot on the ground for effect and pointed with the rifle to where he wanted the dog.

Blacky finally obeyed him, but did not act pleased to be called off. He finally went to the rig and sat down. Satisfied that was over, Thurman looked all around at the emerald green mountains.

The good red horse hadn't been among the ones the outlaws had ridden. Had Red already been sold?

Where in the hell did Charlie Chickenhead go?

SEVEN

"WHO are those men you brought in to jail last night?"
Marsha asked, busy fixing Herschel's breakfast.
The oldest girl, Kate, the twelve-year-old, was at the barn
milking the cow. The other two Marsha had let sleep in, so
she and Herschel would have some privacy to talk. It was
long past midnight the night before when he had arrived
home.

"I suspect they're horse thieves," he answered. "I'm
checking them out. But in the cabin we also found a slicker
that belonged to the dead man with two bullet holes in the
back and dried blood on it, plus, I suspect, his hat. There
was a letter in the slicker pocket that was addressed to a
Wallace Hamby."

She refilled his cup with flavorful hot coffee. "What did
it say?"

He fished it out of his shirt pocket, and read it aloud.

"Dear Wallace, I am sorry to tell you because I know
you do not know this, but your mother died last fall and so

I have sold the farm, and I will wire your share of the money to whatever bank you tell me. Please write or wire me what bank and what town it is in so I can do that and close this matter. Sincerely yours, Titus Hamby."

"Oh," she said, standing straight-backed, holding the enameled coffeepot. "Maybe then this Wally was robbed, too?"

"That's what Art and I decided riding in last night. I left word for Phil to check today with all the banks and see if they paid this Wally a sum of money. Also the telegraph office."

"So what do you have to do today? Is all this going to cancel our going up to Soda Springs for the dance?"

"No, no, but there's been word of a shooting over at Gayline's Store yesterday. I'm riding over and checking on it. But if you will start out for the Soda Springs school-house in the buckboard this morning, I promise I'll be up there for supper with you tonight."

She shook her head in dismay. "They're working you to death, Herschel. Can't your deputies do some of this?"

"They've got all they can do. I promise—"

She set the pot on the table and squeezed his head to her breasts. "I know you like this job, but you need more help."

"There are no funds for more deputies. Maybe when the taxes come in, I can hire a few. Right now, it's pretty well up to me. Marsha, you know I took this job because the last man wasn't doing anything."

She stood back and straightened her apron. "Herschel Baker, you better not stand me up at that dance."

He half ducked and grinned. "I won't, Marsha, I promise."

On the back porch, he hugged his oldest stepdaughter, Kate, who was coming in with the pail of milk. The aroma of the hot milk and cow clung to her as she smiled at him. "Are you two going to the dance?"

He looked at the back door and nodded, releasing her. "Your mother is meeting me up there."

Kate shook her head with a mischievous look. "I bet she's real happy about that."

He stopped at the bottom of the stairs. "Just things I've got to do today."

"Next time we all want to go to the dance," she said after him.

He stopped again, turned, and pointed his finger at her. "You have a deal."

"I won't forget—remember, you promised me."

At mid-morning, Herschel arrived at Gayline's crossroads store. It being Saturday, there was an assortment of parked rigs there and several hipshot horses. Women in bonnets were going in and out the front door on the high porch. Some horse-swapping was going on. Boys were playing mumblety-peg with knives.

Tanner Rademaker was shoeing a team of light horses. He had his forge going and a son working the bellows. He was a big burly-shouldered man who did blacksmithing and farmed, and he looked up holding a hoof in his leather apron-covered lap when Herschel dismounted.

"Howdy, Sheriff. What's new?"

"I heard there was shooting up here yesterday." Herschel looked around. He knew his presence had people talking behind their hands.

"I heard the same thing," Rademaker said, busy measuring a shoe on a trimmed hoof. He dropped it and straightened. "You up here checking on it?"

"What did you hear?" Herschel walked over with him to his iron basin, which held the glowing coals and emitted a bitter-smelling smoke.

Using tongs, Rademaker shoved the shoe in the red-hot coals and pulled off his thick leather gloves. "That's enough air, Carl," he said to his son on the accordion pump.

"Well, Herschel, I heard it was over a pig. Another man said—" He turned to his son of twelve. "Carl, go play awhile."

The boy took his leave with a pleased grin and a nod for Herschel.

Rademaker waited until the boy was beyond hearing. "He didn't need to hear this. But I think it was more about Tompkins' wife than a pig."

"Oh?"

"I don't know if you know it, but Tompkins' wife, Etta, does not have the shiniest reputation anyway. Been several maverick newborn calves taken over there by ranch hands. So the word was out to them that an orphan doggie . . . well, you know what I mean."

"I think I am following you. How did the pig figure in?"

"Tompkins come home and found Earl Howard in his house. You know Earl?"

Herschel shook his head. "But go ahead."

"Earl claimed he was over there looking for a missing pig. I guess they had a fistfight. I'm not sure who won. Yesterday, they got into it again here and Earl shot Tompkins."

"Tompkins have a gun?"

"Yeah, he had one." Rademaker made a face. "He wasn't no match for Earl."

"How's Tompkins now?"

"Fine. Earl's bullet hit a Bible that Tompkins had in his overall bib. Guess you could call it the Good Lord saving him. He was knocked down. But folks first thought he was dead. Earl rode off. Guess he left the country thinking he'd killed him."

Herschel shook his head. And he'd ridden almost twenty

miles to find out it was two dumb men having a gunfight that turned out like that. At times, this job proved to be trying.

"Thanks. You see Earl or he comes back, tell him to ride into Billings and see me in my office."

"You won't ever see him again." Rademaker laughed. "He's G.T.T."

Gone to Texas. Herschel understood that abbreviation.

He thanked the big man and led Cob over to the hitch rack at the foot of Gayline's Store's stairs. Tipping his hat to the ladies coming out, he strode into the busy store. What he needed was a gewgaw for Marsha. Some little thing that would show he cared, especially after making her drive the buckboard up to Soda Springs by herself.

He roamed around, looking in the glass cases and not seeing a thing. A straight-backed woman with silver in her pinned-up hair, Mrs. Gayline, finally confronted him.

"Sheriff Baker, what do you need?"

He removed his hat, looked across the case, and smiled at her. "Something special for my wife."

"Combs for her hair?"

"No, she wears it in a Dutch bob."

"I don't know her, but we do some pawning with people. And if they don't come back for it, it is ours to sell."

"Yes, but I can't afford—"

"The item I am thinking about would not be expensive to you. We all know you have tried to be fair in how you handle the law. So if I did not make a profit, then whose business would that be but yours and mine?" She reached in and brought out an ivory cameo on a chain and held it in her open palm.

"That's too expensive," he said.

She leaned over the counter. "What number is E in the alphabet? Count them off."

"Five."

"That was our cost. You may have it for that."

On the cameo was carved a delicate dancing girl. A ballerina on her toes. He opened it and there was no photograph inside.

"The lady who pawned it took the picture out."

"You sure that's all it cost you?"

"If I am lying, put me in jail." She held out her hands with the long slender fingers and a gold wedding band.

"Don't guess I'll do that," he said, feeling a little embarrassed by her confrontation. Digging down in his pocket, he found several silver dollars and paid her.

"Wait," she said. "I have a small velvet box to deliver it in."

"How much is it?"

"Sheriff Baker, I am giving it to your wife."

He set the necklace down on the counter and dried his palms on the front of his pants. While he did that, she put the cameo in the red velvet box.

"I guess the shooting's over up here. I came and talked to some folks today and they think the main troublemaker left the county."

"I knew why you came today. That's why I bragged on you. It doesn't have to be a large corporation-owned cattle company to get your attention. I hope your wife likes it."

He nodded and put on his hat. "Marsha will like it fine. Thanks again."

Tipping his hat to the ladies, he exited the store, spoke to a few men, and shook their hands. With the box in his vest pocket, he swung on Cob, waved to some kids, and rode northeast. He didn't want to be late for supper—not this night.

Roscoe Hatch—that was the man he wanted to talk to at the Soda Springs dance. It was apparent from the letter that Wallace Hamby might have received a sum of money from an estate. That he might have been executed in that old abandoned cabin. The question was by whom? And how could Herschel prove it in a court of law?

He pushed Cob, short-loping him across country. This was not the day to be tardy. It was supposed to have been a day for him and his wife to leisurely drive up there, enjoy the company of each other, dance the night away, and camp under the stars. So far, he'd already missed the drive. He wanted to have time to put up the fly for her, although the Montana sky looked clear blue. Anxious to simply be there with her, he pushed the big roan horse on faster through the sage and bunchgrass.

At mid-afternoon, he pulled the hard-breathing horse down. They were on the road near the spot where the body had been. He looked to the south and saw a team coming—they were his wife's matched buckskins.

He'd timed it right. Even better than he thought he could. He was off Cob and loosening the cinch when Marsha drove up.

She wrapped the reins, jumped off, and ran to hug him. "You sure rode hard to get here."

"Feel anything in my vest between us?"

She frowned, and then she felt it on the outside with her hand.

"Better look at it."

"What is it?" With shaky fingers, she opened the velvet box and seeing it, sucked in her breath. "Oh, Herschel—it is wonderful. How much did it cost?"

He hugged her. "Not much. We can get a photograph made of all of us and put it in there."

"No. I already have those photos. I will get one of you to put in there. You gave it to me and I will always wear it. Then I will always have you with me."

"Mrs. Baker. Let's tie Cob on the tailgate and I'll drive you to the Soda Springs dance."

"Oh, whoever said that cowboys are not romantic?" She hugged his arm to her.

"Why, we're the knights of the range."

"You are, aren't you?"

"My pa told Travis and me that years ago when we were boys. 'You boys are knights of the range.' He said we'd never raise cotton. So far, I haven't had to."

"You miss Travis, don't you?"

"Yes, I do. I always thought the two of us would have built a big ranch together."

She pushed him onto the spring seat. "I think you have done very well for yourself, Herschel Baker. Let's go dance." On the seat, she removed her straw hat and put the cameo chain around her neck, and then the locket down behind her dress front.

"Ready?" he asked.

She hugged his arm. "Yes, I am ready for a wonderful evening, my knight."

"You boys will be knights on horseback, not knaves that chop cotton," their pa told them long ago. Maybe Thurman Baker had been right.

EIGHT

THURMAN stood with a camp ax in his hand. One he'd used to split cooking wood for Mary. It was late afternoon when Youree, sitting on the wagon seat, and Morris, on horseback, arrived at the clearing beside the road where Thurman and Mary had set up their camp.

"Thought you'd be way up the road—who's he?" Morris blinked at the sight of the Indian boy seated on the ground with his leg in a splint.

"Name's Needles. I figured he's worth a fifty-dollar reward. He's one of Chickenhead's men. They tried to hold us up back down the road, but they were full of firewater and left when I went to shooting at them. Except Needles' horse threw him off and broke his leg."

"Yeah, Morris," Youree said. "I seen Needles' name on that list."

"Well, now the court owes you a hundred dollars," Morris said to Thurman. "That's more than I'll make this month."

"Yeah, but you can wait around for your money. I'll have to discount mine."

"What in the hell're we going to do with a broke-leg Injun?" Morris squeezed his unshaven chin and shook his head.

"You've got plenty of labor. Get them to load and unload him. Write me a receipt."

Morris agreed, but only begrudgingly. "Was Chickenhead riding your red horse?"

"No, or I'd've got that horse back. I shot a black hat off one of them to send them running. If he'd been riding my horse today, he'd be lying dead in this road."

Morris made the receipt out in pencil on the seat of his saddle and handed it to Thurman. "Expensive-looking hat even with a hole in it."

Then he nodded at Mary, who was bent over the fire, wearing the silk-bound black hat with the high crown creased in the front as she stirred their supper. She took it off and tipped it to them. Putting it back on, she wore it with its trailing eagle feather and a smug look on her face.

The lawmen took the prisoner and then went to the far side of the meadow to camp.

Thurman was seated cross-legged on the ground, drinking coffee. Bareheaded, Mary came and sat beside him. Looking upset, she pulled the short grass up and tossed it into the hot evening wind. "I never told you *everything* about me."

"So. I haven't told you much about me."

"But I have a dark secret you must know before we get to Fort Smith."

He blew on the coffee. "What is that?"

"I carry another man's child."

He nodded. "And?"

"And it was forced on me."

He nodded again, busy studying how the small red-blue flames licked the bottom of her black kettle.

"Did you know?" she asked.

"I thought so the first day I saw you."

Her brown eyes filled with tears as she looked at him hard for his answer. "It does not bother you?"

"I guess we can raise it to be better than its father. It will be all yours. You think that is why those men tried to stop us today?"

"I never told him. I promised myself I would kill him if he ever touched me again."

"In few days or a week, we'll be beyond him and he won't find us up there in the vast prairie country between here and Montana."

"Hold me?"

He took her on his lap and despite the pain in his side, he rocked her. She dried her eyes with his handkerchief and sniffed a lot. There was no need for words between them. They already had a strong bond. The simple security of his arms and him holding her settled her down.

"Should we hurry to Montana before you have the baby?" he whispered in her ear.

She straightened up and looked in his face. "No, I am strong. I have had two children. One by myself in a lodge. I have good medicine."

"All right. I think the food must be ready."

She agreed and jumped up.

Before the marshals' prisoners stirred the next morning, the two of them were on the dark road for Fort Smith. Using the full moon and stars, they jog-trotted the mule through the shadowy groves and past the rail fences while the sun struggled to come up over some mountains in the east. Thurman could tell she had found a new spirit. Good. Who was he to judge someone else? He'd made the greatest mistake in his entire life riding off to San Antonio for a life he simply knew was going to be more exciting.

When it all shattered, then he couldn't go back. He'd shut the gate on that part of his life, too. Later on, he began to find some solace in reading the Bible. God forgives, it said. He'd marry this woman in time. But he'd already broken more commandments than he could count. In his case, God had lots to forgive. But he hoped His forces led him to Herschel and then helped him convince that boy he needed to join him on the 7 Bar.

They crossed the Canadian River on a ferry in late afternoon. The dingy brown water lapped at the side of the barge. The black man cranking the winch to carry them across sang gospel songs as they started across the high river. Thurman was grateful he wasn't staring at that high water with a herd to cross it.

Many a son of Texas never came up from the first ducking they took in swift water like this—swept away by the strong current that made the thick rope, which the man was working his great muscles on to propel them across, bow. Halfway, he stopped singing and used all his strength to wind the rope up.

Mary moved against Thurman and clutched his leg. "I don't like this."

Ira shook all over, rattling the harness standing in the traces. Then he snorted so loud, she jumped. The towrope groaned. The river rushed past faster underneath the barge. Heavy grunts from the black man lasted until he began to break the river's force and they were inching again for the far bank.

Thurman would have gone to assist him, but he knew the broken rib was still too tender for him to be much help.

When they approached the north bank, he squeezed Mary's leg through the dress. "We're about there."

Then she struck his right arm. "I hated that."

"No, you never had to swim it with a horse. It was ten times worse, and then the cattle were swept downstream and your cowboys were drowning. No, no, Mary, it was an easy crossing."

He took her in his arms and kissed her hard on the mouth.

When he settled back, she stared at him as if lost. Her fingertips touched her lips as if he had burned them. Then, she finally smiled at him. "I will complain more often if that is your punishment."

"Ma'am, you's can drive off now," the black man said, standing in the front of the docked ferry.

"Oh, yes." Startled, she took up the reins and drove Ira off the barge.

"Let's make camp," Thurman said, looking around. "I think we can reach Fort Smith tomorrow."

"We are not stopping until I don't have to smell or hear that damn river," she said, and made Ira go faster.

Thurman twisted and looked back. Not near as bad as some of the crossings he'd made. Then he looked to heaven, grateful for their safety.

Late afternoon the next day, they reached a shantytown on the west bank of the Arkansas River. A settlement of Indians, 'breeds, and riffraff that lived in dugouts, crate shacks, and canvas-covered lodges with their skinny, slinking black dogs and dirty, naked children looking blankly at the wagon's passing.

Thurman drove the mule down the steep cross-tie road laid in the alluvial sand to the waiting ferry. Mary closed her eyes and held his leg tight.

He nudged her with an elbow. "You can look now. We're on the ferry."

"Two bits," the ferryman said, and Thurman paid him.

Then the man in a sailor's cap went inside the small doghouse and blew a steam whistle that made Ira spook in his tracks. The paddle wheeler began to churn the brown water, and they were off for the far shore. Several red brick buildings stood against the skyline across the Arkansas. A half dozen river paddle wheelers were docked on the bank, unloading or taking on cargo. The town showed off its success despite the setbacks of the war.

Thurman drove Ira up on Garrison Avenue, then turned right to go to the federal court building. He stopped in front, then undid his gun belt and left it on the seat.

"I need to go in here and see about my rewards. Then we'll put Ira and Blacky up at a livery. Find us a room in a hotel and go have supper in a café."

She looked warily at the three-story brick barracks. "That is where Parker's court is held?"

"Yes."

"They won't keep you, will they?"

"No."

"Good." She hugged her arm and looked around the near empty brick street. "I'll be fine."

"I hope so."

He took the stairs two at a time and went inside the right-hand door. A clerk looked up at him. "Can I help you?"

"I have two receipts for federal rewards."

The young man held out his hand. He read them and handed them back. "Go to the second door on the left. They can help you in there."

In the second office, a middle-aged man at a desk removed his glasses and came over to the counter. "What do you need?"

"I have two receipts for rewards."

"Hmm," the man snorted. "You've been busy shooting 'em, huh?"

"No, they were busy attacking me."

"I can't sign these warrants and my boss is gone for the day. You'll have to come back tomorrow."

"Then give them back to me or issue a receipt for them."

"Well, don't you trust me?" The man swaggered up to the counter and tossed them down.

"That ain't the question." He put them in his pocket, bit his tongue, and started for the door. "Good day."

At the buggy, Mary frowned at him. "Did you get the money?"

"No, I didn't get the warrants that they issue for them. The man who signs them was not there."

"You weren't this mad when they tried to rob us."

"Sorry." He collapsed on the seat and smiled at her. "We'll do better tomorrow."

She clutched his arm and laughed. "Ferries make me upset. Judge Parker's men make you mad. We were lots happier in the mountains."

"It will all work out." He clucked to Ira and gave Mary the reins to turn him around as he put his gun belt back on his waist. He whistled to Blacky and the dog fell in with them. No need to let him get into a fight with some town dog.

"Where do we go next?" she asked.

"Dearborn's Livery, go two blocks, then turn left and a right on Garrison."

She looked uncertainly at him and finally nodded, clapping Ira on the butt to go faster.

Inside the livery, a whiskered man came out of the office, licking a lead pencil with a tag in his hand.

"Name?"

"Thurman Baker."

"Well, I'll be dogged gone. Captain Baker, that you?"

Thurman stepped down. "Who're you?"

"Why, Sergeant Reilly O'Brien, sir." He clicked his heels and saluted.

"I'll be damned, Sarge, how are you?"

"Fine. It's been a long time, sir."

"Yes, it has been. I need to leave Ira and my dog Blacky here, and we have several things in our buggy I want looked after."

"Cap'n, I'll be damn sure it's all here when you get ready to leave. Cross me heart."

"Good enough. Also, Mary and I need a clean hotel."

O'Brien scratched his ear. "The Palace is good as I know."

Mary rolled up some things of hers including her new dress. Putting on the moccasins, she smiled at Thurman. "You knew him?"

"In the war."

"You were an officer?" she asked as he guided her outside and to the edge of the busy street.

"I've been many things." Then he took her by the elbow past the beer wagons and riders to the far curb, then inside the lobby of the Palace.

He went to the desk and asked the clerk about a room.

"I have a room for you, sir. But she can't go in—"

Thurman's right fist shot out and he jerked the young man halfway over the counter to talk in his face. "She's my wife. You say one word and I'll cut your tongue out. Savvy?"

The man's face went to putty and he tried to swallow. He finally managed a croaking "Yes."

Thurman released him, and he about fell off the counter he'd been taken halfway over. Straightening his suit and tie, the clerk swallowed hard. "If you will sign in for both of you."

Thurman did that. "We will stay four nights."

"That will be ten—I mean eight—dollars for four nights, sir."

Thurman paid him, and the man marked paid on the four dates in the register.

"The room is on the second floor—206." The clerk put the key on the countertop.

They went up the stairs in silence.

When they got to the door marked 206, she stopped, looked up at him, and wet her lips. "I see why you were a captain."

Then her shoulders began to shake in mirth. In the room, she laughed aloud and in a falsetto voice said, "No damn Indians can be in here."

Amused, he went and opened the two windows. "Peel back the sheet. If you see one black bug we're leaving."

She pulled the spread and sheet aside and examined the bed closely. "No bugs."

"Good," he said, then grabbed her around the waist, lifted her up, and swung her around. "Is this better than the last time?"

Looking down at him, she smiled and removed his hat. "I think you should kiss me again."

Late that night, from the open window, he studied the traffic on Garrison Avenue and took a sip of whiskey from the new pint. The sounds and smells of the city wafted on the warm night air. Buy a stout horse and let her drive the buggy. In three days they'd be headed for Montana. He needed to find that boy.

NINE

THE music of a fiddle being tuned carried on the air. The atmosphere inside the schoolhouse tingled with excitement. Late arrivals rushed inside with pots of food and loaves of bread for the potluck. On a bench against the wall, Herschel sat with Marsha. They were eating their supper off tin plates and nodding to well-wishers going by.

"Nice to have you up here, Sheriff. Ma'am, you, too."

He thanked them and took another bite. Every woman there had wanted him to try something they'd brought, so his plate was covered with food for him to sample. He'd probably bust eating it all.

"You're looking for Roscoe Hatch?" Marsha asked in a whisper.

"Yes, he's the one supposedly knew Hamby, or maybe Hamby worked for Hatch. Shultz and that cowboy both mentioned it the morning we brought in the body."

"I thought so. Would you eat some cherry pie if I got you a piece on my plate?"

"Might save me from having to eat some of everyone's dessert."

"I'll do that." She squeezed his forearm. "I'm really enjoying you doing this, and the lovely cameo was such a surprise."

"I guess at times, Marsha, I get so involved in what I must do, I plumb forget it's the little things that count."

"No, no, you do fine." She rose and winked at him. "But sometimes you shock me."

Good thing. She and the girls had turned his life around. From an oatmeal-eating bachelor to a comfortably married man with a family. He felt that way, too. Having a wife had never seriously entered his mind before he became involved with her. He was lucky that Marsha saw something worth having in him. Why, he'd about run away from any other woman that even tried to get close. They gave him the jitters whenever he thought things were getting serious. But with her, it turned out different.

She returned with his piece of pie and traded him plates.

"Looks good."

"It was the best one I saw over there."

She took up the seat beside him. "I may have forgotten how to dance," she said.

"Naw. It comes back when they play the music."

After he ate the pie, she carried their cups and utensils outside to wash them in the hot water tub set up, and then put them away.

Shultz soon took a seat beside Herschel. "I heard you learned his name."

"Hamby, Wallace Hamby. And he was shot wearing a slicker."

"How did you find that out? He didn't have one on that morning."

"Oh, I know lots more things about that dead man now."

"Why would someone have murdered him?"

"I'll know more about that when I get back to Billings."

Shultz nodded, looking impressed. "Most folks don't know how hard you work to solve these crimes."

"Save that for reelection time." Herschel looked around the room. "I don't know Roscoe Hatch very well. Have you seen him here tonight?"

"That's what I came over to tell you. When I was unsaddling my horse outside a while ago, Roscoe and three of his hands rode up. I heard someone say the sheriff's here. Roscoe said something to his boys, then they turned and rode off."

"That's a shame. I had some questions to ask him about Hamby."

"I figured you'd want to talk to him."

"Who said the sheriff is here, do you recall?"

"By Jove, let me think. I never thought about it at the time, but he might be in on something with Roscoe."

Herschel nodded. "Might be. I'd like to talk to him anyway."

"Oh, shoot, I'll remember his name after a while and tell you. Oh, do you mind if I dance with your wife a few times?"

"Better ask her. She'll be back here shortly."

Shultz thanked him and started off to talk to some others.

"Learn anything?" Marsha asked when she returned.

"Shultz asked to dance with you."

"Oh."

"He also said that Hatch came tonight and someone told him I was here and he left."

"Was he afraid of you?"

"I don't know, Marsha. But it would be strange for him to avoid me unless he'd done something wrong."

"Excuse me, Mrs. Baker, they're going to play some slow music first. Would you dance with me?" Shultz asked.

Herschel nodded and smiled, amused because she was taller by five inches than the cattle buyer.

"Oh," Shultz said to Herschel. "I think it was Hans Olsen told him you were here."

"Thanks." Herschel looked though the crowd for the blond Dane. Shultz led Marsha off for the first dance. The sheriff stood up and stretched, then realized that the man he wanted wasn't inside and headed for the front door.

He knew there would be several men outside nipping on a bottle or jug. That was what some of them came for. In the dying sundown, a handful was gathered around a bonfire more for light than heat in the warm spring night.

"Would we offend you, sir," a man said, "if we offered you a drink?"

"Thanks, but not now. I'm looking for Hans Olsen. Is he around?"

"What's he done?" someone asked.

Herschel shook his head. "Nothing. I just need to talk to him. I'm up here with the missus to enjoy the fine weather and dance a little."

"We'll tell him you're needing to talk to him."

"Thanks."

He went to check on his horses on the picket line by the wagon off at the edge of the large school yard. They were standing hipshot and all looked fine. He started back for the dance, and two men approached from the bonfire area. Obviously, they had business with him or wanted to talk with him privately.

"Sheriff Baker, my name's Clem Shaefer and this is my

neighbor John Dart. You know we have a problem up here?"

"Oh?" He shook their calloused hands.

"I call it"—Shaefer looked around to be certain they were alone—"dealing with a bully. I had a springing heifer. She was staying up on small creek and I was keeping an eye on her. Rode up there every day and checked on her in case she had trouble calving."

Herschel understood calving heifers and the problems associated with them.

"Well, I rode up there one morning and she was gone. I found where someone had gutted her. Blood was all over the ground. Hide and all, they took it everything with 'em."

"You know who did it?"

"Wagon tracks went east."

"Who lives in that direction?" Herschel asked.

"Roscoe Hatch."

"You think he butchered your heifer?"

"Accuse him and face his wrath?" The man shook his head. "I couldn't do that. I've got a wife and three kids to think about."

"That goes on all the time up here," Dart says. "He sells his beef over at Miles City."

"That's a ways to take it."

"Yeah, but if beef don't cost you anything, it will sure make money," Shaefer said.

"I can't accuse him of stealing without proof. Let me work on it. He's stealing beef, we can catch him at it."

"It's hard enough to make a living up here," Dart said. "Someone stealing your stock makes it even harder."

"I agree and we can stop it. May take me some time. He sounds pretty smooth. Either of you seen Olsen around here?"

"Earlier. Ain't seen him in a while. You need him, I'll tell him if I see him again," Dart said.

Herschel shook his head. "Don't mention it. I'll find him."

No need to spook him, too. This cattle rustling business sounded serious. The question was how many others were doing it. Somehow, there must be more than Hatch if they were selling beef clear over at Miles City.

Monday, he'd telegraph Sheriff Don Harold and ask him to look into the sales if there were any he could learn about. That would be a start. This job never ended. He shook the men's hands and thanked them, promising to do some investigating. No sign of Olsen. Strange that the man would come to a social function, warn someone, and then leave. They were some things that needed close scrutiny in this part of the county.

Herschel rejoined his wife, and they danced to a waltz. As she swirled around floor to the fiddle, she smiled up at him. "Find Olsen?"

"No, he seems to have evaporated. Strange there is no sign of him."

"What do they have to hide from you?"

"I'll tell you later what I think."

She smiled and nodded, obviously enjoying the opportunity to have a dance with him. With her in his arms, he could waltz across Montana—at least the smooth schoolhouse floor part. He nodded to people he knew as they circled around the room. For a few minutes with her in his arms, he was on a cloud above the rest of the world. Far away from the problems of his office and life itself—it was heady. He should do this more often.

After the waltz, she went for some cold lemonade, a sugary mixture of the sour fruit and chunks of river ice floating in the vast bowl like icebergs. She returned with both cups filled and he thanked her.

"If this is sheriffing, we need to do this more often," she said.

He sipped his drink and smiled at her. "Make this job look too easy and everyone will want it."

"I doubt that."

"There are always folks want your position in life. Take Shultz, he wants a wife."

"Not me, I hope." She suppressed her amusement as best she could. "He'd need a ladder to even get in our bed."

"That don't keep him from wanting the job."

They both laughed. How long since they'd laughed together? Too long. Maybe they should move back to her ranch. He could break and trade horses again—they'd make a living. Sleep every night in their own bed together. Let someone else take over all the worries about lawbreakers in Yellowstone County.

Sure, and eat oatmeal again. The girls would really love that. No, he was probably where he belonged—in politics and making enough money to pay for their place in town as well as their lifestyle.

After the dance, Herschel and Marsha camped in the cool night air and snuggled in the bedroll with her silky skin pressed against his. She wore no nightgown, so his hands could explore every inch of her with his palms. He closed his eyes, hugged her tight, and thanked God for her.

"What will you do next week?"

"Go find Roscoe Hatch. If he wasn't in on murdering Hamby, he may be guilty of rustling."

She snuggled to him. "What if we have to get up in the night?"

"Guess we better dress then or the stars will see our bare butts."

"Herschel." Then they giggled.

Morning came too quick. He built a fire and she made coffee while the Dutch oven heated. Shultz came by and she invited him to breakfast. Before long, she was making more coffee and feeding the hat-in-hand single friends of Herschel who had supposedly just dropped by to say howdy.

"You don't need to feed every dog-eyed cowboy in camp," he said under his breath, putting more fuel under the grill.

"Maybe they'll vote for you." She shared a mischievous grin with him as she bent over checking on her biscuits. "Stir the gravy and the potatoes."

"How close are the biscuits?"

"A few more minutes."

Shultz was grinding more coffee for the next pot. A cowboy named Poke was peeling spuds, and Marsha had more dough mixed for the next batch. She was enjoying the attention, Herschel could tell. Everyone ate till she finally ran out, and then they stayed, helped her clean up, and packed everything in the buckboard. Because of having to feed her army, they were almost late for church services in the schoolhouse. Voices were raised singing the first hymn when they went inside and, along with her "eaters," finished filling the classroom.

After services, several folks invited them to come back and they promised to return. The two of them drove out with four cowboys trailing along, each dropping off at various side roads with a big thank-you and a high wave.

"Nice folks up at Soda Springs," she said as the buckskins jogged along at a brisk pace. A cooler wind swept over his face as he agreed. Montana was full of nice folks—it was the un-nice ones that were his problem.

He only had one regret—he had not learned one thing about Hatch's connection to Hamby. That meant he'd have to ride back up there and find out more. And see what else he could learn about Roscoe Hatch.

TEN

THE next day, Thurman's trip to the federal courthouse went more smoothly. The supervisor was there and after looking over his receipts, issued him two warrants for fifty dollars each.

"Now of course, these can only be redeemed when there is money in the federal coffer to pay them. However, several folks in Fort Smith will redeem them at a discount."

"Marshal Morris warned me about that."

"Good, then you know."

"Yes. Thank you, sir."

Thurman left and walked back to Garrison Avenue and the Palace. In the hotel room, Mary was busy sewing, so he went out, found a barbershop, and got a haircut and a shave.

"You new here?" asked the mustachioed barber.

"Passing through. Had a couple of rewards to collect."

The barber laughed and said to his colleague, "He's got some rewards."

"What'll he take for 'em?" the other barber asked.

"Forty apiece," Thurman said.

The barber quit cutting his client's hair and shook his head. "You're too damn high."

"That's twenty percent interest." Under the sheet, Thurman shuddered at the notion of giving that much away.

"You borrowed any money lately?" his barber asked.

"No."

"The going rate around here's twenty-five percent."

"That's risk money—this is U.S. script."

"Governments fail, too."

Thurman knew there was no way he would win the argument, so he let it go. He listened to their talk that the federal government was going to open up some of the unused Indian lands for white settlers.

Finished, he paid the man a quarter and headed down the sidewalk past the panhandlers, the expensive ladies of the evening in their rustling satin gowns laughing about the night before, and the ordinary folks. Swampers dumped slop buckets and spittoons off the curb from inside the stale-smelling joints. A few blacks with handcarts were sweeping up and shoveling horse manure off Garrison.

He reached Dearborn's stables and ducked inside.

A familiar rusty voice welcomed him as Thurman petted Blacky, who was tied to a rope.

He turned and asked, "How're you doing, Sarge?"

"Fine. What do you need? You ain't leaving already?"

"No, I need a good saddle horse. I've got a far piece to ride."

"How fur?"

"Montana."

"Woo-wee, you do have a long ways to go. I know a man's got a good Morgan horse. He's a chestnut the color of good polished furniture. They used him as a stud for a while—but that only made him a more muscled horse."

"How old is he?"

"Four going on five."

"What's he asking for him?"

Sarge scratched his bushy sideburns and gave a pained look. "Hundred and a half."

"Wow, he must be some horse."

"Cap'n, he's as stout and sound a horse as I know about. He's a little spooky of things, but I think you riding him hard, he'd lose lots of that."

"When can I try him?"

Sarge paused. "The man owns him is pretty well stuck on that price."

"I want to ride him before I even say any more."

"I'll have him here in the morning for you."

"Good, I'll look for him then."

"Yes, sir, Cap'n. I wondered a lot about where you went after the war and all. You go home and ranch in Texas?"

"I did that for a while." He scratched Blacky's ears. "Traded cattle and horses. Took some herds to Kansas."

"Your children grown up now, ain't they?"

Thurman nodded. "That's who I'm going to Montana to try and find. My oldest son, Herschel."

"Oh, both my two boys are dead, Cap'n. One got killed in a gunfight over in the Nation. The other drowned. My daughter, Effie, married an outlaw and Parker hung him. She takes care of me—got a couple of kids. You never knew, of course, but my wife, Eleanor, died before I got back home from Mississippi. I just always somehow figured you and your family was doing good at ranching in Texas."

Thurman nodded. "Been some bumps in the road for all of us since that time."

"Sure have, sir. I'll have that good hoss here in the morning."

Thurman told him thanks and went to see about Mary. The day was warming up and it had the muggy feeling of a storm building. Grateful he wasn't worried about holding a herd in the face of one of the furious storms that could sweep across the Indian Territory, he moved along the busy sidewalk toward the hotel.

"Baker. Baker, wait up."

He turned and saw a face that looked familiar. A man in his forties dressed in a cheap suit was hurrying to catch him.

"How have you been?" The man stuck out his hand. "Nelson Manner. You remember me from Fort Worth? I set up the Carlille Cattle drive you ramrodded."

The man's face appeared tired, and from the look of his dress, he must have fallen on hard times. His gaze even appeared hollow.

"Yes, I remember you now. What are you doing here?"

"Working on a contract to sell beef to these Indian agencies. Man, the red tape!" Manner glanced up at the saloon sign. "You have a minute? I might have a deal that would interest you."

When they stepped inside, Thurman noticed the saloon was empty save for two grizzly swampers cleaning up. The bartender drew them two drafts, and Thurman paid for them. Manner guided him over to a side table where enough light came in from outside over the short curtain that kept the street passersby from having to look into the sin pot.

"At last I have a valid contract for delivery of a thousand head to each of three Injun agencies." He spread the papers out on the table. "Now, before I go to Fort Worth and find me a partner, I wanted for you to take a look at this opportunity. It'll make us both rich."

Thurman glanced over the papers, set them back down, and took a sip of the beer.

"It's a deal, ain't it?" Manner said.

"If the roads were open and there was no barbed wire in the way, yes, you could make some money. But the only way to get those cattle up here anymore is by rail, and that will kill this deal."

"Oh, no. No, you have it all wrong. Some tough hands and a good trail boss could drive a thousand head up here, say, from San Antonio."

"I wish you luck, my friend. I just covered that country. There is no way to get a thousand head up here. The trail's closed to cattle. It's a freight route. Jessie Chisholm would turn over in his grave if he knew that—his namesake reduced to a freight road and all the Indians he used to trade with now on reservations with nothing to swap for but government handouts."

Manner drew his head back in shocked disbelief. "You've lost all your nerve?"

Thurman looked over at the man mildly. "I'm not the man I was ten years ago. But I just rode up here from south Texas. The western routes are all that's left to drive cattle over."

With the back of his fingers, Manner rapped the contract on the table. "There's twenty thousand dollars in this deal. I'd split it with you. Having a professional like you in charge, I can raise the money and then we can buy the cattle—buy them cheap in Mexico."

Calmly, Thurman shook his head. "I ain't going back there either."

"Aw, hell, where's your guts? I'm offering you over ten thousand dollars to head up this deal."

"Gawdamnit, it's not there. The cattle ain't down there in Mexico anymore. The roads are fenced. There's not any free range to drive them over. I can't help you." He rose over the chair and then downed his mug of beer. Wiping his mouth on the back of his hand, he asked, "You need some money?"

Red-faced, Manners looked up at him. "I didn't come to beg money off you. I have a valid deal here."

"I'll stake you to thirty bucks. That's more than the train fare to Fort Worth. Maybe there's men there more foolhardy than I am." Thurman tossed the three tens on the table. "Good luck, but I've warned you."

Collapsing in defeat, Manners slid the bills between his fingers, not looking up. "Thanks, Thurman."

With a nod, Thurman left the saloon.

Out in the warm daylight, he felt free. He had a deal of his own. A project he wanted to complete. He stuck his head in a delicatessen and spoke to a square-shouldered, blond Dutch woman. "I want a picnic basket with fried chicken, fresh bread, butter, some sweet rolls or pie, silverware, plates, and two bottles of good wine. I'll bring the basket and silverware back."

"I have it ready at eleven o'clock," she announced. "And what is *dee* name?"

"Thurman Baker."

"Fine, Mr. Baker. It *vill* be delicious."

"I'm counting on that." He waved and went back on the street. Outside in the bright sunshine, he caught an older street urchin by the sleeve. "Can you drive a horse and buggy?"

The youth swept the dark lock of hair back from his face and looked hard at Thurman's hand holding his sleeve. "Sure. Why?"

"Go to Dearborn's Livery and talk to Sarge. Have him hitch Captain Baker's mule to the buggy, put my dog in back, and drive him down here to the Palace Hotel. You park in front and wait for me."

The boy's brown eyes bugged out when Thurman tore a dollar bill in two, giving him half of it. "You get the other half when you deliver my buggy."

"Yes, sir, Cap'n Baker, sir."

The brat did have manners. Thurman nodded and looked at the sun time, then spoke again to the boy "Walk, don't run. You have an hour to get back there."

"Yes, sir."

"Repeat what I told you."

He flipped back the hair. "Tell Sarge at Dearborn's that I am to drive Captain Thurman's buggy down to the Palace Hotel for him—and get his dog."

"Not bad. See you in an hour."

"Yes, sir," And the boy was gone down the crowded sidewalk.

Thurman went into the hotel and up to their room. Mary sat on the bed, sewing on the new dress material he'd bought her for the more loosely fitting dress she'd need on the trip. He removed his hat and placed it on the dresser, crown side down.

"I have a surprise. We are going on a picnic," he announced.

"A what?"

"Lunch on the ground." He went to the window and looked down at the traffic. Poor girl, she had no idea what a picnic was. For his part, he hadn't been on many. The better ones were with that other woman in his life on the river outside San Antonio. Maybe she'd taught him picnic etiquette.

"We're going over to the free ferry side of town and spread a blanket on the ground, eat some lunch, sip some wine, and watch the paddleboats go by."

"That sounds nice. What about the saddle horse?"

"I am supposed to look at him in the morning. Today is your day."

She nodded, gathered the dress-to-be from her lap, and scooted off the bed. "Would I look less like a squaw if I cut my braids?"

He hugged her by the waist and rocked her. "Don't cut your braids. You're fine for me. Where we are going, it won't matter anyway."

"The horse?"

"My old sarge says he's a helluva horse."

"Picnic?" She looked up at him. "Are they fun?"

"With you along, it will be heavenly."

She laughed aloud, then hugged him.

Long past noontime, the toot of a riverboat going past accompanied him as he sliced the hard-crusted French bread. On her knees, she was eating a crisp fried chicken leg and laughing. "Now I know what a picnic is all about."

He buttered some bread and fed her a bite. "This tastes good with wine."

"The wine tastes good anyway. All I ever had before was made from possum grapes, and it wasn't near this good."

"We could get on that boat, go to Memphis, and ride a riverboat clear to Montana."

"No. It would be too much like a ferry." She tossed the bare white bone in the bushes and Blacky ran to recover it.

"Fine, we'll drive Ira, lead my new horse, and go across country."

"You aren't mad at me for not taking the boat?"

"I get mad, you'll know it."

She looked at him and then she nodded. "I'll try not to do that. Make you mad at me."

He raised up and kissed her.

When he released her, she nodded and smiled. "Can I ask you a question?"

"Sure, what is it?"

"If your son won't join you in this ranch business, what then?"

He tossed some pinched-off grass in the air. No wind. It was growing hotter. He put his index finger inside his collar for some more room to swallow. "I'll deal with that when it happens. Do you know anything more from your visions?"

"No."

"Then I guess we'll find out when we get there."

She nodded, rose on her knees, and threw her arms around him. Her sobbing pulsated in his tight hug and tears ran down her copper face. "Thurman Baker, where have you been for all my life?"

Off chasing elusive sundowns like Manner was today, but not anymore.

ELEVEN

WHEN they arrived home from Soda Springs in the late evening, Herschel let Marsha off at the house, kissed her, and promised to be back after he checked on the jail. With her waving after him, he drove the buckskins the four blocks to the courthouse and hitched them out in front.

To his dismay, he found Art half asleep in his chair. He cleared his throat and Art sat up. "You back?"

Herschel glanced over at Phil, asleep on the floor. "Can't you guys go home? Your wives mad at you?"

"No, sir. We've had some problems last night, but they're all wound up now. We think."

Phil sat up cross-legged and rubbed his sleepy face with his palms. "About ten o'clock—" He yawned and covered his mouth. "Last night, we had some folks that wanted to swing the store robber and anyone else in the jail."

"What did you do?"

"We did what we thought you'd do. We went down to

the Antelope Saloon and shot a hole in the ceiling to get their attention."

Art nodded. "We told 'em to disperse and go home or we'd jail the whole lot of them."

"Must have worked."

"It did, but there's still rumors going around they'll be back for the necktie party."

"You boys go home. One of you needs to get Marsha word on the way that I'm staying up here. Oh, and take my team home as well."

"Hell, this was supposed to be your weekend off."

"You're both worn out. Go home."

Art stood and rubbed the back of his neck. "You learn anything up there?"

"Yes, there may be more than a murder going on up there."

"What else?" Phil asked.

"They say this Roscoe Hatch is butchering other folks' cattle and selling the meat in Miles City."

"How do we catch him at that?"

"I'm working on that. I also learned that, when someone told him I was at the dance, he tucked tail and ran."

"Sounds like he's acting guilty to me," Phil said.

Herschel shook his head. "No telling, but there's lots of small folks upset over his bullying them out of reporting anything."

"What do we need to do?"

"I'll take the stage to Miles City and talk to Don Harold, the new sheriff. He may have some ideas on Hatch's operation. Oh, Phil, did we get a description out on the other two store robbers?"

"Yes, sir, but it's so vague, you could find six other guys in this town fit it."

"I suspected that. What about money—did Hamby have any we didn't know about?"

"Seven hundred dollars was wired here from Michigan to the Cattleman's Bank."

"When?"

"He picked it up the day before you found him dead."

"He spend any of it in town that we know about?"

Art nodded. "He spent some of it the next morning in Madame Shiner's Parlor House."

"Who was with him?"

"Some Dane lives up there near Soda Springs."

"Olsen his name?"

With a questioning look, Art nodded. "You know him?"

Herschel made a face. "He's the one that warned Hatch I was there, according to Shultz, and then took a powder himself. Who's the loudmouth caused all the lynch problems last night?"

"Link Colter," Art said.

"Was he acting on his own?"

"Some folks think he's being paid by those big ranchers that's left. They like quick justice—it scares out all the criminal element, they think."

"You two start watching and listening. I want to know who Colter works for."

"He don't have a job and he always has money to buy beer," Phil put in.

"Why not give Joe Black Feather ten bucks? He could tell us everywhere Colter goes in a week," Art said.

Herschel looked out at the darkening street bathed in the fiery sundown. "I may do that. Thanks. Get some rest. We need to settle some of these cases."

After the two left, he went back to talk to his jailer, Wally Simms. The big man was cleaning and oiling some of the rifles out of his armory. The smell of gun oil hung strong in the office.

"About a half hour from now, I want to slip out the back door. I won't be far from the jail in case anything breaks loose or if I learn anything."

Simms nodded. "You want me to let you out and then lock the door again, right?"

"Yes. And bar it."

"I will. I thought them deputies did a great job last night."

"They did. But I figure it ain't over yet."

Simms nodded. "It's in their blood, ain't it?"

"The lawlessness in Montana caused a ground swell, I guess. Now it's going to be hard to go back to the right ways of handling the law. Hanging a man without a legal trial is anarchy. And as we've learned around here, some men are hung because they got in someone's way."

"Aye, Hersch, but you be careful. Them boys are good, but they ain't like you out there. This county needs you."

"We'll see, Simms, come the next election."

"Why, if you don't get reelected, there's a bunch of damn fools running around out there."

"Thanks. I'll need every vote I can get." He headed into his office to look over his paperwork to kill some time—it would be dark outside in thirty minutes.

Forty-five minutes later, he slipped into the alley, thanked Simms in a low voice, and headed west. He liked checking saloons from the back door. Slipping in and out the same way caught people off their guard. He needed every edge there was in times like these when trouble from the public threatened to erupt. Maybe, he thought as his boot soles ground on the gritty surface and alley cats accompanied him, the boys had done a good enough job to shut it down.

In that case, he could go home and go to bed with Marsha.

The Sunday night crowd in the Red Horse was thin, and there was no trouble in sight. Patrick, the burly, red-faced bartender, gave him an all-clear nod, and Herschel went back out to join the alley cats. The Antelope was next, and he eased inside the back door. Standing at the end of the dark hallway, he listened to two men talking to each other at a table in the back.

". . . that don't make any sense."

"You . . ." The man lowered his voice so Herschel couldn't hear him.

"Ah, hell."

"I swear to God, he told me that—"

"What's Anton doing?"

"He says he ain't going. But I know he don't want to sit in prison again."

"Can he do that?"

"He's the damn sheriff, I guess he can."

Herschel eased out the back door and closed it quietly. In the next half hour, he found nothing happening in any of the saloons—Sunday night and all. So they were worried about his authority to evict Pleago. All he really cared about in that deal was that the gentleman better be packing his bags.

He checked in with Simms, then walked under the stars the four blocks to his place. At a distance, he could hear the bench swing creaking in the shadows of the porch.

"Past your bedtime," he said to his wife from the bottom of the porch steps.

"I was just letting the wonderful time we had this weekend simmer into me. You settle the lynching situation Art told me about?"

"Art and Phil must have. It gets worse and the troublemakers figure out that wounded man is over at doc's and not in my jail, I might have more problems."

She nodded and patted the place beside her. "Join me."

He sat down, put his arm around her shoulder over the shawl she wore against the night air. Then, with his feet on the porch floor, he shoved off for a swing.

"I love this place. The house, the whole setup. We have everything so nice here, I don't want you to think I'm upset in any way, but—" She snuggled against him. "Is this where we're going to be forever?"

"You restless?"

"No. Herschel, I want to be where you are. You know I'd support you in whatever you wanted to do. I just wondered if you ever thought of anything else you wanted to do."

"Not really. I like this job—*today*."

She clapped the top of his leg beside her. "Do you miss ranching, breaking horses?"

"Some."

"I wondered—" Then she gathered her dress and climbed up to straddle his lap. She looked him in the eye. "Are you happy with me and my girls?"

He reached out and hugged her. "Best damn thing I ever did was hitch up with you and the girls. I still laugh about the time I told Nina that I ate oatmeal all the time when I was a bachelor."

"Shocked her, I remember. Did you have supper?"

"No."

"I'll fix you something."

He hugged her, smelling the faint wisp of lavender. "Not yet. I can eat a bowl of oatmeal later."

In a deep embrace, they both laughed. It was sure easing for him to just hold her and savor all the good things in his life.

* * *

He was up at daylight the next morning, and drank his coffee on the porch and took note of the clouds. Felt like
moisture in the air. They might have rain. Range grasses
and the crops this time of year could use all the sky could
squeeze out.

"Your breakfast is ready," Marsha said from the doorway.

He nodded when he saw her standing in the coolness of
the first light. "I'm coming."

"What's on the sheriff's agenda today?" she asked, de-
livering the flapjacks and fried eggs on his plate. The
golden brown biscuits and the gravy bowl were close by on
his side of the table.

"Wire Miles City and see if Sheriff Harold knows anything about Hatch's beef business. I also need to find out
more about the money Hamby collected the day before his
death."

"You think he was murdered for that money?"

"I suspect that. But proving it may be harder. This whole
deal up there needs to be straightened out. A murder, a
possible robbery, bullying people, and the beef-stealing
business."

"What about the horse rustlers?"

"I can hold them another ten days. Maybe someone will
contact us. Phil put wires out on them. Many of these
places may want them for trial but don't have the money to
send someone after them."

"So they can go scot-free then?"

"It's possible. I can't prove they stole those horses. They
can't prove they bought them."

Refilling his coffee cup, she laughed. "That is a di-
lemma."

"Oh, there's more of those kind of deals in this business

than you can ever imagine." Lots more than he'd ever dreamed there would be.

Later at his office, a boy from the telegraph office brought him a wire.

SHERIFF BAKER STOP HOLD TWO MEN DOFF PORTER AND CLYDE SNYDER STOP THEY ARE WANTED IN MY JURISDICTION FOR VARIOUS CRIMES STOP UPON RECEIPT OF YOUR WIRE THAT THEY ARE STILL IN YOUR CUSTODY I WILL DISPATCH DEPUTY TO BILLINGS MONTANA TO BRING THEM BACK TO STAND TRIAL HERE IN NORTH PLATTE NEBRASKA STOP SHERIFF RAYMAN STOUD END

"Any reply sir?"

"Yes. I'll write it out and you can take it back with you." He took up a pen and wrote out the telegram back to Sheriff Stoud. "There, you can send that for me."

"Yes, sir."

After the boy left, Herschel told his assistant Darby he would return shortly and went back into the jail. He found the two prisoners lounging in their cell.

"I just got a wire from North Platte and Sheriff Stoud."

"Huh?" the taller one said, and came to hold the bars in his hands.

"Stoud says you two are wanted down there and he's sending a deputy up here to take you back for trial."

"What else did he say?" Porter asked, lying on his back on the bunk.

"That's all. I want some answers about that cabin."

"Hey," Porter said, sitting up and swinging his legs off the bed. "We didn't do one bloody thing in your district."

"Was there anything else in the shack?"

"That slicker and hat was all we found."

Herschel nodded. "No money that you stashed?"

"Huh, what money?" Snyder asked.

"The man that you shot had over six hundred dollars in cash on him."

"Man! We shot? We didn't shoot anyone. You think if we'd got six hundred bucks we'd been hiding out there?" Snyder asked.

"Yes," Herschel said. "Keeping low. Anything else you saw in that cabin when you got there?"

"I could still smell the gun smoke inside," Porter said, and his partner agreed. "But there wasn't anyone around or we'd have ridden on. The slicker was lying on the floor and the hat was under the table. We saw the bullet holes and the blood and wondered about it."

"We kinda thought they'd started a grave in the dirt floor, and gave up 'cause maybe they didn't have a shovel," Snyder said.

"There wasn't any other thing you noticed?" Herschel waited.

"We didn't want no part of that slicker with two bullet holes in it and that blood," Snyder said.

"What time did you get there?"

"Oh, about four in the afternoon the day before. We're telling you the truth."

Herschel nodded. "Who was coming to buy those horses?"

Both men looked shocked, and quickly frowned at each other. He'd obviously discovered a chink in their story.

"No one," Porter said as if to rectify their mistake.

"I want his name," Herschel said. "The man who was coming to buy those horses."

He turned on his heel, not wanting to listen to their denials. He felt certain that they were up there at that place to do business with a buyer.

"We weren't meeting anyone there!" Porter's voice screeched after him as he walked out of the jail.

He'd have to see about that.

TWELVE

THURMAN squatted on his boot heels and watched Sarge saddling the stout-looking bay horse. Earlier that morning, a black youth riding a flea-bitten mare had delivered the fine horse and now acted like he knew all about him.

"You ever ride him, boy?" Thurman asked.

"No, sir, that hoss he belongs to *de* boss man. I's never ride him."

"Is he a handful?"

The boy shrugged his thin shoulders under the crudely made shirt he wore.

"Mathew there, he ain't no jockey." Sarge slapped down the stirrup and brought the bay over to him.

"Just wondering," Thurman said, and took the rein, led the horse into the street, and stuck a boot toe in the stirrup. Hand on the horn, he proceeded to swing up and sit in the saddle. No surprise when the horse ducked his head and went off into the early morning traffic crow-hopping. There were halfhearted jumps and stiff-legged hops out through the drays, carts, and startled pedestrians. Some were yelling for Thurman to succeed. Others were cursing both him and the horse.

He didn't care, sawing on the bay's mouth. There was a name for this horse that fit him—Buck. The horse was still upset at the end of a block's worth of bucking, and Thurman brought him to a stop and patted his neck. "I bet by the time we get to Montana, Buck, you'll have all that foolishness out of you."

"What do you think now?" Sarge asked when Thurman rode back to the livery and dismounted.

"Tell the man I have a hundred dollars in warrants from Parker's Court and twenty-five dollars cash I'll pay for the horse."

"I don't know about them warrants, Cap'n."

"This way, he'll get his money eventually and not have to feed the horse while he's looking for another high-powered buyer."

"I have to admit there ain't many buyers looking for that much hoss."

"If he don't want to make the swap with me, look for another pony. There's bound to be others for sale."

Sarge nodded and began to unsaddle the bay. "I'll let you know by this afternoon."

"Fine."

Thurman went by and petted Blacky. He hadn't been attracted by a dog in years. Blacky suited him and minded well enough. In time, he'd have him trained even better. A good dog, like an attentive horse, could be your best eyes and ears. He looked back at the thick-necked horse—he was damn sure powerful.

Thurman played poker for a few hours in the Border City Saloon. Cards weren't coming his way. So he excused himself and picked up his money, making a mental calculation that he'd lost about thirty dollars.

"Come back again," a tinhorn named Kyle said after him.

"I will if I'm still in town."

"Where you headed?"

"North," Thurman said over his shoulder from the batwing doors.

"Don't let one of them polar bears bite you in the ass. I hear they got sharp teeth."

He waved, and went on out hearing everyone's laughter.

In the hotel hallway, he unlocked the door. Mary looked up from her sewing when he came in.

"How was the horse?"

"Good. He bucked a little. But he was upset about the traffic and things going on around him. I made an offer. The owner's liable to accept it."

"Blacky all right?"

"Anxious to get the hell out of here."

She laughed. "So am I."

"I find a horse, then we can go. How is the dress coming?"

"Fine."

She held it up in front of her and he agreed. "Nice job. It's been keeping you busy."

"Yes."

He hugged and rocked her in his arms. "We'll be on our way shortly."

"Good. I could never live here. There are too many spirits in this place."

"Good or bad ones?"

"Some are very bad."

She shuddered in his arms, as if repelled by the thought

of them. With the side of his hand, he raised her chin. "I'm sorry. We'll move on."

"I will be glad."

That evening, Sarge sent him word the seller had accepted his terms. So they prepared to leave Fort Smith at first light the next morning. He'd studied a map and decided to head northwest to Fort Gibson. The Marcy Road westward didn't seem to be the best way for him to go to Council Oaks or some other intersection on the Chisholm Trail.

Under a cloudy predawn, they crossed on the ferry, and Thurman stood by Buck in case the whistle or paddle wheel spooked him. When the ferry docked, he hitched Buck on the back and drove the rig off for her. When they reached the top of the cross-tie ramp, she reached over to squeeze his arm and then nodded in approval. He glanced back to see the outline of the taller buildings and nodded. Blacky minded him while they passed the shantytown and kept close to the rig.

The traffic on the road west consisted of wagon trains powered by oxen. Thurman drove past freighters on foot who waved, cracking whips and swearing at the lazy animals. The acres and acres of cotton fields they drove past were hardly out of the two-leaf stage. The sight of them only made him want to drive the mule faster—if there were boogers in Fort Smith for her, there were more in this farmland for him.

That evening, they camped in a small grove of persimmon and oaks. He gathered enough wood for her to cook with. While she fixed supper, he curried down the horse and mule tied on a picket line between two post oaks. He fed them both corn in feed bags, and the sundown was dipping low when she called him to eat.

He washed his hands in the water that was heating to wash her dishes in, and smiled taking the tin plate from her. There was cured ham, fried potatoes, and big biscuits. Seated cross-legged on the ground, he thought about all the meals of hard jerky he'd shared with himself at sundown. How fortunate he was to have her along on this trip.

"I'll be glad when we are beyond the Nation," she said, pouring his coffee.

"It won't be long till we're there. You still worried about Chickenhead?"

She nodded, taking a place to sit on the ground facing him. The flames of the small orange fire reflected off her olive complexion in the gathering darkness. Hatless, she held her head high, and her thick braids swung behind her back like willow limbs in a soft breeze.

"What is this ranch in Texas like?" she asked.

He thought about it. "It is a green place with water seeps, marshes, and springs. There are tall cottonwoods and cattails all in the middle of the range, which is strictly prickly pear cactus, mesquite, and grass."

"Range?"

"Means dry land."

She nodded.

"The house is not much more than your cabin. But I'll build you a better one."

"If I have a roof, food, and—you, I will be fine."

He closed his eyes while chewing on a bite of hot biscuit. She'd probably tramp through Hell with him—different anyway than most women.

It was Blacky's growl in the night that made him open his eyes and close his fingers around the redwood grips of the .44. He glanced over. Mary must have heard it, too. He nodded at her. Someone or something was out there. With care, he eased the blanket back and rose to his knees to peer in the starlight to try and see what had the dog's hackles up.

"Easy, Blacky," he said under his breath, not finding anything out of place in the silver-tinted night. But the dog was facing the south and some scent on the soft wind had him upset.

"It's him," she hissed, picking up his rifle and easing a cartridge in the chamber.

"Stay down so you don't make a target. They must be across the road." He bellied himself on the ground to face that direction. "Blacky, get back here."

A horse snorted in the night. It wasn't one of their animals. The sound came from the grove of trees across the road. Beside him, Blacky's throaty growl showed his anger over the intruders.

"Have you seen them?" she asked.

"No," he said, straining to look for any movement in the darkness.

Then Blacky whirled and Thurman did the same and cocked the pistol as he did. The outline of a person stepped from behind a small tree not twenty feet away. The .44 roared in Thurman's fist, and he saw the orange flames from the other person's handgun pointed at the ground. Good, he was down. Thurman rolled back around, wondering about any others.

Before he could do anything to stop him, Blacky charged the man he had shot. The dog's angry growls went with him as he tore apart anything that his teeth caught on—clothing or flesh.

Thurman holstered his pistol and took the rifle from Mary. "Stop him. I'm going to see if there are any more."

She agreed, hurrying to her feet and talking sternly to the furious dog.

On his bare feet, Thurman walked across the open ground to the road with the rifle ready. Sticks and stiff stems all tried to puncture his soles, but his intense focus was on the dark woods for any movement. Then he saw a figure move in the trees, and dropped to his knees. He could only see a flash in the iron sights, but he put three fast shots where he thought the person was.

After the third shot, someone screamed. "I'm hit. Don't leave me."

Despite the objects jabbing his feet, he ran across the road and searched in the night for any other intruders. A horse raced away, and someone cursed loudly on the hill about its escape.

There were others still over there. Gulping for his breath and feeling cold chills run up his cheek from the pain in his feet, he leaned on a great tree and listened. He could hear a tethered horse or two stomping their hoofs close by. That meant their mounts were to his right.

Maybe he had them cut off from their horses. Placing his steps with care, he moved toward their ponies. Blacky joined him. Still upset, the dog slipped against his leg looking for a scratch on the head, then threw up his nose and immediately began to growl.

"Easy, boy," he said to the dog and petted him. He crossed a small open spot, and could see the hitched horses twisting and moving around. Where were the riders?

Then, from his left came a man's loud roar, and Thurman whirled, firing the rifle from his hip. The attacker folded up and a large knife fell from his grasp. With the acrid gun smoke smarting his eyes, Thurman searched for any other threat—but even the night bugs had quit their chorus.

"Thurman? Thurman? Are you all right?" Mary cried, coming up behind him.

"I'm fine," he said, still searching around and gathering her to his still tender left side. "But there is still another one around."

"How do you know?" she asked.

"I shot one at camp. One here. There's two horses here and one horse ran off."

"Where is he?"

On his knees, he patted Blacky on the head. "Dog, where did he go?"

He didn't really expect an answer, but so far, the collie had saved his life twice. One more time wasn't too much to ask of him.

"Did you see who I shot over there?"

She shook her head. "It wasn't him. This isn't him either."

"Then he's still out there?"

She nodded. He got up. "Let's take these horses back to our camp."

She went and unhitched them while he covered her. Then he eased over to the prone man. He was dead or close to it. Then, backing out, Thurman followed Mary to camp. With the horses on the line, he went to sit on the bedroll and tried to brush off his soles and put on his socks and boots.

He noticed that Blacky lay on the ground close by without growling, so he felt satisfied the third man wasn't close at the moment.

"What will we do with them?"

"Come first light, we'll decide."

At last, with his back to a tree where he had a chance to see plenty of the starlit area around them, he reloaded the rifle and sat back to wait for the damned outlaw.

"How did they know where we were?"

"I'd bet when I told Sarge the night before that I'd leave in the morning, there was an ear to hear that and then he beat it to Chickenhead's camp."

She nodded, seated beside him. "I thought we'd be rid of him."

His eyes became slits trying to see though the night for any threat. "He wants revenge. I've stolen you from him."

"I never—"

"He must think you belong to him."

"He has no right to me!"

"Don't be mad at me."

"I'm sorry, Thurman. Why don't we hitch up and go on?"

"There are times in life you need to make a stand. All he would do is follow us. When the sun comes up, I want this over."

She scooted closer. "I don't want him to kill you."

"I don't intend to let him do that, nor hurt you either."

"How will you find him?"

"I think come sunup, Blacky will lead me to him."

She furrowed her dark brows. "He's not a hound."

"No, but he knows a good man from bad. He'll find him."

Dawn came, and Thurman gave Mary the small pistol from his gear. She nodded and wet her lips. "I can use it."

"Never hesitate. He'll think you will and charge you."

"I won't. I promise."

He kissed her and whistled to the dog. In the growing light, Blacky bounded across the road. On the far side, he stopped and tested the air. Thurman nodded. "I'll be back."

In the woods, he soon found the second dead man's body. An Indian, or at least a 'breed, in his twenties. He carried a cap-and-ball pistol and some ammunition. No money. Satisfied, Thurman pushed on through the brush and trees. Every step of the way, he watched the dog's actions. Blacky trailed something or someone, marking trees as he went. His zig-zag travels soon centered on a game path, and Thurman could see some rock-faced bluffs ahead.

When the dog reached the base, he began to growl, and Thurman cocked his .44/40 Winchester, searching around for what Blacky had found.

"You son of bitch—" Next came the cold snap of a pistol striking on a dud. Thurman returned rapid fire with the rifle at the figure of a man high above him. Hatless, and struck hard by several rounds, the third gang member pitched forward. The six-gun's muzzle in his hand dropped down. His knees buckled and he fell forward off the twenty-foot bluff to crash on his back in the talus at the base.

"Thurman. Thurman," Mary cried, running up. "It's him—Chickenhead."

He gathered her under his left arm and looked hard at the prone outlaw. Just a dead man dressed in dirty ragged clothes, with his long hair back in a ponytail. In death, he looked more like a bum than a notorious badman.

"It's over," he said softly to her.

"Yes. What can we do now?" she asked, looking like she wanted to avoid being near the body.

"There is three hundred and fifty dollars lying here in these woods. I aim to wrap their bodies, find you a safe place, and then I'll go back to Fort Smith to collect my warrants."

She shook her head. "No. I will go back with you."

"You'll have to cross on the ferry."

"I am your woman. I'll go make us some food and then we can go back." She hurried off toward camp.

He watched Blacky go by, hike his leg, and mark Chickenhead's run-over boots. Good enough for a killer and rapist.

THIRTEEN

"Art, in the morning you ride up and see about Pleago," Herschel said. "If he ain't loaded up, I'll get a warrant from Judge Carney and we'll jail him. He's had all the warnings I'm giving him."

His deputy gave him a nod. "Nebraska sending someone after our horse thieves?"

"He's supposed to be on his way up here after the wire I sent telling him I'd hold 'em for them." Herschel motioned for his man to take a chair in front of his desk. "Questioning those two yesterday, I think I stumbled on something. I think they were going to meet a buyer up there."

"Who was that?"

"They aren't talkative enough yet to tell me who it is."

"That's interesting—a buyer from around here? Any word on the two store robbers?"

"No, they vanished faster than I could even imagine."

"I bet they're hiding down south in the Prior Mountains," Art said.

"Why there?"

"Backcountry, not many folks go up there. Got them some small trapper's cabin and are waiting for things to cool off."

"Maybe you or I should ride down there and check on them."

"It would be better if we took Black Feather. It's pretty well Crow land anyway."

Herschel agreed. All he needed was six more deputies and two more hands of his own to do everything this job entailed.

"See about Pleago in the morning. Any word on this troublemaker from the other night?"

"Link Colter? He kinda dropped from sight."

"That could be good or bad. Phil," he called out to his other deputy, who had came into the outside office.

"What's up, guys?" the younger man asked, walking in.

"How's our patient doing?" Herschel asked.

"Got a high fever. He ain't coming around very fast."

"Good thing he's over there."

Phil nodded. "He's tough, but he may not be tough enough to survive this."

"We're thinking his buddies may be hiding in the Prior Mountains until things cool down."

Phil took the other chair. "It's a good place to hide. If they went up there, some Crow saw them going in. Nothing happens up there they don't know and see it. Why not have one of us go ask them if they saw anyone going up there?"

'I'll send Black Feather," Herschel said. "Save us a trip."

"We've been going to use him for days," Art said, and laughed.

"I'll go find him this afternoon," Herschel said. "Oh,

Nebraska is coming after those two horse thieves. But I think they were going to meet a buyer up there." He explained what had happened the day before.

Phil agreed.

"Now figure out how to get them to tell me who that individual was." Herschel dropped back in his big chair, which squealed in protest.

"We might separate them for a few days," Art said. "Then one won't know what the other one told us. Put one in that single cell down the hall. Then they couldn't communicate."

"Great idea," Herschel agreed. That might work fine.

He ate an early plate lunch at the Real Food Café. Buster Cory came out, sat down, and talked to him.

"Any news I need to know about?" Herschel asked.

"Looks like they've got the railroad coming again. I hear they'll be in Miles City in no time."

"Oh, it's coming. It is just slower than I figured."

"You know, them railroad camps draw more whores and crooks than flies on a dead cow."

Herschel nodded.

"Well, you know, the railroad expects all that to be in place. They want them workers dead broke after every payday. That way, they keep them on the job and they don't have any money to run off or go home."

"I expect that's the truth."

"You'll have more crap to tend to than you have now for sure."

Herschel nodded, savoring the sweet smoked ham on his plate. "I think that's happening now over there at Miles City."

"It won't be fun."

"Anything else?"

Twisting up a cigarette, Buster stopped before he put it in his lips. "Word's out that this dead man you got the other day was rich."

"He inherited some money. Took a buddy to the whorehouse and had a small party with him. After that, he probably had seven to eight hundred dollars left. It wasn't on him when I found his body."

"That was all?"

"That's lots of money to me."

Buster laughed. "Me, too, but it sounded from the rumor like he had lots more than that."

"Maybe that's why they killed him. Thought he was holding out on them."

"*Them* mean anything?"

"Naw, Buster. Still parties unknown."

"Well." Buster clapped his upper legs under his apron. "I better get back to work or she'll fire me."

"See you." Herschel grinned. No way Maude would fire him. She'd found him as sincere a man as she'd ever met. Probably then he'd been close to sixty or a little older, and he'd proposed to her. She was a long ways his junior, recently widowed, and by a man they said never treated her with any respect. Buster'd never been married before, and when she accepted, all the trail hands in the country that knew him threw a high old Montana wedding for both of them.

He stood stiff-like and looked back. "You ever hear from your father?"

Herschel shook his head. "He must not know my address."

"Damn shame. I always liked him. Couldn't believe what got into him back then to make him just up and leave."

"That war changed lots of folks. People said when he came back, he wasn't the same person. I don't know. I was just a big kid who'd run the ranch the whole time he was off fighting. I was so glad when he came home. I figured he'd build up a big ranch. But somehow, it was like he just didn't belong there. He'd go off and trade for cattle, and come back home six weeks later and approve whatever I'd done."

"No idea where he went?"

"I haven't really cared. He chose to ride off. I never did anything to him to make him do that."

Buster nodded. "A man's mind can get all twisted sometimes. I always wondered about him. He was the best captain a man could have."

"Thanks for the information."

Herschel paid for his lunch and walked the six blocks to Black Feather's tepee in his camp by the river. The man's oldest wife was hoeing in the garden plot, and two black dogs ran out to greet him barking their heads off. A younger wife stuck her head out and shouted at them to stop. Then he heard her say, "The sheriff is here."

Wrapped in a colorful red and blue wool trade blanket, Black Feather came out bareheaded and nodded. The Crow stood six foot tall, a giant among other red men, and he wore thick braids. He had come to live among white men, he told people, to learn their ways. But his polygamous situation and living in a tepee hardly made him blend in.

"Some men robbed Taylor's store a few days ago," said Herschel. "I wonder if the two who rode off with the money are hiding in the Prior Mountains."

"That is a vast land. Many places to hide."

"Can you see them all for me for ten dollars?"

"Is there a reward for these men?"

"I'll ask Mr. Taylor for one. They are mean men. You better come get me if you find them."

Black Feather nodded. "I go in the morning. What if they are not there?"

"I'll still pay you ten dollars in silver."

"You and I speak truth to each other. I come tell you what I find when I get back."

"I'm counting on it. I have another job for you when we finish this one."

"Plenty good. Nice weather. The grass is strong for my ponies."

"I'll see you when you return. Be careful. They are dangerous men."

Black Feather solemnly nodded.

Herschel hoped the tall Indian understood those men would be armed and desperate. But Indians had their ways—he needed to ask the Taylors about the reward in case Black Feather did find them.

On his leisurely walk back to town, he saw lots of garden planting beginning in earnest. Marsha was busy planting at home. He should be home helping her, but he still had several things he'd call duties to do.

At the Taylor store, he rang the bell overhead and pushed inside.

"Why, Sheriff Baker," Mrs. Taylor said, coming down the aisle to met him. "What can I do for you today?"

"They return the slicker and blanket I was so grateful for the other day?"

"Yes, the very next day. What do you need?"

"Is Ted here?"

"No, he's home planting our garden. Can I help you?"

"Ted ever mention offering a reward for those two outlaws?"

"No, but I am certain he would. Do you have a lead on them?"

"Not for me or my deputies. But another man who may locate them. I'll need a reward for him."

"Does he know where they are now?"

"No. But he's going looking and may find them."

"I'd say we could pay twenty-five dollars each for their capture."

"You could pay that in groceries. I'm sure he wouldn't mind."

Her face brightened. "Why, of course."

"I only have two deputies and serving papers, getting jurors, investigating crimes take up all our time."

"Most folks know you work very short-handed and they appreciate all you do for us. The town has no money for a police force either."

"We handle that, but we'll sure need a police force when the railroad gets closer. I don't think any of us are ready for that."

"Be a boomtown, won't it?"

"Things will be different, that's for sure. Thanks, I hope my man can find the robbers."

"How is the missus? She was in here getting garden seed earlier."

"She and the girls are very busy putting them in the ground today."

"Tell her I said hello."

"I will." He walked back toward the office. One more place he needed to stop. Miss Sally's Place. He climbed the long flight of stairs and found the door open.

"Anyone here?"

"The girls are all asleep." Sally came sweeping into the living room wearing a satin robe with white fur trim. "Oh, Sheriff Baker. My, what brings you upstairs?"

Removing his hat, he stepped over the threshold. "How's things, Sally?"

"Good. Is someone complaining about us?"

"No. I need some information on a client." Her strong perfume filled the air.

"Come in the kitchen and we can discuss it over hot tea."

He followed her in to a large table with twelve place settings. The smell of cooking made his mouth water. A black woman named Hatty nodded at him.

"Tea, Hatty, for the high sheriff and myself." She showed him a chair and took the next one for herself.

"Yes, ma'am. You's be all right, Mr. Baker?"

"Fine, Hatty."

"Now," Sally said, retying her robe, crossing her bare legs, and showing more of her cleavage. "Who do you need to know about?"

"A couple of days ago a man named Hamby brought a friend named Olsen up here and they had a party."

"You mean Wally Hamby?"

"Yes."

"I was so sad to hear the poor man was shot shortly after that." Her thick eyelashes closed as if in respect for his demise.

"Did Hamby and Olsen argue while they were here?"

"I didn't hear of anything. Hattie, go wake up Ruth and Nalda. Tell them the sheriff is here to ask them some questions. There is no problem." When the woman had gone out of the room, she reached over and shook his leg. "You can come up the back stairs any time you want to. You know that, don't you?"

"Thanks, but I don't reckon I will."

She shrugged. "The past sheriff found our services satisfactory."

"What I need worse than anything is to solve a murder right now."

The sleepy-eyed girls came in, yawning and wearing too large gowns.

"Sheriff Baker is here to ask you about Wally Hamby and the Olsen boy."

Herschel nodded at the girls. "When they were here, did they ever argue?"

The black-headed one shook her head. "They was just having them a real good time."

The brunette with the long nose agreed. "I thought they was big buddies. He—Hamby was paying for it all, and Olsen, he was sure whooping it up."

"How much money did they spend?"

"Champagne and all?" Sally asked.

"Yes."

"Thirty-three dollars."

"Did Hamby tip you girls?"

They shook their heads, but they would deny that anyway because they had to hide that money from Sally. He hadn't learned much.

"Well, Sheriff, anything else you need to know?" Sally asked.

"Where were they going from here?"

"Page's place."

"What for?" He was unfamiliar with the name.

"They never said." Nalda shrugged. "But they had to ride hard, they said, to get there to meet someone." She turned to her "sister."

"Yeah, they mentioned someone's name, but I forgot it."

"Thanks," he said. "You recall that name, send me word at once."

"You girls may go back to bed," Sally said. "Anything else, Sheriff Baker?"

"No, but you hear anything, let me know. I want this murder solved."

"I cross my heart I will."

She showed him to the door and blew him a kiss when he turned back to tell her thanks. Seduction was her game, and while he never felt tempted in her company, he still knew he'd just met a real pro at the game. Besides, men sometimes confided in doves—sometimes the doves knew too much for their own health.

He walked into the office and Darby looked up. "The store robber died today."

"The infection?"

"No, Doc wasn't certain. He just quit breathing or had a heart seizure, I guess."

"Thanks." He'd lost a witness. He wondered how Art was doing with the eviction. Time would tell. Who knows? And Black Feather might find those men.

Who were Hamby and Olsen in such a hurry to meet? He might never know that either.

FOURTEEN

I T was past midnight in a light drizzle when they crossed on the ferry. The three bodies were slung across the horses. Mary was under the big black hat and wearing a slicker as she drove the mule and filled Thurman in about the outlaws. Thurman was wearing his rubber raincoat and sodden hat. They made a right turn and went to the courthouse, which had some lighted lamps on the porch and inside.

He hitched the horses, walked up the sidewalk, and then took the steps. Inside, a clerk looked up, shocked at seeing him.

"Can—I—help you, sir?"

"I have three dead outlaws outside. Where should I take them?"

A tall man with a big mustache came down the hall, his boot heels echoing in the building. "Did I hear you right, sir?"

"Yes, Charlie Chickenhead, Burl McDougan, and another man known as Squirrel with buck teeth."

The man's brows furrowed he blinked in disbelief. "They're all dead?"

"They've been that way since last night. They raided our camp over in the Territory."

"Mister, my name's Bill Bowlin. I'm the second in command here. Our marshals have been after those outlaws for over a year." He shook his hand. "I never caught your name."

"Thurman Baker. I'm on my way to find my son. The sooner I can get my warrants, the sooner I can be on my way."

"The newspaper will want a story from you."

"Maybe you could do that. One of those outlaws shot me ten days ago down in the Kiamish Mountains. I got one that night. They stole a good horse I never got back. Then later, I captured one called Needles when they tried to hold me up on the way up here. They wouldn't leave well enough alone and tried to jump us in camp last night. I still don't have my expensive horse back."

Bowlin smiled. "Three hundred fifty dollars in reward should buy a good horse."

"Whenever I get the cash. Will a bank hold it for redemption and mail me the money?" he asked.

"Costs ten bucks. The River Bank or the Cotton Planters will do that."

"Which one is the best-run bank?"

"Planters probably."

"Thanks. I guess I have to come back here and get them?"

Bowlin nodded. "Eight A.M."

"Fine. Where do you want the bodies left?"

"Green Funeral Parlor on Garrison. I'll go along and help you."

"Fine. You can ride in the buggy with Mary. Better get your slicker. It don't have a top."

The buggy wheels cut through the sheet of water as Mary drove the mule sharply up to the funeral home. Bowlin hitched the mule and helped her down, then came back to help Thurman undo the ropes.

They carried the first canvas-wrapped corpse inside the mortuary, while she untied the next one from the horse. When they came out again, Thurman told her to go inside and dry out, they'd get the rest. At last, all three outlaws were laid out, and Bowlin had the two funeral home employees unwrap the bodies for identification.

Once they were out of the wraps, he looked at their pale faces and nodded in approval. "It's them all right. You know, it is not often that one man brings an end to an entire outlaw gang."

"I didn't look for them. They came looking for me."

"You ever consider making law enforcement your career?"

"No, I'm a cattleman and I'm going back to being one if these outlaws let me alone."

"These three sure won't trouble you again."

"I sure hope not. Now we're going to get some sleep."

"I'd buy you a drink."

"Ordinarily, I'd jump at the chance, but I better get Mary to bed."

"You're entitled to their horses and gear," Bowlin said as he walked Thurman outside.

"Good, they aren't worth much. But they'll bring something."

He helped Mary onto the buggy seat and they drove to

Dearborn's. The hostler said Sarge was at home asleep, and said he'd put up all their horses and their possessions would be fine on the buggy. He tied up Blacky.

Moments later, they stomped inside the Palace lobby and Thurman told the clerk he wanted a room for the night. The young man never hesitated, and Thurman signed the register, paid the two dollars, and in few minutes they were inside Room 220.

He hugged Mary as they stood in their wet slickers, and then he pushed the heavy hat off her head to kiss her. She giggled.

"We sure didn't get very far this time."

He held her tight. "Yes, we did. That son of a bitch is dead. No more dreams of him coming back."

It was past sunup when he washed himself using the washcloth, pitcher, and bowl. He dressed, then told her to sleep, that he'd be back $350 richer.

He walked the three blocks to the courthouse. A half block from the old barracks, he saw a blinding flash from near the stairs. The photographers were already there.

"Mister, look over here. This is last of the famous Chickenhead gang. Some guy brought them in last night— single-handed they say."

"I see." He refused to look at the three corpses propped up in their open coffins, and took the stairs two at a time, grateful to be inside.

The clerk recognized him. "Second door."

Thurman nodded and when he walked into the office, a blinding flash went off.

"Stand right there," someone ordered, and another flash went off.

Blinking his eyes, he threw his arm up. "That's enough."

"Sir. Might I have a word with you?" The reporter had his pad and pencil ready.

"What I did was what any law-abiding man would do. They attacked me and I returned fire."

"But three against one?"

"That's three bullets. How long did that take?"

"Did they say anything?"

He shook his head. "Oh, they growled like bears and came after me. Worthless humanity is all I can say."

"What will you do next?"

"Go get my wife and find some breakfast." He folded the warrants the clerk handed him, then put them inside his coat with a thanks. "I'll be leaving now."

"Wait. Tell me your business in the Territory."

"Getting across it."

"No, I mean where were you going?" The reporter was hurrying alongside him.

"Kansas, unless they moved it."

Thurman was really striding down the hall and hoping to lose this question-asking devil.

"Can you tell me—?"

"Go ask Charlie Chickenhead all your questions."

The reporter frowned at him. "But he's dead."

"So am I. Good day, sir."

Thurman took Mary to breakfast, and then they went to the Planters Bank. She waited in a chair in the lobby while he spoke to a big man in a fine brown suit in his office behind a frosted-glass door. Troy Donovan was his name, and he had the aloofness of most bankers Thurman had dealt with in the past. But the suit that Thurman wore made the banker less standoffish than if he'd come in there wearing his vaquero clothing.

"I have warrants for three hundred and fifty dollars from the federal court," Thurman said. "I've been told that for a fee you would cash them for me when that money is available."

"You know that can be as long as a year."

"I know they are slow to pay."

"Our usual fee for doing that is ten percent of the face value, or we can discount them for cash for thirty percent."

"Seems like everyone in Fort Smith is in the discount business. No, I'll do ten percent, Mr. Donovan, and you can hold it until I telegraph you where to send it."

"Very well, sir. Do you have heirs?"

"Yes, my lawyer in San Antonio, Texas, Charles T. Watson, can handle that."

Donovan wrote that down. "What else may I do for you today?"

Thurman shook his head. "That's all."

"If you will sign them over to the Planters Bank, I'll handle the matter when the money comes in."

"I can do that."

"Excuse me. I'll have my secretary write up a short agreement and then you can sign it, too, sir."

In a few minutes, Donovan returned, and he showed Thurman the agreement for a ten percent fee. It all looked official and he signed both copies. Donovan did the same and gave him one of the copies.

When he shook the man's hand, Thurman wondered if he'd ever see his money. His distrust of banks and bankers ran deep.

He gathered Mary and they went to the livery. The outlaws had less than thirty dollars cash on them when they'd turned their pockets out. So besides their black powder pistols and some crudely made knives, there wasn't much besides their old saddles and two common horses, a paint and a bay mare.

Sarge figured they'd bring ten, maybe fifteen dollars apiece.

"How old are your grandkids?" Thurman asked Sarge, with a notion on his mind about the horses' disposal.

"The oldest boy is twelve."

"You got a place to keep these horses?"

"Sure, I've got a small farm, but you want me to keep them for you?"

"No, I'm going to loan them to your grandchildren to keep."

"Why, Cap'n, that's about the nicest thing I can ever imagine."

Mary hugged his arm and winked in approval.

He clapped his ex-noncom on the shoulder. "Tell 'em to ride and enjoy them."

"Aw, hell—" Sarge sniffed. "That's just wonderful."

"We'll be ready to go again before sunup."

"I'll have that mule harnessed and everything ready. Boy, I can't wait to go home and show them ponies to the kids. Thanks, sir."

"Thurman Baker, is this May or December?" Mary asked as they strode down Garrison Avenue.

"I hope it ain't December. I've got a boy of my own to find before then."

"His grandchildren are really going to think it is Christmas. Two horses and saddles. They made a fine gift."

"I was real poor once myself. A man gave me a horse one time. Preacher Tom Clary was his name. She was a clumsy two-year-old. I broke her myself. My father got drunk in town one Saturday and sold her for five bucks."

"How old were you?"

"Twelve, thirteen. Him and I were never close after that."

She put her cheek on his shoulder. "It was a nice way to heal that scar."

"Scar?"

"Yes, the scar will always be there, but giving those horses healed it for you."

"My profound Cherokee woman." He shook his head in amazement. "I never thought of it that way."

"What does that word 'profound' mean?"

"Means you have lots of insight into the ways of people's minds and hearts." When he glanced over at her, she looked embarrassed.

"Maybe I do. Maybe I do."

They would leave again in the morning. This time there would be no Chickenhead lurking on the road.

What else would happen? He could drive cattle herds faster than he was going north. Then he considered Mary and nodded to himself—he was grateful for her.

FIFTEEN

"ANTON Pleago ain't to be found," Art said, and dropped heavily in the chair in front of Herschel's desk. "His Indian woman told me he'd left a couple of days ago. She had no idea where he went."

"Anyone else know anything?" Herschel asked.

"No, I talked to several folks. They don't know anything about where he went."

"Phil's doing some checking, too. He might have murdered Taunton yesterday."

Art scowled at him. "Why do that?"

"He figured that Taunton would testify that he put them up knowing about their plans to rob the store. Doc thinks he smothered him with a pillow."

"Any witnesses?"

"That's what Phil's doing. Trying to find someone who saw him in town about the time of the murder. Doc was gone to deliver a baby, his nurse was gone to see about a man hurt at the sawmill, and his housekeeper was off buying groceries. It would have have been easy to slip in and silence Taunton forever."

Art shook his head in disgust. "We sure keep racking them up, don't we?"

"Yes. I also learned that Hamby and Olsen were going to Page's place to meet someone."

"Where's Page's place?"

Herschel tented his fingers. "Damned if I know or can learn. It may be in that country east of the Soda Springs schoolhouse."

"There any Pages on the tax rolls?"

Herschel shook his head. "I checked on that. Can't find a thing by that name or anyone who's heard of the name."

"What next?"

"I wonder if Pleago knows where those other two are hid out."

"You mean he might kill them, too?"

"No, I mean he might join them to get some money now he's on the run, too." Herschel pressed the side of his fingers to his mouth and used the two of them to punctuate his words. "One of us needs to go check out this Miles City deal, too. If Hatch is selling stolen beef over there, we need to stop that, and I believe those ranchers. He's got them buffaloed."

"Maybe I need to camp out up there."

"Naw, he's got too many lookouts. I couldn't even confront him at the dance without him being warned. But at this party Hamby had at Sally's, Olsen was with him. They said they had to ride hard to be at Page's place and meet someone. The dove forgot the name of the man they were to meet."

Art shook his head. "You learn the horse buyer's name?"

"No, they ain't been apart long enough to worry about what the other one said to me."

"Strange thing that they were at the same place that those rustlers were. Who'd need some stolen horses anyway?" Art asked.

"The only way it would make sense was if you were going to do a robbery and didn't want your horse recognized."

"They didn't steal those horses to give them away. They're nice horses and worth some money in Canada."

"Let's suppose they were stopped by a party and told to go to that old ranch and wait 'cause there would be a buyer coming to meet them. Why else would they stop and get caught there? If I was going to Canada, I'd've kept on riding.

"I may go back there and talk to that cocky one. You take the rest of the day off. I'll go up to Miles City on the stage in the morning. You'll have to do my job and patrol the town tomorrow and until I get back."

"Phil and I can handle it," said Art.

"I know, but we'll need to at least triple our force before the tracks gets close. I think Don Harold has his hands full up there."

"You get lots of bad ones in those boomtowns. I'll work on the Page situation while you're in Miles City."

"Thanks. I'm also going back to the dance Saturday. I promised the girls they could go, too."

"Can't never tell, that oldest one might find her a beau."

"I don't think her mother is ready for that." Herschel chuckled.

Art shook his head. "They aren't ever ready for that. See you when you get back."

Herschel took his saddle along in case he needed it, and the stage driver, Rip, put it in the back under the tarp. It was early and two women were waiting. Rip had told him there was one more ticket holder coming. Then Rip checked his large pocket watch.

"He ain't here in ten minutes, he can walk to Miles City. Go get a seat, Sheriff."

Herschel thanked him. It was Wednesday, and he'd promised Marsha he'd be back by Friday night. No way he needed to miss that return. Besides, what could he get into in Miles City to hold him up? But simple trips had a habit of becoming complicated in his life.

The mother and daughter soon joined him in the front seat. They introduced themselves as Mrs. Carson and her daughter Magdeline. Magdeline was probably in her twenties. Her mother was gray-haired and a very well-preserved lady. Both women were dressed in very stylish outfits. They did not look like homesteaders.

"The driver said you were the sheriff here?" Mrs. Carson asked.

He doffed his hat again. "Yes, I'm going to Miles City to see about some criminal activity in that area."

"Oh."

"You ladies headed east?"

"Yes, we're going to St. Louis."

"Well, the train ride will be much easier than the stages."

"We're looking forward to it."

Herschel agreed. A red-faced man who smelled of whiskey climbed up, looked them all over, and blinked at the sight of the two women. "*Wall,* ain't'cha the prettiest things in the land."

"Mister, you're drunk and if you want to ride to Miles City, you'll be riding up there with Rip."

He blinked his bleary eyes. "I paid for *plassage.*"

"Rip," Herschel said out the window. "This gentleman can ride on top or stay here."

Rip pulled him back. "You can ride the next stage, mister."

"Why you—"

The drunk drew back, and Rip hit him with a right uppercut that drove him back on the porch, where he collapsed on his butt.

Ignoring him, Rip climbed in the box, undid the reins, and kicked the brake loose. A loud whistle and a "Heeyah" to the horses and they were off. It was an all-day trip, and Herschel sat back to enjoy the brief reprieve from the week of problems.

"You have a wife?" Mrs. Carson asked over the clatter of the wheels and the horses' hooves pounding the road.

"Yes, a wife and three daughters."

"Magdeline was to have been married a week ago. Her fiancé was killed in a mining accident a week before we arrived."

"Oh, I'm sorry."

"It has been a very exhausting three weeks."

"I would imagine so."

"He was such a nice young man. Came from a good family back home. I am certain his family is as distraught as we are."

"Was it his mine?"

"He held an interest in it."

"Well, ma'am, I hope you can find something to take your mind off it."

"Thank you," said Magdeline.

"Are there many Indian problems out here?" Mrs. Carson adjusted her full skirt in her lap.

"No, most of the troublemakers are on reservations or in prisons."

"We found Idaho very wild. They no doubt have very little law enforcement."

Herschel nodded. "Most places in the West don't have enough tax base to support a large law enforcement effort."

"I never thought about that."

Mrs. Carson talked on about her life in St. Louis, her plans for Magdeline, and what all they must do when they arrived home. Magdeline wrung her hands in her lap, looking very uncomfortable, contributing nothing to the conversation.

When they switched horses at the next station, Rip spoke to him on the side. "Sorry, I didn't notice he was that drunk."

"No problem. I didn't want those ladies putting up with him."

"You know, I may need a job pretty soon. You need any deputies? This stage business is getting swallowed up by railroads."

"Come see me when that day comes."

"Thanks. I will."

Back in the coach, they headed east, boiling up dust in their wake. It was late in the afternoon when they arrived in Miles City, and Herschel helped both the women down. He could see by all the traffic that things were booming.

"Ma'am," Rip said, taking off his weather-beaten felt hat. "It's about five miles out to where the train will be. They'll have a cab to take you in thirty minutes."

"Thank you. And thank you, Sheriff Baker. We enjoyed your company. I can tell my friends in St. Louis I met a real man of the West."

"You have a drawl still," Magdeline said, stopping and using her hand to shade the sun to look up at him.

"I was born in Texas, miss."

"Yes, I could tell. Your mother raised you right, sir. And

thanks for listening to my poor mother. She's been worried ever since we learned James had been killed that she would have an old maid on her hands."

"Oh, I doubt that."

"Really?"

"Stay in Montana and teach school. There will be more moon-eyed cowboys coming around to court you than there are jackrabbits."

"Really?" She looked as perked up as he'd seen her in eight hours. Whirling around, she looked over the traffic. "Will they need one here?"

"Try the courthouse. They usually know about such openings."

"But we'd miss the train." Lines of concern creased her smooth forehead.

He shrugged. "There'll be another one tomorrow."

A slow, sly smile crossed her mouth and she nodded. "Thank you."

He tipped his hat to her. Some cowboys would sure owe him if she stayed and taught school. "Good luck, Magdeline."

It was two blocks to the sheriff's office, and when he came in sight of it, he was shocked. Two deputies armed with shotguns stood guarding several men seated on the ground in leg irons. It was obvious this was where they were being housed.

A hatless Sheriff Don Harold sat looking haggard behind a cluttered desk in the outer office, talking to two handcuffed men under the guard of an older man.

"Put them on the chain gang," he said to the deputy.

Then he went to looking through papers piled on the desk.

"Yes?" He never looked up.

"You look bad."

"What?" His eyes tried to focus for a second. "Damn, that's you, Baker."

"You stop eating and sleeping both?"

He shook a finger at Baker. "Wait till you get the damn railroad in your county. Folks were calling it great progress. I call it bullshit."

"Can you take a ten-minute break? I'd even buy your supper."

Harold put both hands on top of his legs and nodded like a wooden Indian. "Let's go eat something. I'm so tired of this."

"I can't say I'm ready for it either." Herschel didn't want to think about the mess outside being in his town.

"Let's eat at the Grand Hotel. We can get a private dining room and talk."

"Sounds fine."

"You just get here?"

"Ten minutes or so. Came on the stage."

"Well, if we all survive it, we'll have train service here in two months."

"Why so long?"

"Can't get enough rails. Everyone in the world is building railroads. They run out all the time. Lay off the hands for a couple of weeks and they all get drunk and rowdy. It's bad."

"I have two murders and a store robbery and I think I'm overworked."

They stomped up the steps of the hotel, and Harold opened the left front door with the glass in the window. "Two murders? I have two murders a night on a slow one."

"You still single?"

"Yeah, why?"

"There's a young lady on the stage today from St. Louis who went to get married in Idaho and her fiancé was killed in a mine accident before she got there. I tried to talk her into teaching school in Montana. She went to see about a job at the courthouse. She sticks around, you might like to meet her."

"If I ever have time. What's her name?"

"Magdeline Carson."

"Nice-looking?"

"Yes, and a lady. She won't talk your ear off either."

Harold looked hard at him with his clear blue eyes brighter than they had been since he'd arrived. "That would be wonderful." Then he signaled to the man who was seating people in the dining area. "Put Sheriff Baker and me in a small room in the back."

Harold repeated Magdeline's name three times.

"Just bring us some food," Harold said, waving off the menus. "He drinks coffee, I drink whiskey on days like this."

Exhaling, he collapsed in his chair. "You didn't come to help me find a wife. You need something."

"There is a man over in the eastern part of my county named Roscoe Hatch. He's killing beef and hauling it over here and selling the meat."

"Smart man. We have all kinds of folks want to eat. Most wouldn't look at a piece of meat and ask was it his, would they?"

"He's of course a bully. Keeps some toughs around him so the little ranchers won't complain much."

"What's his name again?"

"Roscoe Hatch. There may be others. A Wally Hamby, looks part Indian, high checkbones, and a blond-headed Dane named Olsen."

"You can ask around. I never heard of them."

The waiter brought Herschel's coffee and a bottle of bonded Kentucky whiskey for Harold. "Stan, you know

anyone named Roscoe Hatch that sells butchered beef?"
Sheriff Harold asked the waiter.

"Oh, I can ask Earl. He does the buying."

"Thanks. Send him around." Harold held up the jigger
toward Herschel. "Here's to much better days."

"Yes, we can use them."

"There are more pickpockets, con men, cheating tin-
horns in Miles City than I could even imagine existed in
the entire West." He downed the whiskey and made a loud
"ah."

"Sir?" said a new man who came up.

"You must be Earl, the meat buyer. Sheriff Baker from
Billings is over here looking for some men who might be
selling stolen beef."

"What are their names?"

"Hatch?"

The man shook his head.

"Olsen?"

Again, the man shook his head.

"A dark-haired, high-cheekbone guy—"

"Named Hamilton. He is one of four men sells us beef.
A big man calls himself Smith and a blond-headed Dane
who calls himself Kaufman."

"That's my boys. Who's the fourth one?"

"A well-dressed man of means. His name is—well,
what he calls himself is Thompson."

"It sounds like they do have a gang," Harold said as the
food arrived. Sliced beef, potatoes, and peas heaped on a
plate. Also, hot French bread and butter by the bowl.

"Thompson live around here?" Herschel asked, never
hearing of the man in his county.

"I can ask," Earl said.

"No, don't tip them off. Business as usual. I don't want
them thinking I'm on to them."

"I had no way to know they were rustlers, Sheriff."

"Hell, Earl, we didn't know either. Don't worry. Do business like you always do."

Harold nodded at Herschel. "Let's eat. We've solved one crime already."

"I'll be damned if we haven't. Food looks good and it tastes better."

"What did they used to say, eating stolen beef is the best meal?"

"I recall that growing up."

How would he ever catch them at it? That was the next part. Oh, well, this way, he'd at least be home in time to take his girls to the next Soda Springs dance.

SIXTEEN

R AIN struck in mid-afternoon of the second day. Two ferry crossings and they were at the old outpost of Fort Gibson. A cluster of log buildings in disrepair, with a few small businesses that all looked as dismal as the dripping countryside. Thurman found a livery and spoke to the man who owned it.

"You can get a meal at Marty's over there and sleep in my bunkhouse," the gray-headed man said. "There ain't no one else here, so you and her would have it by yourself."

"Things pretty slow?" Thurman asked.

The man laughed. "Worse than that. It's dead. Railroad got to Muskogee and shut this place down."

"That's what happens, they say. Grain the mule and horse."

"I will. Pull your rig inside. It'll be safe and dry in here."

"Thanks. I'll tie the dog up while we go to eat."

"He won't hurt nothing loose."

"All right." He went out in the drizzle and told Mary to drive inside.

Once the rig was inside, the man sent them off to eat. They found the café across the street, warm and smelling of good food when they came in. There were pegs to hang their slickers on the wall, and a smiling buxom woman told them to take any table.

"Nice place," Mary said softly, looking around at the tableclothes and curtains.

"Thanks. Beef stew is what we have to eat," the woman said. "What to drink?"

"Coffee," he said. "Beef stew's fine." He winked at Mary. "We're stew eaters."

"Good. The rain's got every one holed up, so we didn't cook as much as usual today. Oh, we've got plenty for you two. Have to watch things close to stay in business."

"I imagine that is so," Thurman said.

"Times are hard, aren't they?" Mary asked him when the woman went back in the kitchen.

"I guess. Things seemed all right in Fort Smith, but they sure aren't up here," he said. "Maybe folks will make some good crops and things will look up. Just so I don't have to tend them."

She chuckled. "I had started a garden."

He nodded. Since he left south Texas, he'd lost almost a month, been shot, collected reward warrants on five outlaws, and found Mary. She was the brightest thing in the whole deal.

They left Fort Gibson the next morning and set out for Wichita. Passing around Tulsey and going across the rolling flint hill grass country, they camped in the open and enjoyed the meadowlarks' song at dawn. He'd been to Wichita during the heyday of the cattle business. In place of the wild cow town, he now found a large industrial center with grain elevators, blocks and blocks of homes, and railroad yards. The land the trail crews once spread their herds over while waiting for cattle cars less than a dozen years before was all under the plow. The contrast of what he'd seen then with what he saw now struck him forcefully.

"Where are the trees?" she asked.

"They grow on islands in the river where a prairie fire can't get them. From here on, trees are rare."

"What do we use for cooking?"

"Dry buffalo chips. No, they're gone, too. Dry cow chips."

She wrinkled her nose.

"It will work. The cooks with cattle outfits used 'em for years to feed entire crews. They get real dry out here."

"Oh, I won't ever say a bad thing about trees again."

"Why not? Hell, out here they couldn't hear you anyway for the wind."

Laughing, she gave him a shove. "You can be mean sometimes."

"To who, the trees?"

He drove downtown to the stockyard district and found the Baltimore Hotel. He looked at the four-story brick structure and nodded to Mary. "This is supposed to be where the cattle buyers hang out. I'll only be a few minutes."

"Fine."

He put Blacky on a lead and went inside. When he inquired about the bar, the desk clerk sent him to the left and he walked into an ornate sitting room. When he found the door locked, he knocked, and someone opened a small slot and looked at him, then told him to come in.

Discretion and more stringent laws no doubt forced the gamblers to be back there. He entered and stood to let his eyes adjust. A half dozen men were around a table large enough to accommodate a dozen. Cigar smoke curled in the air. Kansas was dry, he recalled.

"Can one of us help you, sir?" the man preparing to deal the cards asked.

"Rip Salton here?"

The man shook his head. "He got religion and a new wife. She won't let him gamble." Then he deftly dealt the five cards around the table.

"Russ Barker?"

"Omaha. Got too slow for him in these parts. Who else?"

"I was just passing through. I brought some herds up here years ago. Thought I might know someone."

"Thurman Baker?" a man on the far side said, taking off his wire-framed glasses. "I remember you. Only man that ever wore a clean white shirt all the way from south Texas to Kansas."

The others laughed.

"I guess I'm short your name."

"Abraham Reames."

The name came back to Thurman. "I think I loaned you a dozen horses when some renegades down in the Territory stole your entire remuda."

"A lifesaver. Saved my ass, that's for sure." Reames came over and shook his hand. "How have you been?"

"Fine. I want to stable my horses and get my wife a room. Then, if you all don't mind, I'd like to join you."

"Come on. We love new money," the dealer said, and the rest voted yes.

So he got a room from the desk clerk and moved Mary into it. She kissed him and he left her there. Then, the clerk sent for a young man from a nearby livery and he took the mule and horse as well as Blacky to his livery.

In twenty minutes time, he was back in the gambling room ready to play cards.

"What've you been doing since the cattle drive days?" the dealer asked as he dealt him his first card.

"Acquiring horses in Mexico."

"That profitable?"

Thurman nodded. "There's some fine original Barb horses in parts of Mexico. Expensive ones."

"What's a real barb worth up here?"

"I sold the last herd of sound and green-broke for a hundred fifty apiece."

"Whew, that's too high for me."

Thurman counted out five dollars and bet it on two queens in his hand.

Cost him a two-dollar raise to stay, but the third queen came in his draw.

"Where you headed?" he was asked.

"Montana."

"That's a long ways."

He bet five again and in the end, his ladies won the hand.

"Why Montana?"

"I'm looking for my son. He's supposed to be up there."

"What's his name?' a thickset man across the table asked.

"Herschel Baker. Do you know him?"

The man nodded. "What would you give me if I tell you right where he's at?"

"What've you got to have?"

"Naw." He shook his head as if he'd changed his mind about something. "If you saved Reames' butt back then by just flat giving him horses when no one had too many, I'd have to tell you where he's at. Time I usually got up here to Kansas, we were damn near walking."

Thurman never picked up his new cards. Was he about to learn where in Montana his son was located?

The man fanned his cards and smiled smugly behind them. "The Yellowstone County Jail."

"What for?" His heart quit. In jail . . .

The man grinned back at Thurman. "He's the elected sheriff up there."

Everyone laughed.

"What else do you know about him?"

"He's married. Has a nice wife and three stepdaughters. Two years ago, he took on all the politicians in that county and got elected as an independent. Cleaned house and set all those big outfits on their butts. Nobody owns Herschel Baker. I can tell you that for a fact."

"What town is that in?"

"Billings."

Thank God. He's alive. "Excuse me, gents." He rose. "I need to go share this news with my wife."

"Barmaid?" He called the girl over. "Give them all a round of drinks. Here's twenty, they can have all but the dollar that's yours."

"Well. Thank you," she gushed.

"See you guys." Thurman waved to them. He couldn't wait to find a map and see what end of Montana Billings was at.

SEVENTEEN

WHAT else did you learn in Miles City?" Art asked.
"They all used an alias up there. Hamby they called Hamilton. Hatch was Smith and Olsen was Kaufman. But the mystery man in the deal is the fourth one. They called him Thompson and said he was the boss, not Hatch."

"That surprises me. I'd of thought Hatch was the ringleader."

"They do a brisk business with the fanciest hotel in town. Keep them in beef."

"Who is this Thompson?" Phil asked. "You see him?"

"No, he wasn't around. In fact, they know little about him in Miles City. I don't think he lives there."

"No idea where he lives?"

Herschel shook his head. "They're a pretty well-organized ring as far as I can tell."

"Where do we go next?" Art asked.

"I think get the state brand inspector down here and get a search warrant. Then make a raid on Hatch's place. He may have a telltale hide in his possession. It only takes one."

"When will we do that?"

"The district man, Carl Ruger, wasn't at home. I left a letter with his wife concerning it. And for him to contact me."

"Any description of this new guy?" Phil asked.

"A big man, wears a suit and a black hat. Brown hair and eyes, talks like he's very educated. A man of means, the hotel man said."

"He runs the deal?"

"The hotel kitchen man said he did. The other three made the deliveries."

"How do they order it?"

"Someone comes by each week and leaves some beef and takes the new order. They're so dependable, the hotel counts on them."

Art shook his head in dismay. "That means they must butcher something every week."

"That's fifty head of beef in a year's time."

"That many beef, they ain't getting them all out of that district up by the Soda Springs schoolhouse," Phil said.

"You're right about that. They've got to be stealing them elsewhere, too."

The spring-loaded chair squeaked when Herschel leaned back in it and nodded. "But where?

"How about those separated horse thieves?" Herschel asked next.

"They ain't said a word."

Herschel nodded. "I'm going to walk down there and try something."

"What's that?" Art asked.

"You two can listen in."

He strode through the jail, and when he approached Doff Porter's cell, he cleared his throat. "Your old buddy Thompson said to say hi."

Porter, who was reading a dog-eared magazine, set it down and sat up. "What did that sumbitch say?"

"Said he was sorry he couldn't get them horses you brought him."

"That no-good outfit. He'd been there—where in the hell did you talk to him?"

"I want to know all you know about him."

Porter stood and gripped the bars. "I guess he told you something else."

"Tell me your side of it."

"We were down in the Wolf Mountains staying in some trapper's cabin about to starve. Thompson came down there and cut us a deal."

"What kind of a deal?"

"Horses for cash."

"No questions asked?"

"They could not be Montana horses."

"What else do you know about the man?"

"Not a damn thing, except we found some horses that fit and brought them up."

"How did he know you were coming?"

"We sent a letter to him a week before."

"Make you nervous waiting around before you rode up there?"

Porter shook his head. "Hell, I was always nervous. There's damn renegade Injuns down there in those mountains. It's a tough place to be in by itself."

"Where does he live?"

"Got his mail in Beaver Creek."

"He have a first name?"

"Yeah, initials W.C.. What's he doing?"

"Same old stuff as always."

"If that sumbitch had been there when we arrived like he promised and paid us, you'd not have us in here."

"Maybe he was busy killing someone that morning and couldn't stay."

"You mean that slicker and hat business? Snyder said it was a bad sign." Porter rubbed the back of his neck. "Guess we should have seen it as one."

Herschel nodded and turned on his heel. "Maybe so."

He held his finger up to silence the other two, and they went back to his office. Art went and looked at the street from the window. "This guy must be some crook."

"Beaver Creek's over in the Milk River country," Phil said.

"That's why we or the sheriff in Miles City don't know him. I imagine his neighbors are missing cattle, too," Art added.

"More than likely. What was he doing with the horses?" Herschel asked.

"He must have had a place in Canada to sell them."

Herschel wasn't certain, but he wanted to know more about the man.

"What do we do next, boss man?"

"Art, why don't you scout this W. C. Thompson out. Kinda drift in that country and out. Don't make any moves against him. A day to ride up there and a couple days to look around for work, and then get back here."

Art nodded. "I don't know many folks up there. That should work."

"The missus be all right for that long by herself?" Herschel asked.

With a dismissive nod, Art acted as if that was no problem.

"Just look in on him. But watch your back. Where is Pleago?" Herschel asked them.

"A guy told me he was slinking around town," Phil said. "But I haven't seen him."

"Does Doc think he suffocated Taunton?"

Phil shrugged. "We don't have any proof."

"He's still around, let's arrest him and try him for implication in the store robbery. He's used up his time to leave."

They both nodded.

"Billings would be better without him. But I don't know what we'll do when the railroad gets closer. They're pouring in up there like a flood. Don Harold has so many prisoners that some are chained outside. We'll need lots more deputies. Lots more, and Billings will need a police department. I'll meet with the mayor and the county commissioners." He shook his head, thinking about all the problems ahead.

After lunch and a visit with Buster, he walked down to the Yellowstone River. He wanted to check on Black Feather and see if he'd returned. Also look for Pleago—if he was hiding, that might be the place—there were lots of 'breeds and riffraff around the shantytown. He stopped at Black Feather's tepee, and his oldest wife came out with a small brown boy in tow to greet him.

"Any word from him?" he asked her.

She shook her head. "No word."

"If he comes back, tell him to be sure to see me."

She agreed, and Herschel went on. He asked a young couple camped with a wagon if they knew Pleago. They didn't, and wanted to know where there was some good land to homestead. They'd wintered in South Dakota and were still looking for the right place.

After some suggestions for them, he moved on and stopped at a half dugout where an older man sat repairing a saddle. His beard was white and untrimmed. When he looked up and saw the badge, he nodded curtly.

"Afternoon," Herschel said and squatted down. "My name's Baker and I'm the sheriff. I'm looking for a man named Pleago."

"He owes me two dollars. You find him, collect it."

"For what?"

"I damn near rebuilt his old kack and he wouldn't pay me a cent, said he had to sell some horses first."

"When was that?"

"Two days ago. I ain't seen hide nor hair of him since then."

"Say where he was going?"

"No." The old man shook his head and went back to his sewing. "He's worthless."

"I know that. I told him to clear out and he ain't done it, so he can serve some hard time. Anyone around here know any more about him?"

"There's a woman down there—" He never looked up while he was sewing. "He was staying there."

"What's her name?"

"Grace. She's in that covered wagon with no wheels under it down the way."

"Thanks."

"Don't mention it."

"I won't."

Herschel ambled down the ruts, spoke to a man making himself an ax handle. Said he'd busted out the old one and his old lady wasn't cooking anymore until he fixed it.

Beyond the wagon box, he found a buxom woman making a garden. She looked up from her planting. "Good day."

"The same to you, ma'am."

"You the law in this land?"

"I am."

"Is it against the law to plant carrots?" She moved ahead a few feet, sowing her seeds in a shallow indent.

"Only if you force some folks to eat them."

With a flip of the hair in her face, she laughed and started to straighten up. Standing straddle-legged, she waited for him to say something.

"I'm looking for Anton Pleago."

"Well, he ain't here."

"Any idea where he went?"

She shook her head, still standing over the new row.

"You see him, tell him to turn himself in."

"I won't see him again."

"Is that so?"

"He stole seventy-five cents from me. I won't put up with thieves."

"Yes, ma'am."

"So don't expect to find him around here, Sheriff."

"Thanks, ma'am." He tipped his hat, satisfied he knew all she'd tell him.

"My name's Grace, too, not ma'am."

"I'll try to remember that—Grace."

When he was back in his office, Phil came by and stuck his head in the door. "Anton may be out at the old Sutter place. Sandy Barr said he saw an old skinny horse out there this morning. Like the paint he rides."

"Get your horse and I'll get mine. We can get out there before dark."

"Meet you in thirty minutes?" Phil asked.

"I should be back with Cob by then."

He hurried to the house, and was saddling Cob when his middle daughter came running around the barn to confront him with her hands on her hips and blocking the doorway.

"Didn't your mother say no pony riding till the strawberries were weeded? Are you through weeding them, Nina?" He drew up the cinch and dropped the stirrup.

"Last row. Where do you have to go?"

"I have to go arrest a man."

"For what?"

"Conspiracy."

"Where he going?" little Sarah whispered, joining her sister.

"He's going after a man that's constipated," Nina said.

"No." Herschel broke up laughing. "Con-spir-acy. It's different."

"Anyway, you're going after a man that broke the law, right?"

"Who's constipated?" Marsha asked, herding the girls back from the horse. "Cob is not your pony. Get over here. Will you be back for supper?"

"I doubt it. We're going down to the Sutter place looking for an outlaw. But I'll come home as soon as I can."

"Be careful."

He nodded and outside the barn, he stepped in the saddle, threw her a kiss, and Cob went sideways ten feet. Nina ran a few feet toward him, waving her hat, shouting, "Buck, Cob, buck!"

"Nina, get back here this instant. You want our daddy hurt?"

She shook her head. "No, I just wanted to see him make a good ride."

Herschel rode off laughing, not convinced that he still wouldn't have a show with his big roan until he was two blocks from his house. From there on, Cob settled down and went on to the courthouse in a fast swinging jog.

The picture of Nina swinging her straw hat at him and

Cob made Herschel grin. She'd be the real one to raise when she got into her teens.

Maybe they'd settle this Pleago situation before dark. No telling.

EIGHTEEN

Thurman and Mary drove into Pine Bluff, Nebraska, on the Texas Trail for the night. Thurman reined the mule up at the wagon yard and climbed down. Then, with his hands on his hips, he stretched his stiff back, "We'll be in Cheyenne in a couple more days."

"Good," she said, working her way over to his side of the rig to climb down.

He lifted her off and set her on the ground. She smiled and laughed at him. "One day, you will fall down doing that."

"Oh, but you'd be on top."

"Not so funny either." But despite her scolding, she had a hard time suppressing a grin. Her figure had really become large, showing off the baby she carried.

It looked cloudy in the west, so he was anxious to hang up the fly. Late afternoon showers weren't unusual coming off the Rockies.

"Ask if they have cooking wood for sale," she said as he went to check in.

He nodded, and went to the weathered unpainted building that served as the office.

"Howdy," he said when the bell rang overhead above the door and a small gray-haired woman came up to the desk. "Staying one night."

She nodded and turned the register around. "Twenty-five cents."

"You have any firewood for sale?"

"Yes, it's around back. All split and ready for a cooking fire. You can have a big armload for ten cents."

"I'll take twenty cents worth."

She smiled. "My grandson will like to know that. He cuts and splits it."

"You don't get many freight wagons anymore, do you?"

"No, but we still get some drovers and a few folks moving and like you on the go. Railroad got the rest."

"Thanks," he said, then paid her and went outside.

"They have firewood," he said to Mary, and her face brightened.

"Where will we camp?"

"Back under those pines. I'll hook up our fly. It may rain here soon."

"Good idea," she said, walking along beside him.

He strung a rope between two good-sized pines, and soon had the canvas slung over it. She was on her knees pounding in stakes to tie it down. By the time it was tied and tight, a small dust storm had gathered and thunder rolled across the western sky. With the crates, bedding, and his saddle under the tent, he went to unharness the mule.

Small ice pellets began to peck on him, and the taut canvas shed hundreds of them. He tossed the harness inside, and quickly led the mule to the picket line with Buck. Then the hail increased in size and really began to beat on him. Under the tarp at last, he smiled at the concerned look she gave him while she was seated on one of the crates.

"Just a little storm. Why, I saw hail in Kansas big as cannonballs." He hugged her shoulders, grateful it was high enough in the center for him to stand up.

Thunder rolled across the high prairie and rain began to replace the stones. But it was cold, too. In a short while, it would pass and all would be well.

In the dim light, he saw her rubbing her swollen belly. "That guy getting close?"

"I think so."

"Hold off three more days and we can have him in Cheyenne. There will be a doctor there."

"Indian women have babies all the time by themselves."

"I don't want to take any chances. You're pretty precious to me." He stood by the open end and watched the sunlight begin to return to the rolling brown grassland. The storm moved northeast, and diamonds sparkled on every blade of grass.

She came over and gently shoved her bulge against him. "Even as clumsy and awkward as I am?"

"More so."

"Why did you leave your first wife?" Her face was nestled on his chest as he held her.

"Probably the damn war." He ran his upper teeth over his lower lip. "I came home beat, tired, and disgusted. I guess she was tired of running the place, and she acted jealous that I got to go and she had to stay there." He dropped his head and shook it.

"She had no idea. No idea of the hell there is in a war. It wasn't the same when I got back. I'd never cheated on her in those four years. But when I came home, the bed was cold.

"I found another woman who made me laugh. I couldn't see things clear. I'd been drug through purgatory, and I felt I deserved to laugh and enjoy life. I even spoke to my wife of more children—she wanted no more. My time away from the place grew longer, buying and trading stock, and my drab gray days at home, where I guess she wanted me to do penance forever, became less and less.

"I couldn't explain it to the kids. So I left them debt free and a thousand dollars in the bank and I rode out for San Antonio. I left her a note saying I wouldn't be back."

"That was a lot of money."

"Yes, but money won't ever replace being there. In fact, I cut myself too short and soon fell on some hard times. Quicker than a jackrabbit can bounce up and run off, the woman I chose left me for another man with a pocketful of change."

"What happened to her?"

"My first wife is buried on that place in Texas. The other one was working in a whorehouse in Denver last I heard about her."

She hugged him tighter. "You never found anyone else?"

"To be quite honest—no. I wasn't looking for you or any woman, but I'm glad you came along." He gently rocked her in his arms. "I really am so pleased. I want this baby to be raised right. I want to have a life—a place of my own. When I find my son, I'll marry you."

"You don't have to do that."

He closed his eyes and laid his cheek on the top of her head. "Yes, I do."

"I am glad that we laugh," she said. "I never laughed after I married him. We were like spirits when he courted me, but after the honeymoon, he turned sour. I was his—his slave. He accused me of being unfaithful and beat me the week before my daughter was born.

"He drank lots and treated me badly when he came home drunk. I lived under his shadow. He was also friends with Chickenhead. That was why I think *he* noticed me. I cried on my children's grave, but I never shed a tear for him."

"Why pick me?"

"I told you before, I have powers to see things. I knew that evening you came to buy supper, and took your hat off for an Indian woman, you were a good man—but I thought you might be married. I could see, too, that your heart was big and you had strong medicine. I couldn't let him kill you."

"I owe you my life."

"Oh, you better go get that wood or we'll starve to death."

He came back in the glow of the fiery sundown with the first armload. She was sitting on the ground on his bedroll cloth waiting for her wood.

"How far is Billings?" she asked.

"Maybe two weeks. You getting tired?"

"No, me and the baby are fine. But I sure hope my carrying him on this trip doesn't make him a restless person."

"I don't think we're restless. I think he should grow up and be serene."

"What is that sur—reen?"

"Means like us—happy and content."

"I hope so."

He went back and got his second armload of cooking wood to take back. As he returned across the prairie, the lonesome whistle of a train moaned in the twilight and a dozen coyotes raised their heads and howled. Steel against nature. Things had changed so much in his lifetime, he could hardly believe it.

Back in camp, he bound the firewood in smaller bundles

with string while seated by her on the ground. The aroma of the smoke was much better than the cow chip fires they'd used coming across eastern Colorado.

"Cheyenne is a big place?" she asked.

"Oh, I think so. I was only there once and that was six years ago. I went through there to go to Deadwood and get rich."

"What was there?"

"Gold."

"You find any?"

"Lord, no, or I'd still be there."

She laughed. "What was it like in Deadwood?"

"Canyons and high mountains. It rained a lot the time I was there, and that turned it all into mud knee deep in the streets."

"It was that bad?"

"It was worse than that." He shook his head. Deadwood was a hellhole.

"Was Cheyenne muddy?"

"No, they had lots of brick streets."

"Like Fort Smith?"

"Yes, but no ferry to cross."

"Good." She laughed while frying the bacon.

The baby didn't come that night. The third day, they reached Cheyenne and Thurman checked them in to a hotel. Once in the room, she held her belly and smiled at him. "I may name the baby after this place."

"Monarch Hotel?"

"No, silly, Cheyenne."

"He coming tonight?"

She shook her head. "I don't think so."

"We may have to call him Billings."

"No. Cheyenne."

"Fine. You want supper?"

"No, I brought some crackers and cheese from the wagon. I am not very hungry. I don't want to walk those stairs again tonight." Hands on her hips, she looked uncomfortable.

"I'm going to check on a few things and I'll be back."

"Promise me you will eat supper while you are out."

He raised his right hand. "I promise."

She hugged him. "I will be fine. Go out and eat. You are tired of my cooking anyway."

"No, I'm not."

She pushed him toward the door. He kissed her and left. Outside, he crossed the street and went down two blocks west to the Longhorn Saloon. He took a table where he could see the front door and ordered a steak and some whiskey.

A man came in dressed expensively, and Thurman wondered as he poured some whiskey in his glass if he didn't know him. Then the man saw him and recognized him with a small smile.

"Captain Baker?"

"Yes. Colonel Feltner?"

The man nodded. "I haven't seen you since the war."

Thurman rose and shook his former superior officer's hand. "Have a seat. Waiter, bring us another glass, please."

"I thought you were a Texan."

"I am, sir. However, I am looking for my son."

"Is he up here?"

"He's in Montana."

"And the rest of the family?"

"They're in Texas," he said to save explaining. "What're you doing in Wyoming?"

"Well, there was nothing in the South to do after the war, so I came West and was in some land development.

There was a large ranch out here owned by some Eastern investors being run very shabbily. I contacted them and offered my services. They made me general superintendent."

The glass arrived and he offered the colonel supper, but the man refused. Thurman poured him a drink.

"So I fired all the crooked help that had been rustling the ranch cattle. Hired new help, and we are making a serious profit. But I could always use a good ranch manager for one of my divisions."

Thurman shook his head. "No, I have a ranch in south Texas waiting for me."

He noticed two Mexicans walk in and go to the bar. For a moment, he froze at the sight of them. They had never made eye contact with him. Both were dressed like cowboys, not vaqueros, but their clothing was new. It was them—Corrales's two pistoleros.

How in the hell did they know he was up here? He must have left some trail behind him. A buggy and an Indian woman weren't that hard to track.

"Something wrong?"

"Two hired guns just walked in. Don't look. They're standing at the bar."

"They after you?"

"Yes. They're pistoleros out of Mexico."

"You have their names?"

"Petrillo and Sanchez."

"No problem. I'll simply have the Cheyenne police hold them for the Texas authorities."

Thurman frowned. "I don't think they have any warrants out for them in Texas."

The colonel smiled at him. "They do now. Two weeks a good enough lead?"

"That's plenty of time."

"Sit tight. They won't try anything in this place."

"That'll be pretty hard to do, sitting in the same room with two rattlesnakes."

"Baker, I can handle it. Trust me."

Thurman nodded. But still not that convinced the colonel's plan would work, he slowly ate his steak.

NINETEEN

Herschel and Phil dismounted and held their horses as they rode the ferry across the Yellowstone. The old man wasn't there, and a pimple-faced boy in his teens cranked the winch that afternoon. Phil called him Shad.

"He's Matty Kendal's boy," Phil said later.

Herschel gave him a nod. His mind was set on capturing Pleago and on wondering why the stupid man did not leave when he had the chance. Would have saved the cost of prosecution and prison time as well.

The day had been nice. A gentle wind out of the south—great springtime weather. They thanked the boy when he docked on the south shore, and they rode on in a short lope. The Sutter place was on the main road and only a few miles from the ferry. Still amused at Nina's efforts to get Cob to buck, Herschel shook his head.

They reined up at the pole fence that surrounded the fields and looked at the dark log house, sheds, and corrals that were in a shabby condition. The place was tied up with out-of-state heirs, and except that the hay had been mowed and removed the year before by neighbors, nothing had been done to it in several years.

"I don't see his horse," Phil said.

"He may have hidden it. Keep in mind he might get desperate."

"Yes, sir."

Herschel checked the six-gun on his side and moved it to a more accessible place on his hip. They rode side by side up the driveway. If Pleago was in there, chances are he knew by now they were coming for him. Herschel rubbed his right palm on the top of his canvas pants. He was forced to check Cob, who must have sensed the tension and had began to dance, but his gaze remained on the house for any sign of movement.

Seconds ticked by and they dismounted at the rack. With his .44 in his fist, Herschel scanned the small windows upstairs and the ones under the porch. Nothing.

"This is Sheriff Baker, Pleago. Come out hands high or else."

No answer.

"Phil, go around and cover the back door. Watch yourself."

"I will." His deputy took off in a run.

Under Herschel's boot sole, the porch board creaked when he stepped up on it. A quick check and he pulled the latchstring and kicked the door open. The revolver ready, he stepped inside. The house's interior was dark save for the little light coming in the windows.

He searched around and went to the fireplace. The ashes in the hearth were cold. Too late.

"I didn't see his horse anywhere out back," Phil said, coming in through the back door.

"He hasn't been here in several hours," Herschel said. "The ashes in the fireplace are cold."

Phil nodded and squatted down on his heels. "What next?"

Herschel holstered his gun. "We can hope he left the country."

"Lots of dead ends in this business."

"There sure are. We better get back to Billings. My wife'll have supper waiting."

Herschel and his man made a sweep of the sheds and pens. From the fresh manure, it was obvious that a horse had been kept in the front pen—the one that had been seen from the road.

"You don't sound convinced that he's left," Phil said as they mounted up to return to town.

"I'm not sure about anything concerning him. He stole seventy-five cents from a woman who'd been keeping him."

"He must be desperate."

"That's why he worries me."

Phil nodded.

The sun was sinking fast when Herschel rode into the lot and dropped heavily from the saddle. He tossed up the stirrup and stripped out the latigo. A strong smell of horse sweat leaked out of the saddle and pads when he swung both off Cob's back. With the kack in the rack and the blankets spread out to dry, he led Cob to the stall and hung a pail of water in there for him.

He'd given him a measure of oats when he heard the sound of Marsha's footsteps and her dress swishing. His chores done for the time being, he turned and hugged her, swinging her around.

"Did you arrest him?"

"Nope. He was gone when we got there."

"So he's still maybe constipated?"

He laughed and shook his head. "That Nina."

"I have supper in the oven," she said.

"Good, the ride made me hungry."

"When *can't* you eat?"

He winked at her and set her down. "Aw, I'd rather not say when."

She looked at the loft for help. Then they went hand in hand to the porch, where he washed up.

"We're going back to Soda Springs, but—" He dried his hands on the towel.

"The girls are also going. They have reminded me several times about that this week."

"Hey, it won't hurt. There's a bald-faced horse those rustlers stole somewhere that will soon be up for sale if no one claims him. I'm thinking on buying him for Kate."

"Well, don't tell her or you'll get ragged to death."

He smiled and hugged Marsha's shoulder. They went inside and Nina came to meet them, "Con-spir-acy means for two or more people to plan to do something together."

"Very good."

"The other you take prunes for it."

Marsha's shoulders dropped and she looked defeated.

Herschel snickered and hugged the girl's shoulder. "Nina, you've got that right."

Kate read a book to the other girls in the living room while he ate his supper.

"What next, High Sheriff?" Marsha asked.

"I need to work on this murder case some more. Tomorrow, I'm going to take the two bullets the coroner got out of Hamby down to Andy's Gun Shop and see what caliber they are for certain."

"He can tell?"

"Yes. He's the expert I have to rely on."

"What then?"

"Well, if they match the caliber of the casings Art found, then we have another link. Not a strong one, but a link to the cattle rustlers."

"That old ranch was sure well used of late."

"Yes, I'd say it set there for years just waiting to become the outlaws' headquarters." He cut up some more of the sliced roast beef on his plate. "I still aim to find Hamby's killer or killers."

"No word from Black Feather?"

"No, but I think he may be on a honeymoon."

She frowned at him.

"He took one of the younger wives with him."

She laughed and shook her head in disapproval.

"He'll show up one day," Herschel said.

"I'll be ready Friday morning to drive up to Soda Springs, and we can camp out two nights if that's all right."

"Good, I can talk to more folks then."

"I thought that's what you wanted to do."

"Yes, it is."

"Your piece of the apple pie is next," she said, and slid off the chair to go get it.

Boy, he sure had moved up marrying her.

The morning sun shone in the gun shop's front windows. Andy looked hard at the two bullets under a magnifying glass. "They look like 38s."

"Anything else?" Herschel asked.

"I'd say a Smith and Wesson cartridge. That's the commonest round in this caliber. He was obviously shot at close range, so the bullets are not flattened like a longer shot would be. Most folks have .44- or .45-caliber ammo."

"Good. Art found two Smith and Wesson casings not a hundred yards from where they dumped the body."

"I can fire a few of them in some material like his body and have them as proof if you want them."

"I'd like to have them for the trial. I think the killer will be packing that pistol when I arrest him."

"I'll do it this week."

"Thanks, Andy."

"Any time, Sheriff. Any time."

Herschel left the gun shop and started back to the office. He stopped for coffee at the café and talked to Buster about the Pleago situation.

"Pleago wasn't there, huh?" Buster said.

"No, he was long gone. You know where he might be? Heard any word on him?"

"If he stole seventy-five cents from that woman down on the river, then he's too broke to simply leave. I bet he went to find his partners in the robbery."

"I've got Black Feather down in the Priors looking for them."

"Oh, he should find them."

"He's been gone for over a week."

Buster grinned. "That's white man time."

"I know all about Indians and their lack of keeping time. He also took his newest bride with him."

"See, you answered your own question." Buster slapped his knees and laughed.

He left Buster and started down Main Street again, headed for the office. The peaceful traffic of incoming farmers, some freight wagons, a bicycle or two, along with a few ranch hands sure was much less than Miles City's stampede. But that would soon descend upon him, he knew, and end all the tranquillity of this small town.

He needed to talk to the county commissioners about what they faced. If he didn't do something before the situation exploded, the railroad might send in its own regulators. That would be more like anarchy in his book than doing it by the law. Their form of law would revive the big ranchers' style that he'd ended with his election. Maybe he could convince the railroad to help the county fund some of the expenses. He'd need to see about that.

When Herschel entered his office, Darby, his deskman, spoke up. "The deputy from North Platte is coming in today to get those two. I got the telegram that he was in Sheridan this morning."

"Good, save feeding them," Herschel said, and shook his head. "Bring both of them in my office. I need to talk to them."

"Yes, sir."

While he was engrossed in his expenses, he heard the leg irons dragging on the floor and looked up from the papers.

"Have a seat. You two are about to depart my establishment. I wanted to have a little heart-to-heart talk with you. I promise you that you will not be prosecuted for anything in Montana if you level with me. Fair enough trade?"

They looked at each other and nodded.

"This Thompson found you down in the Wolf Mountains?"

"Yeah, we thought he was law. Came wearing a black suit like some badge toter, and Porter held a gun on him for a while."

Porter agreed. "Wasn't no reason other than to arrest us when he came down there."

"What's he like?"

"Hell, he's tougher than you first think. I figured he'd kill a guy and never bat an eye."

"He pay you some money?" Herschel asked.

"Five bucks to buy food," Snyder said. "We were busted and except for some deer meat, we'd've been starving."

"Tell me the deal."

"He wanted four good horses. No junk, and he'd pay us thirty bucks a head less the five he'd advanced us," Porter said.

"So you got the horses and came up on that date in the letter. He called it Page's place."

Herschel nodded for them to continue—he'd solved one mystery.

"We had four good ones. I know that bald-faced horse showed out, but he's solid as a drum. Thompson never said no fancy ones," Porter said.

"You two were set to collect over a hundred dollars?"

"Exactly."

"What was he going to do with 'em?"

"Damned if I know, but we got them far enough away, they weren't local horses someone would recognize."

"He mention anything else, like work he had for you after the horse deal?"

They looked at each other and Snyder spoke. "He kinda acted like he was testing us."

"He ever mention rustling cattle?"

Porter shook his head. "He asked the questions and we answered 'em."

"Tell me one thing you saw about him that was different."

"He must be married—he wears a gold wedding ring," Snyder said.

"He carries a pearl-handled pistol."

"What kind?"

"Looks like a Smith and Wesson."

Herschel tented his fingers and touched the end of his nose. "What else?"

They shrugged and shook their heads.

"Good luck in North Platte. You guard's coming today."

"Hey, Baker," Porter said, standing up with a rattle of chains. "For a lawman, you're about as fair as a man can get."

Snyder agreed.

The two were taken back to their cells. Herschel slumped in the protesting chair and wondered how and when he'd meet up with this Thompson. Soon, he hoped, and with enough evidence to convince a jury of his peers the man killed Hamby.

TWENTY

THURMAN unlocked the hotel room and looked in shock at Mary's face in the lamplight. It was laced in rivers of sweat as she sat back on the bed, obviously in labor.

"Is the baby coming?"

"It's—trying."

"I'm going for a doctor." He didn't wait for her refusal, and raced out of the room, down the stairs. Halfway down, he shouted at the clerk, "Get a doctor at once. My wife is having a baby."

"Yes, sir," the pale-faced clerk said, and ran out the front door shouting for a doctor.

Thurman had no idea if that would work, but headed back up the stairs. A heavyset woman met him on the second floor. "I can help her."

"Good. Heaven only knows if he'll get anyone."

"My name's Martha Goode. I can help her." She hurried beside him.

"Thurman Baker. Her name's Mary."

"Is it Mary's first?"

"No, she's delivered two before this—one on her own."

"Good."

They were back in the room and Martha took charge. "Lie down, darling," she said, washing her hands in the bowl on the dresser and drying them. "Now, how close are you? Oh, my, he's coming."

Thurman knelt on the far side of the bed and Mary squeezed his hand. Soon, Martha was up in the middle of the bed and coaxing her to push.

After what seemed like an interminable amount of time, there was a final push and the woman held a slick-looking infant up by the heels. She slapped it twice and it tried its lungs.

"Why it's a dandy boy," she said, rocking him in her arms.

"His name is Cheyenne," Thurman told her.

"Well, Cheyenne it will be. Here, Mary, is your precious boy." Martha gently handed the baby to Mary.

"Thanks," Thurman said in a state of dulled shock.

"Don't thank me. Thank God, sir. A baby always is a miracle. Ah, and he's such a fine strong little fellow, too."

There was a knock on the door and Thurman went to answer it.

"Dr. Williams. This where the lady's having a child?"

"Yes." He swung the door open to the man. "But he's already here."

The doctor fussed around, and soon declared her and the baby to be fine. Thurman was at the open window, looking at the street below in the gathering darkness. He turned back and thanked them both.

"What do I owe you?"

"Me? Laddie, you don't owe a dime. I just wanted to be

a help." Martha shook her head, gathered her skirt, and curtsied before she left.

The doctor piped up. "My usual fee is ten dollars, but since I did so little, I'll settle for five."

"Record his birth, too?"

"I can do that for another fifty cents."

"You do that. His name is Cheyenne Baker."

"I'll send a copy back here in the morning."

Thurman paid him six and told him to keep the change. The doctor spoke to Mary briefly, and then thanked Thurman as he left.

"Those two pistoleros are in town." He went back to the window to look at the street. "They showed up in the bar where I was eating tonight. Lucky for me my former commander in the army was there. He had the local law arrest them on warrants from Texas. They can hold them for two weeks—"

"What do you mean warrants?" Mary asked.

"They can say they looked like men on wanted posters and wire those law agencies that they have these men they think are their wanted fugitives. The colonel is very influential in this city. I found that out tonight."

"What must we do?"

"I think we should take the stage to Billings. I can get you and the baby settled up there, then I can handle those two."

"I'm sorry to be such a burden."

"You aren't. I wanted you and him. But Cheyenne is not the place to play cat and mouse with two killers."

"Will they quit here?"

"No. They can't go home to Mexico without my head. Hell, they've tracked us from Texas to here. They don't know the word for quit."

"So it's either your death or theirs?" she asked him in a soft voice, cuddling her new infant.

"If there was a better way, I'd do it. You know I told you how between San Antonio and Fort Worth I set them afoot, no boots and no horses . . ." He dropped his chin while looking at the floor and shook his head. "I should have killed them then."

"Oh, I'm sorry. This baby has made things worse."

"No! This is something I can handle. I want you, Mary. He's our son. I gave him my name."

"Yes, that pleased me."

"I am sorry to upset you at such a trying time. I'll get you out of here. If you get too tired, we can lay over on the trip."

"I can leave tomorrow."

"You sure you will be strong enough?"

"I walked twelve miles the day after my first one was born."

"I'll go see how I can get the horse and mule handled. Blacky, too. And check on the stage schedule. What can I get for you and him?"

"Some diapers and a couple of small blankets. I can make him clothes when I get there."

"Food?"

She shook her had. "I am fine."

"I'm sorry we have to move. But this is not the time or the place."

"It will be fine. He is here."

"I'll be back in an hour."

"We'll be all right. Take your time."

He agreed, but wasn't satisfied at all closing the door and hurrying off. But he cut a deal on boarding the dog, horse, and mule with the liveryman, and paid him for two months' care with word not to sell them, he'd be back. The man agreed.

A short while later, he learned the railroad passenger service ran to Casper and bought tickets on it. The station man said there was a daily stage that ran from Casper on to Sheridan and then to Billings. If she could stand it, they'd make it in a three-day trip. Angry that his plans to simply let her rest up awhile when the baby was born had evaporated, he hurried off to buy what she needed.

He was feeling very protective of her as they started out the next morning. Besides her bag, he took his saddle and rifle along. They rode in a cab to the depot. She looked tired and that worried him, but she pushed him to go ahead. On the train, she marveled at everything.

"This is much better than the ferry," she said, looking out the window at the passing Wyoming country.

"Why, hell, you've never been on a train before. I'm sorry."

"It is fine. The baby comes in the world and the very next day he rides a train. When he is old enough, I will tell him about this trip and the adventures we had." She laughed.

He sat back on the passenger seat and felt relaxed for the first time in a day. She had a way of soothing him. He didn't really know how she did it, but all his piled-on anxiety drained away. His mission's conclusion was only days away. *Lord, help me convince that boy. And thanks for her and the little one.*

In mid-afternoon, they reached Casper and stepped down onto the depot platform. The porter brought his saddle and her things. Thurman found a cab and they went to the hotel that the driver suggested.

They ate in the hotel restaurant, and then ordered a tub

and hot bath in the room for Mary. While she bathed, he sat in the stiff chair and held the baby wrapped in a blanket. The baby's tiny fingers were so small, it was hard to imagine he would ever grow up to someday be a man.

The fourteen-hour stage ride proved tougher than the train. Part of the way, he cared for the baby while she tried to sleep in the rocking coach. Late that night, they were at last in a hotel room in Sheridan.

"We can stay here an extra day," he offered.

She agreed.

The next day, he had his white shirt washed, starched, pressed, and his suit brushed in a Chinese bathhouse. Then after a bath, shave, and haircut, he went back to the hotel room to check on her.

"I feel very rested today," she said.

"Good. It won't be as far up there as it was from Casper."

He stood at the second-story window and hugged her shoulder when she joined him. "You seen anything in the future?"

She squeezed him from the side. "No, I don't dread anything right now. Maybe my visions will come back now my son is here."

"Did you have some earlier?"

She laughed. "I wasn't sure about the train."

"You know, I never thought of that until we were on it."

They both laughed.

He spent the afternoon playing poker in a saloon on Main Street. A small game between four men: a local rancher, a freighter, a builder, and Thurman.

"Where you headed, Baker?" the fortyish rancher named Trisk asked.

"Billings." Thurman folded his hand.

"Damn railroad's headed there next," the Scottish

freighter said, and then turned to spit tobacco in the nearby spittoon.

"You going to settle up there?" the builder, who called himself Earl, asked as he raked in the small pot.

Thurman shook his head. "My son is up there."

"Who's he?" Trisk asked.

"Herschel Baker."

"We know about him. He's the sheriff that tracked a killer down and arrested him here. Tough guy. Borders are just lines to him, they didn't bother him one bit. You just visiting him?"

"For now." He anted two dollars and watched the fresh cards coming.

"What's your line of work?"

"I ranch down in south Texas. Wanted to see my son this summer."

"Whew, laddie, you must have wanted to see him bad," the Scotsman said. "Coming all this way."

"It was time."

The others nodded, and Thurman won the next hand.

Thurman, Mary, and Cheyenne boarded the northbound stage in the cool predawn. They stopped at a stage stop at midday, and the drummer riding with them pointed to the nearby hill. "That's where they got General Custer. Sitting Bull and that bunch killed them all right up there."

After using the facilities out back, they went inside the low-walled building to find some food. Thurman noted two men dressed in buckskin and with unkempt beards who were talking loudly at the bar to the side of the dining table. The woman waiting on Thurman and Mary noticed Cheyenne, and was delighted when Mary held him up for her to see.

Thurman had his back to the wall, and he saw the two

loudmouths talking about something that had attracted their interest. The larger one, towering over six feet, then started toward the dining table. Thurman eased out of the seat and Mary blinked at his move.

"That's close enough." Thurman held up his left hand to stop the man.

"Hell, all I wanted to do was look at the merchandise. I may wanta buy her."

"You better get back to that bar and mind your own business."

"Aw, I'd give you a sack of gold for her. She's a cute little pup." His words were slurred by the whiskey, and he rocked on his moccasin heels.

"She's my wife. She's not for sale. And I'll accept your apologies and you get back to the bar."

"Adobe, get back here. That man's serious. Serious as hell," his partner said from across the room.

But Adobe either didn't hear him or refused to heed him. His hand went for his cross-draw holster. The man's fingers barely had closed on the grips when the .44 in Thurman's hand spit lead and boiling gun smoke from the muzzle. The bullet struck Adobe in the chest like a thud on a watermelon.

The mountain man dropped to his knees, and his partner rushed over screaming, "I told you—"

"This your fight, too?" Thurman asked him, herding Mary and the baby aside. His gun was still cocked in his hand.

"No—no. Adobe, talk to me. Adobe, talk to me." He looked up with tears in his eyes. "He's—he's dead, mister."

"I'm sorry. He went for his gun."

The man nodded and broke into sobs.

Thurman and Mary went outside in the bright sun along with the stage driver.

The woman who'd waited on them came to the door. "I'll bring your food out. No way you can eat in there."

"Shame," the driver said. "But he was too drunk to listen. You did the only thing you could do."

"What'll the law want to do?" Thurman asked.

"Nothing. I'll have someone here bury him."

"Thanks."

"No problem."

When the waitress brought their food on tin plates, she also gave them silverware from her pocket.

"I'd pay for burying him," Thurman said softly to her.

"Naw, Big Mike'll take him up in the Big Horns and bury him near their cabin."

"Sorry about the trouble."

"No need. He should have known better. I'm sorry he embarrassed your wife."

Mary shook it off.

Thurman looked off toward the distant purple Big Horns. Damn shame. While Mary ate her food, he held the baby. No doubt Cheyenne was still upset from the gun's loud report, squirming and whimpering some, but the little guy seldom cried.

Before they climbed back on the stage for the last leg, the woman's man and the other trapper brought the dead man's body out wrapped in a blanket and loaded him over the saddle across a riding mule. When the body was tied down, the trapper mounted a crop-eared paint buffalo pony and rode off.

Next stop was Billings. Why did he dread that notion so? It roiled his stomach.

TWENTY-ONE

BLANKETS, the canvas fly, three poles with iron bolts in the ends for tent support, a shovel, ax, food for an army—Herschel considered it a major deal when he saw it.

"We're ready to go," Nina told him before he dismounted. "We been working all day like slaves."

He nodded to her when he dropped off Cob and began to undo the girth. "I guess it's lots of work getting ready to go to a dance."

"Yeah, but I don't plan to get married at this one."

"Oh?" He lifted the saddle and blankets off Cob.

"I made up my mind."

"How is that?"

"Since Kate's the oldest, she'll have to get married before I can."

"I guess. Is that a rule?" He put the saddle on the rack.

"Of course it is. And since she ain't looking very hard, why, I'll probably be an old maid."

"What's happening out here?" Marsha asked, joining them.

"Oh, we were talking about not getting married this weekend."

"Well, I should hope not."

"Mother, it is a conspiracy between Daddy and me."

"Very well. We are loaded and ready to go."

"I see that," said Herschel. "Reckon those buckskins can tow that load and all of us up there?"

"They'll make it."

"We better get headed up there then."

"I didn't bring anything I didn't think we'd need," Marsha declared.

He smiled and winked at her. "I'm just used to an old greasy sack tied on the saddle horn."

Nina made a face and they laughed.

When the girls were loaded and they found themselves a place to sit among the load, Herschel helped Marsha up and they drove off. The long tent poles were under her feet and presented no problem, but he was amazed at all she'd brought along. They wouldn't starve for certain. Of course, there'd be more freeloaders coming around at mealtimes since the word would be out.

The drive went fine. They took some breaks. And Kate was soon braiding daisies into a crown. She made one for Sarah to wear instead of the sunbonnet she hated. Nina wore a boy's derby for headgear, and refused to be involved in any flowery attire. Instead, she skipped rocks across the streams they stopped at, or tried to hit meadowlarks with rocks while going down the road.

Close to sundown, they pulled up to park on the edge of the school yard. The girls were worn out. Marsha started a fire to cook supper, and Herschel began unloading. A few folks were already camped there. They came over and helped, making small talk about the nice weather and the cattle markets. Soon, the Baker camp was set up and the horses were on the picket line eating oats from nose bags.

Sarah fell asleep before finishing supper, and he carried her wearing her daisy crown to her palette. His little princess tucked under the blanket, he walked back to the fire's glow, grateful Marsha had thought to bring some wood along. In the morning, he'd find some to chop up.

"I'm not going to sleep tonight," Nina announced.

"Why not?" Marsha asked.

"I might miss something."

"But then you'd be too tired to play tomorrow."

"Oh, well, I may sleep a little."

"Did you go to dances when you were a boy?" Kate asked him.

"Yes. They had dances at folks' houses, they had them in town, they had them out at schoolhouses."

"Who taught you to dance?"

"A girl named Gretchen."

"Did you want to marry her?"

"No."

"You don't have to marry whoever you dance with," her mother said, looking at the stars for help.

Kate shrugged. "I just wanted to know about Daddy's life before we knew him."

"That's being nosy."

"Naw, Kate's all right. Back then, I got my tongue all tangled up talking to girls who I thought I liked. And I reckon I never impressed them much on account of that."

"But you don't act like that now."

Marsha gave her an exasperated look as she washed the dishes.

"I guess, Kate, I was slow growing up about that," Herschel said.

"If I'd been a girl back then, would you have wanted to dance with me?"

"I sure would have. But I'd've stammered and sounded plumb clumsy."

"Why did you dance with Gretchen?"

"Because she always asked me to dance with her."

Kate snickered. "Was she pretty?"

He sucked on an eyetooth and shook his head. "Not near as pretty as you girls are."

He had an image of the straight-backed, flat-chested Gretchen in her very homemade dress dancing stiff-legged with him. One and two and one and two. Then, one night, he must have heard the music, and they were soon whirling around the floor and her brown eyes got big enough to pop out. After that, he always danced with her—because he didn't know how to dance with the other girls. It only worked for him with her. She even laughed sometimes when they had to quit to get their breath. And one day, he wasn't dancing with a flat-chested girl, but a woman with a nice figure, and he never knew when it all changed.

Gretchen's big brothers caught him outside the schoolhouse one night, and demanded to know his intentions toward their sister. What did he do for a living? How could he support her? When would he ask her to marry him?

His answers did not suit them and they beat up on him. Travis wanted to get back at them when he found Herschel spitting blood on the ground by the outhouses. Herschel called him off.

"Hell, Travis, I can't marry her. I can't support her. We barely get by ourselves. Besides, them three are twice our size."

"When did that ever stop us?"

"Tonight, I think, they caved in a rib or two." He winced at the pain.

"What'll happen to her?" Travis asked, looking out in the dark school yard for her brothers. When the two of them went back inside, there was no sign of her in the schoolhouse either. They'd taken her away.

The next week in town, Herschel learned she was engaged to a much older man in San Antonio who'd lost his wife in an Indian raid. He saw her one time a year later on the sidewalk in Mason. She was big as a house, expecting a baby any minute by his appraisal.

"Damn you anyway," she said under her breath, glaring out of her dark eyes at him. "When you told them you didn't want me, they sold me to him."

"I never said that. Sold you—" He didn't know what to say.

"Yes." she hissed, and put her hands on her belly. "This is all your fault, too."

She tried to blame him for everything, but he knew that dancing with her didn't cause what happened to her. Still, it was one more of his mistakes with women. Thank God he had found Marsha.

That night, when the girls were asleep and he and his wife were in their bedroll, Marsha whispered, "Were you engaged to her?"

"To who?"

She poked him. "You know. Gretchen."

"No, and when I wouldn't get engaged to her, her brothers beat me up and sold her to an old man."

"They did what?"

"You heard me."

"Oh, that was horrible."

"I thought so, too." He rolled over and rocked her in his arms. "But I'm so glad I have you."

"So am I."

The next day, he was hoping to talk to several attendees that might come for the dance. Hatch and Olsen headed his list. He visited in private with a few ranchers he felt were trustworthy enough to ask if they knew anyone named Thompson, but no one did. He guessed that Hatch had some of them too scared to say a word to a lawman. Those other men who'd talked about Hatch at the previous dance were probably the bravest ones.

Shultz arrived in a fresh-boiled shirt and with his suit brushed. First thing, he stopped by to talk to Marsha. Herschel figured that way the cattle buyer would get an invite to take meals with them and also dance that night with her. He wasn't missing a trick.

Bailey Hanks showed up at noontime for lunch. Bailey was another single Texas cowboy who always did rope tricks for the girls when he came by. Wore his pants tucked in his boot tops and was so bowlegged, a hog on the run would get right though them. He came over to the wagon tailgate to wash up.

Bailey looked around and then cleared his throat. "I ain't a man to snitch, but don't Sonny Pharr work for you?"

"Yes, why?"

"Well, I was up in Miles City this week getting a load of salt and seen him last Wednesday." Bailey wet his lower lip. "I'd sworn he was there on business."

"What kinda business?"

"He had something tarped down in a wagon bed. I seen it when I rode past him. Couldn't tell what it was."

"Thanks."

"I figured you'd like to know that."

"I do. And I'll check on it. You seen Hatch or Olsen?"

A dark mask spread over Bailey's face. "Let me tell you a story about Olsen. I was checking on some heifers two weeks ago and I run on to him. There were two heifers kinda boxed up in a canyon, and he was sitting on the ground at the mouth of it, smoking a cigarette. I knew them heifers had been run up there, 'cause they were bawling about it wanting to get back to some others.

"I jumped him and asked him what in the hell he was doing with 'em. He got his back all up and said he was just riding through the country and if I didn't mind my own damn business I'd be sprouting daisies."

"He make any more threats?"

"Yeah, something about nosy cowboys don't live long."

"You better watch your back. They shot Hamby."

"I know, and he was one of them."

"You know anything else?"

"You two come eat," Marsha called to them.

"I'll tell you later," Bailey said. Then he swept off his silk-rimmed best hat and made a deep bow for her that set the girls to giggling. "We're a-coming, my fair lady."

What else did Bailey know about the Hamby deal? What in the hell was Sonny Pharr doing over in Miles City on a weekday?

TWENTY-TWO

THURMAN helped Mary down from the stage and looked around them in the mid-afternoon. A nice orderly-looking place, Billings was a lot like many Western towns. He'd asked the stage driver at the last stopover about a suitable hotel. He'd recommended the Bismarck, and it was only a block away. Thurman stored their things in the stage office except for Mary's bag, and they started down the boardwalk. The Real Food Café was ahead of them on their side of the street.

"Could you eat something?" he asked her.

"I think so. I am not very hungry, but know I must eat to feed Cheyenne."

He nodded. "Looks like we'll eat here."

A good-sized woman came over to where they sat to take their order. "You two must be new in town. I'm Maude and this is my place."

"I'm Thurman and that's Mary."

"Oh, and you have a baby. How old is it?"

"Three days old," Mary said.

"Where you folks from?"

"South Texas."

"Lots of Texas folks up here. My husband, Buster, is from Texas." She looked over at the kitchen doorway where he stood, rolling a cigarette in his fingers. "Buster, these folks are from Texas."

Buster nodded. "I know him. Ain't seen him in fifteen years. Don't you know who he is?"

Maude shook her head and glanced back at Thurman.

"Look hard."

"Is he Herschel Baker's father?"

Thurman nodded, and rose. "Your husband and I were together in the war, too. Come over and meet my wife, Sergeant."

"I'll be damned," Buster said, still acting surprised. "You're the last person I ever expected to see in Billings."

"Why? It's a free country."

"Damn sure is that. Sit down," Buster said, and scraped up a chair. Seated, he struck a gopher match under the table and lit the twisted cylinder. "Captain Baker, I guess you're here to see Herschel."

"I am. I have a proposition to make him."

Buster looked at the floor and took the cigarette out of his mouth. "Reckon he'd listen?"

"I don't know. But I came a long way to simply talk with him."

Buster nodded. "It's been a long time."

"I won't disagree. Lots of water's run over the rocks."

"Cap'n, I got to tell you if you don't know that Travis's dead. They buried him between here and the Little Big Horn over five years ago."

"I heard that. Met a man from the cattle drives down at

the Red River a couple of months ago who knew Travis. Said he made a helluva hand with a horse." Thurman nodded. "Both of them boys could always ride."

Buster agreed. "Why, Herschel rides a big stout outlaw roan horse right now."

"He at the office?"

"No, he's up at the Soda Springs dance this weekend. Been a murder up there and he's trying to solve it. And he will, too. Solves them all."

"The whole family is up there," Maude said, bringing them plates of food. "I get to hold the baby while you eat. Where are you staying?"

"Bismarck, I guess."

She held the baby high. "What's his name?"

"Cheyenne," Mary said.

Buster frowned. "She Cheyenne?"

"No, she's Cherokee."

"Been a long time, Cap'n. That mud in Mississippi I won't ever forget. Got it even behind my teeth—" Buster broke up, coughing. "Worst damn thing I ever slipped in, fell, and even rolled in."

Buster looked like the mud still bothered him. "It was the trip home got me. They let you keep your horse and six-gun. Was there six or so of us got back home together?

"We were on foot and in Louisiana. Then you stole them Yankee hosses for us and we all rode home from there. I always wondered why you took all that risk."

"You'd of done it for me."

Buster dropped his head and shook it. "I ain't so damn sure, as tough as those times were, I would have. You did a good thing for some worn-out soldiers that you didn't have to do and risked your life doing it."

"We didn't come home to much more either."

"That damn war—" Buster dropped his head and shook it ruefully.

"I'm healed of that war, Buster. I don't dream about it no more. I only reflect with my old friends about it."

"That's good," Buster agreed. "Herschel'll be back Sunday evening. I don't know what to tell you. I mean, he don't say much about his feelings. I asked him several times about you and he shrugged it off."

"Well, that's his business. I came a long ways to find him. But if he's not interested, then I guess I can ride back."

Buster ground out his cigarette in an ashtray and put it on another table. "He's got a good wife and three dandy girls. They keep him hopping."

"He really had a tough fight," Maude said, rocking the baby. "When they shot his best friend in the back and the sheriff we had then never investigated it, he went on a one-man campaign that liked to get him killed and almost burned him up when they burned his place down.

"His wife, Marsha, really helped him get elected. He took them all on, even the big corporation ranches who'd ran things up till then."

"Sounds like he did a great job. I learned what he was doing clear down in Wichita, Kansas."

Buster nodded. "He changed things around here. There's real law. He's got lots of that Baker stick-to-it in him."

"Thanks, Buster, for putting in a word. I'm on my own now." Thurman buttered another biscuit, considering the meeting he planned with his son.

"Cap'n, you know I'd about gave up that day when you came riding back for us with them horses?"

"I had no idea."

"My bare feet were bloody raw. My belly button rubbing my backbone. I think if I'd had a gun, I'd of ended my

life right there. Then you came busting into camp shouting, 'Get in the saddle,' and I couldn't believe it."

"I saw O'Brien in Fort Smith. His wife died while he
was off in the war. His sons are dead and his daughter
keeps his house."

"Same old burly guy?"

"Yes, he is."

"I better get back to my dishes or the boss'll fire me."

Maude shook her head at him with a frown about his
remark, and handed the baby back to Mary. "She's such a
terror, she just may fire you," Maude said after Buster.

Then she laughed.

She left them to finish their meal, and Mary smiled at
Thurman. "It was nice to meet your friend and his wife."

"Yes, it was. I think you're feeling stronger."

"I am fine. How long will we be here?"

"I don't know, Mary. Maybe a day, maybe longer. He
may say no so loud to my offer, we can leave in the morning."

"I don't think so."

He stopped cutting the beef on his plate. "You know
something?"

She shook her head and tossed her braids over her
shoulder. "No, but sometimes I think about things that will
happen."

"Keep thinking positive then."

In a lowered voice, she said, "She did not care that I was
an Indian, did she?"

"No, she did not care."

Mary held the boy in the crook of her arm and ate with
the other hand like it was no problem. "How did Buster get
up here?"

"I imagine on a cattle drive."

"You must have been a good soldier."

"I did what I had to. That's all."

"You do that a lot. To pregnant squaws even. To anyone who needs help."

"Well, if you think hauling you across the United States and territories is helping people, you're easy to please."

"I am, Thurman Baker. I am."

After lunch, they took a room in the Bismarck and he went off to find a card game. In the Antelope, he joined some poker players and told them his name was Thurman. The others were a man called Barrow, with hard eyes and deft hands when he was shuffling cards, the town physician, and Carl Reeves, who ran a sawmill.

Barrow kept looking at him like he was trying to place him. "Thurman, you sure look familiar to me."

"I'm a cattle buyer. Took a couple herds up the trail for other folks. You may have seen me in some cow town."

"May have. I've got aces." Barrow showed a pair.

Thurman tossed his cards in and Barrow took the pot. They anted a dollar and Doc dealt.

"Railroad's coming. You getting in on the land boom?" Reeves asked.

Thurman shook his head. "You sawing up lots of lumber for it?"

"Much as I can. I think Billings is going to become the biggest city in the region."

"That damn railroad ain't even here yet," Barrow said. "They've been five years getting it this far out of the Dakotas. If the stock market crashes again, the tracks will end at Miles City for another decade," Barrow said, then fanned out his cards in his hand.

Two hours later, Thurman left the card game up or down a few dollars. As the day lengthened, the Saturday crowd changed from ranch family folks in town for supplies to lumberjacks, freighters, and cowboys.

He'd not seen a lawman on the street, but there was little hell-raising. Of course, it wasn't a cow town with wild drovers fresh off the trail and trying to drink the place dry. Even the ones that looked kinda grizzly sounded almost subdued on arrival. Some firewater might change that further along in the night.

He took Mary back for supper at the café. After the meal, when they stepped out on the boardwalk, he heard shouting in the street. He stopped Mary and stood on his toes in the gathering darkness trying to see if the ruckus posed any danger to her and the boy.

Then he saw a short burly man with the glint of a badge on his vest headed for the trouble across the street. Since the obvious fight was between them and the hotel, Thurman told Mary they'd wait.

Maude came out, drying her hands on her apron. "Can you tell from here what's happening?" she asked.

"Sounds like a fight to me."

Maude looked around.

Thurman interpreted her glance as that she was looking for the authorities. "The law went by a minute ago," he said.

"What did he look like?"

"Short, broad-shouldered."

"That's Art. He can handle a mob."

The crowd in the street had grown silent, and a strong voice cut the twilight. "I'm taking the two of you in. Any more of you want to sit in jail till Monday morning, just get in a fight."

It was over. Maude shook her head and started inside. "Railroad gets here, they won't be locals that kinda behave, it'll be lots of trouble. I can hardly wait."

Thurman agreed, and took Mary back to their room. He had another day to wait to meet his son. After fifteen years, that didn't sound like much more than an eternity. All he'd heard about Herschel he liked, but it wouldn't be an easy family reunion.

TWENTY-THREE

Herschel called them "Marsha's freeloaders." Single cowboys drifted in like migrating ducks to a pond. She had eight extras by noontime for lunch, and even Kate laughed with him.

"I think she likes all of them," Kate said.

He winked at his stepdaughter. "It's the mother hen in her. Besides, she's cooked enough beans for all of them."

Kate nodded in firm agreement.

Elsie Moon came over and asked what had attracted the mob. A gray-haired widow woman in her fifties, she stood straight-backed and looked much younger. "What kinda bait are you using? You have more split wood than you can ever use and you're overrun with handsome single men."

"They're all friends of my husband," Marsha said as she replaced the iron lid of the big Dutch oven with the hook. "Biscuits are about done," she announced. "Tucker, take Elsie over an armload of split wood."

"Yes, ma'am," the stringbean cowboy said, getting up.

He tipped his hat to Elsie, and then went to loading up on the freshly split wood.

"I'm over by the gray team," Elsie said, pointing across the school yard.

'I'm a-coming, ma'am."

Herschel caught him when he started that way. "Don't eat any of her pie over there. It'll ruin your appetite for beans."

"Oh, that wouldn't do nothing to my appetite," Tucker said, and laughed.

After lunch, the cowboys washed the plates and cups for Marsha. Tales of wrecks, crazy horses, and mad cattle filled the conversation. Harry Boyd told about one time going to court the new schoolmarm. He'd bought her some hard candy and riding over there, he'd spotted some pretty wildflowers, dismounted, and the seam of his pants ripped out. With no needle or thread to fix it and being over halfway there, he'd ridden on to the schoolhouse anyway. No one could tell the embarrassing condition of his pants as long as he stayed in the saddle, so he'd decided not to get off his horse.

"At the schoolhouse, I rode up close, handed her the candy and the flowers. She said how touching it was and I about busted my buttons. Sure thought I was in. But shortly thereafter, she got engaged to Tom Edgar. When I later asked her why she picked Tom and not me, you'll never guess what she said."

"What was that?"

"She said, 'I figured you wouldn't get off your horse long enough to marry me.'"

If one cowboy could tell a story like this, there'd always be a better one coming, and Herschel sat on his butt with Marsha beside him enjoying the humor.

Curly was next. "You boys all heard of Charlie Goodnight. He was hiring hands one time for a drive, and this round-bottom boy came riding over on a dink. He got off the horse real clumsy, and a bunch of the hands lounging around wondered why he even came to apply.

"He was carrying something in a tow sack under his arm, and he walked up to Goodnight like you approach a king. Charlie was a big old boy that could make you feel two inches tall anyway.

" 'Sir. I want to be a drover on your drive.'

" 'What's your name?'

" 'Laney Wayne.'

" 'Laney Wayne, you ever been on a cattle drive before?'

" 'No, sir, but I sure want to make a hand.'

" 'Your mother know you're here?'

" 'Yes, sir.'

" 'What have you got under your arm?'

" 'My fiddle.'

" 'Can you play it?'

" 'Yes, sir.'

"That boy could really saw on the fiddle, and even had Goodnight tapping his boot toe. When it was over, Goodnight told him he was hired and to get a bedroll and a slicker.

"That boy was plumb excited, jumping up and down how he was going to be a drover. Goodnight stopped him. 'Laney Wayne, Lord sakes, I ain't hiring you to be no drover. I'm hiring you to be the fiddler. You can make music in the camp every night. Cowboys will like that.' "

The stories went on while Marsha served hot cinnamon raisin rolls that she'd made in her large Dutch oven. The girls served them, and drew lots of proposals to marry the men when they got big enough.

Holding the plate of rolls out to one who asked, Nina shook her head at his offer. "Can't."

"Why not?"

"'Cause I'm going to be taller than you are when I grow up."

The afternoon passed with lots more jokes and cutting up. One cowboy complained his belly hurt from laughing so much. He never drew any sympathy from the others. Finally, one of them went and got his guitar, and others went after mandolins and fiddles. Shortly, the singing began in earnest.

The crowd grew, folks sitting down around the circle and enjoying the music. But it was Johnny Frank's ballad "The Texas Cowboy" that brought them all into singing along.

> *Oh, I'm a Texas cowboy and far away from home.*
> *If I get back to Texas I never more will roam.*
> *Montana is too cold for me and the winters are too*
> *   long,*
> *Because before the roundups do begin, your money is*
> *   all gone.*

And Johnny Frank knew all the words and sang the five verses. After he hit the last strum on his mail-order guitar, there was hardly a dry eye in the crowd.

Herschel hugged Marsha's shoulder as she worked at the table set up on the buckboard, making peach cobbler for the night's festivities. "You've got a big crowd now. Lucky there weren't that many here at cinnamon roll time," he said.

She smiled. "It's sure been fun today."

Shultz edged in and under his breath announced, "Hatch and his bunch just arrived."

"Good," Herschel said, seeing the big man riding a stout bay horse at the head of four other riders. Disregarding his wife's words of caution, he walked out to intercept them.

Hatch reined up the bay. "Well," he said from behind the bushy beard. "How's the fine sheriff of Billings?"

"Doing well, Roscoe. Very well, but a friend of yours met a terrible fate two weeks or so ago."

"Oh, who was that?"

"Wallace Hamby."

"You boys know a Wallace Hamby?" Hatch twisted in the saddle and looked at the others. They shook their heads and he turned back. "What's this have to do with me, Sheriff?"

"Someone shot Hamby in a deserted ranch house and then hauled his body over to dump it on the road."

"Did you ask those rustlers I heard that you captured over there about him?"

"I did. They didn't shoot him."

"What makes you so damn certain?"

"Let's say I know they didn't shoot them."

"Why are you asking me?" Hatch held his fingers up toward his chest.

"I thought you might know since he worked for you."

Hatch shrugged, gripping the saddle horn and rocking in his seat. "Did some day work for me was all."

"Folks say he worked for you."

"Did some day work for me, gawdamnit. I don't know and don't care what happened to him." He started to rein his horse around Herschel.

"See that you're at the coroner's hearing Tuesday—ten A.M. If not, I'll come get you."

"That a damn threat?"

"I don't make threats, Hatch. But riding belly down over a horse back to Billings won't be any picnic."

"You talk mighty big for a man without a posse or any backup."

"Hatch, if I come after you, I won't need a posse and you'll make the decision how you want to come back with me—dead or alive."

A cruel smile parted Hatch's lips and the beard around his mouth. "Come on any day you want—to die."

"Don't miss that hearing Tuesday."

Hatch laughed aloud. "Maybe, but don't cry for me if I do." Then he rode past.

Three of the riders with Hatch were kids. They didn't look at Herschel. The fourth man was a stranger with the cold look of a killer in his eyes when he rode on by. Dark complexion. He looked part Indian, with high cheekbones and too long black hair.

"That's Black Fox," Bailey said, joining him. "He was the other thing I was going to tell you about."

Herschel watched them dismount on the far side of the grounds and hitch their horses to a picket line they put up between two pines. "Who's he?"

"A hired gun. They say he's a son of Crazy Horse."

"He isn't a full-blood."

Bailey shrugged. They were drawing a crowd. Shultz looked at Herschel. "Think he'll be there? I mean at the hearing."

"I gave him an option."

Shultz nodded. But the music was over. Cowboys put up their instruments. The happy festival had sunk to near silence. Concerned-faced women herded their small children into their camps. Men guided their women back to their own wagons.

Hatch'd only come there for one reason, to make these people even more afraid of him. Soon, there were folks hitching up and leaving before anything could get started. Herschel squatted by the buckboard. Where did his authority as sheriff stop? Could he go over where Hatch and his gang squatted and order them out of the school yard?

What law had they broken? If they stepped over the line, he could move. What was that line?

"Are we going to leave?" Kate asked.

"No, honey."

"My best friend Claris and her family have left. Her daddy said there would be no dance tonight."

"I'm sorry. There is nothing I can do."

"It's because of those five men, isn't it?"

"Yes."

"Can't you do anything?"

"They're not breaking the law."

Tears streaked down Kate's cheek. "If I was sheriff, I'd make them go home."

She turned and ran for the buckboard, shrugging off her mother when she tried to catch her.

Shultz came to where he stood. "There's five of us willing to back you. You want to go down there and force their hand?"

"I appreciate that, but I can't justify doing anything against them."

"They ran everyone off. Ruined the dance and supper—"

"There's not a law broken. Marsha will cook some food for us. Stay hitched."

The western sky dripped with a bloody sunset. Hatch and his men mounted up, laughing openly at their success. They rode across the grounds. Then Hatch halted them a distance from Herschel's camp, and the five men with Herschel squatted at the fire ignoring the riders.

"Hell, this dance don't look like any fun at all. Guess folks all got sick of the idea. Huh, Baker? Send me word when you have another one." Hatch laughed and started to rein the bay to leave.

"Tuesday. You be there."

"You know, you're kind of amusing. Come up here and order me around single-handed, like you're some big deal. One snap of my finger and you're dead."

"Snap it then," Herschel said. Cold streaks of lightning ran up both sides of his face.

Hatch shook his head as if scoffing at him. "Not here. Not now. Another day, we'll see. I want you to think on it. She could become a widow all over again."

Herschel didn't bother to answer him. Those five men, including Shultz, might explode. They were poised to have it out with Hatch and his gang. He couldn't have that happen. He watched Hatch's bunch ride out in the red twilight, and soon they were gone.

Kate ran out and hugged his arm. "I'm sorry, Daddy. I hated for all my friends to leave, but I don't want them to hurt you."

He hugged her shoulder. "Those men won't hurt me. I promise."

"Bailey, you peel potatoes, and some of you boys dice them up," Marsha said. "Shultz, you cut biscuits. Kate will help you. Johnny Frank, get your guitar, we want some polka music. No sad songs either."

"Yes, ma'am."

"He ain't ruining our Saturday night," Marsha said, putting on her apron. "Nina, you go around and tell any of the folks left that we're having supper over here in an hour. Bring a dish or just come."

Herschel nodded at her and swelled a little with pride. She'd save a sorry day.

After Nina made her announcements, folks came and brought their dishes. Some of the cowboys brought out tables to set things on. Blankets were spread and the main fire built up for light. More Dutch ovens appeared and the meal grew in size.

In a short while, little girls danced and Nina convinced Herschel to play his harmonica with the others. "Old Dan Tucker" had a whiskered man sawing on a fiddle.

"It turned out good." Elsie said to him privately.

"Marsha's idea."

"We all knew the law was here."

"My hands were tied. They'd broken no laws."

She nodded. "And I'm going to tell all of them that left, if they don't stand up to those bullies sooner or later, then they better leave Montana."

"Don't be too hard on them. They had their wives and kids here."

She nodded and left him.

Later that night, he woke up, coughing on smoke. He sat up hearing others shouting, "The schoolhouse is on fire."

Flames were already consuming the roof, cracking and souring in the air. There was no need to try to fight the fire. Whoever had set it had done too good a job.

"You think Hatch came back and burned that schoolhouse?" Marsha asked him, wrapped in a blanket for a robe in the flaring light of the roaring fire.

"I doubt I could prove it, but I'll always believe he did it or had it done."

She hugged Herschel's arm. "That son of a bitch."

TWENTY-FOUR

SUNDAY morning, Thurman went to the stables that Buster had recommended, Pascal's, and rented a horse. He tossed his saddle on a black horse that looked sound enough and cinched him up. The young man on duty was filling out a form.

"Name?" he asked.

"Thurman Baker."

"You any kin to the sheriff?"

"I'll have to ask him." Thurman dropped the stirrup.

"You kinda look like him. Maybe you're a cousin. He sure rides a tough horse. I wouldn't try that damn roan horse. He's a tough sumbitch. Why, he'd put you in a pile in a minute." The youth shook his head as if in awe.

"Guess he likes the sheriff."

"I guess. You want to cross the Yellowstone, use the ferry."

"Can't this old black swim?" Thurman teased.

"That's the boss's orders."

"I won't swim across the river."

"Good."

Thurman caught the bridle headstall and cheeked the horse's head near his left knee when he swung aboard. No fancy riding that morning. Mary was washing clothing and diapers at Maude and Buster's house. That way, Maude got to rock the baby since the restaurant was closed on Sunday. Buster had offered to take Thurman around, but Thurman knew the man was in pain from his stiffness and declined the offer.

He discovered the assortment of folks living along the river. Tepees and tents and log dugouts pocked the area. One person even had a covered wagon box for a residence. Thurman found the ferryman half asleep, and the man looked put out that he had to crank the barge across the river.

"Where you headed?" he asked.

"Horse Creek." That was where Buster said Thurman's son and wife owned a ranch. He wanted to see the operation so he'd know what might keep Herschel from leaving Montana.

"Hmm, you got business down there?" the old man asked.

"Just looking."

"Quiet down there now. They had a helluva lot of trouble down there a year ago." He used both hands on the reel and grunted with his efforts. "Tried to burn down the guy who's sheriff now. Shot the last sheriff down there in a double cross. Lots of trouble."

"Quiet now?"

"Oh, yeah, real quiet."

"Guess it would be a good place to settle, huh?"

"Might be."

On the south bank, Thurman unloaded the black and remounted. "Thanks, see you later."

"Reckon you will if you want back across." He made a hyenalike laugh.

Thurman recalled hearing one like it at a circus in Austin once. He sent the black into an easy lope down the well-worn road. Later, he passed a crossroads store and saw folks all dressed up for church in buckboards and on horseback. With a tip of his hat to the ladies, he followed Buster's instructions. Crossing the bridge that marked the north end of the ranch, he turned the horse off the road and struck the ridge to find a high point to view the country side.

He hitched the black in a grove of pine trees, dug out his field glasses, and carefully cleaned the dust off the lenses with his handkerchief. Then he walked to the east side of the ridge to view the country that rolled off to the east— grass country for a cowman. Water and rich grass made beef.

Then he caught movement and thought he heard someone shouting—it could have been ravens. In the glasses, he found a man afoot while driving a light team of horses hitched to a sled. It carried a freshly skinned beef carcass. Why butcher in the summer? Then he saw the woman coming behind him, whirling around looking in all directions, holding a rifle on her hip. He could read the turmoil on her hard-set face. It was a dangerous, desperate look that said she'd shoot to kill if she saw anyone.

They disappeared into a draw, only to reappear with the man flailing the team with the reins and shouting obscenities at them that carried on the soft wind. He was running behind the horses to keep up. The woman was doing the same.

Thurman wondered if he could see their destination by

going to the end of the point. He made his way, keeping out of easy sight of anyone below. Finally, he could see the alfalfa and grass hayfield along the winding creek. Nearby were a neat log cabin house and several sheds and pens. Once or twice, he saw the woman in the lens as she moved between the buildings and obstacles down there with her ready rifle.

In a short while, the man drove out with a team of big Belgium horses pulling a farm wagon with something tarped down in the back. Thurman took the road back toward the crossroads. He intended to follow the man and try to learn what would happen to the beef. Not in any hurry, he went back to the black, put the glasses up, and rode off the ridge long after the wagon had rumbled over the bridge headed for the crossroads.

They were singing a hymn in the church when he got on the Billings road following the wagon's tracks. No one else was around. Who'd ever think a man would steal a beef on Sunday?

The tracks turned off onto a little-used lane. Thurman decided to take to a ridge on the right and see if he could find out where the wagon was going. Pushing the black through the brush, he caught a glimpse of something in the canyon. He rode the black over on the south side and hitched him, hoping his presence had not been discovered. Getting as close as he dared, he watched two men hauling blocks of ice out of a dugout and icing down the beef carcass in a newer wagon. Smart move. There was a windlass there, too. That was probably how they moved the carcass from one wagon to the other.

The second wagon was hitched to a pair of large black shires. They would not be hard to locate. Soon, the men had the beef tarped down, and the man from Herschel's ranch drove off in a big hurry. The other man closed up the

dugout door and piled some things against it to keep it in-
sulated. Then he drove the high-stepping team off to the
north. Satisfied there would be no problem finding him
and his big team, Thurman rode the black off the ridge and
rode south again to see more of the country.

The cat's away, the mice will play. Did Herschel's man
know his boss was up north somewhere at a dance?

They were still having church services when he rode on
south this time, and in a few miles he discovered a sign. He
reined up to read it. It indicated the boundary of the Crow
reservation and warned that no alcoholic or spirited beverages were allowed.

He could hear some moaning; at first, he thought it
might be ravens in the distance. Then he decided that it
was something else. An Indian wearing an unblocked
black hat and two eagle feathers twirling on the back
came around the bend riding a black piebald horse. He
wore a fancy beaded vest and looked as solemn as any
buck Thurman'd ever seen.

Behind him came three white men, hands tied behind
their backs with a reata tied around their necks daisy-chain
fashion. They were barefoot, too. They stumbled along behind the Indian, moaning. Then a girl in her teens brought
up the rear on a paint and leading two packhorses.

Thurman nodded to the Indian, who reined up his
horse.

"You have prisoners?"

"They are for the sheriff."

"You are one of his deputies?"

"I work for him."

"What did they do?"

"Rob a store."

"My name is Thurman." He pushed his horse over to
shake the man's hand.

"My name is Black Feather. I live at Billings. I am learning to be a white man."

"Oh, that's good."

"My tepee is down by the river. You must come and see me. We can smoke and talk."

Thurman nodded.

"You will come. I can tell." Black Feather pointed at his own eyes with two fingers. "I see in your look you will come and you will talk with me."

"I'll do that."

"Good." He booted his piebald to go on and the three prisoners moaned in protest, but they rose and hurried to follow him.

"Will you be in Billings tonight?" Thurman called after him.

"Tonight. Next day. Who knows?" Black Feather shrugged as if the matter was unimportant to him.

Thurman understood. What were days to a Crow? He tipped his hat to the girl in her teens on the paint and leading the packhorses. Then he rode around them and headed back to Billings in a short lope.

On the ferry in late afternoon, he asked the old man if he knew the name of the man with the shire horses.

"He's a Dane named Olsen."

"He live in Billings?"

"No, he lives somewhere over east. He's a mean sumbitch. Growled at me to hurry. And when I asked him about the guy who used to drive that wagon who was murdered, he said I'd better mind my own damn business if I wanted to go on living."

"The guy got killed who used to drive it?"

"Wally. They shot him in the back twice."

"Who shot him?"

"Damned if I know, but I'd bet that Olsen does."

Thurman nodded, and rode on to Buster and Maude's house. Buster was sitting in a rocker when Thurman hitched his horse to the picket fence entwined in morning glories.

"Don't get up. I'm coming."

"Learn a lot?" Buster asked.

"It's a nice ranch. Good hay and alfalfa fields, well watered. I met an Indian called Black Feather today."

"He tell you he was learning to live like a white man?"

"Yes, he did."

"He's got two or three wives."

"Maybe this one today made four."

Buster slapped his legs. "He ain't learning fast."

"He's bringing in three prisoners on a leash and barefoot."

"Three, huh? Must be the store robbers. You're saying three?"

"He's got three. He'll be here in another day."

"Got them on a leash?"

"Oh, yes." Thurman shook his head. "You'll have to see them."

"He's a dandy."

"Who runs that place of Herschel's down there?"

"Sonny Pharr. You see him?"

Thurman shook his head. "You know much about him?"

"Naw."

"I just wondered." He shrugged it off.

Mary came to the door and Thurman looked up at her. "You get your washing done?" he asked.

"Yes, dried and folded. We are having supper here tonight. Maude invited us. Would you two like some coffee?"

"Sure. Where's the baby?"

"Sleeping."

He winked at her. "Who was the guy got murdered?" he asked Buster.

"Wally Hamby. No one knew much about him. Shot twice in the back. I think that's why Herschel's up at Soda Springs for the dance. Checking on things up there."

Thurman nodded. He had some bits and pieces to discuss with Herschel in the morning. There was a lot going on he might not know about—a whole lot.

That evening when they were in their bed at the hotel, Thurman raised up and kissed Mary good night. Then he looked at the small bundle between them in the starlight that was coming in the window.

"I had a good day today, Cheyenne. Your brother Herschel has some problems we're going to discuss tomorrow. Hope he listens."

"He will," Mary whispered.

He hoped she was right. 'Cause he had lots to tell him.

TWENTY-FIVE

Sunday morning breakfast at the Baker campsite was lip-biting tough. The stink of the smoldering ashes was embedded in everyone's nostrils. Herschel sipped coffee and tried to imagine what kind of a mean son of a bitch would burn down a schoolhouse for pure spite.

Nina came by and pulled on his sleeve. "Play some music on that harmonica. It might cheer us all up."

"Honey—oh, all right."

He got it out and went to cranking on it. After two tunes, he put it away—it had not helped one bit. No one seemed cheered up.

Marsha and two other wives dished out fried potatoes, scrambled eggs, biscuits and gravy, and crisp bacon. Even the cowboys were beat.

"We having church?" Shultz asked Herschel.

"I reckon we are. We always do."

John Frank stood up with his plate in hand and looked

to the west. "We're having company. Guess they came for church, too."

They came from all directions. Families piled in wagons and rigs. Some rode horses. And Herschel noted one thing—they all bristled with guns. They looked at the blackened ashes solemnly, and then filed by to shake his hand.

"If we'd done our part last night, we'd still have a schoolhouse," one man said, shaking his hand.

Herschel held up his hands. "Listen, folks."

The cowboys hoisted him on the back of his buckboard to speak to them.

"That fire happened after we went to bed. No one could have stopped that. If I could have arrested those hard cases, I'd've run them in. They never broke the law here. We can't take the law in our own hands. I have twenty dollars. I am giving it to help buy the lumber to rebuild. Let's rebuild."

A cheer went up. More people were coming in. Word spread, and soon hats were being used to take up a collection. Preacher Green stood up and asked to give a prayer. It was too long, but it set the stage for some hymns, and soon the congregation was into the services.

So by noontime, a dozen souls had been saved and two hundred dollars raised. Marvin Lynch was made the chairman. He promised to have the site cleaned and ready to start rebuilding by the next Saturday. Told everyone to bring tools the next weekend, they were going to get part of the new schoolhouse up then.

Herschel drove home with lots on his mind, but he felt better. The people had regrouped. Burning the building had not done what those hard cases had expected. Their aim was to show they could burn out anyone they wanted.

Instead, it had raised the backbone in these quiet folks and made Herschel proud.

That still did not solve the matter of Hatch and his bully tactics. Maybe if Herschel could solve this cattle rustling case and implicate the man, that would be the way to get him out of the country. But he needed some hard evidence, and that for the moment was scarce. He clucked to the team and they picked up their trot. Definitely, Hatch needed a lesson. Or removal. But how?

"You're thinking hard, Herschel Baker," Marsha said. "How to get rid of all the mean men in the world is a question you'll never answer."

He turned and nodded at her. "I just want to clear out the ones around me."

The girls were worn out when they got home. They all labored to get everything off the buckboard and back in the house or where it belonged. When they were through, it was close to five, and Herschel drove the team into town and parked at the courthouse to check on things.

Art was in the office. Half asleep in his chair, he started to get up. "What's up, boss man?"

"Stay there. Any problems in town?"

"Nope. Quiet weekend. I didn't learn much either over east. No one will talk to me there. What have you been up to?"

"Hatch came over and played the big bad bully before the supper, and several folks left. Then, about three this morning, someone burned down the school with a can of coal oil."

Art bolted upright. "You think he did it?"

"Someone burned it. I could smell coal oil on the north side ashes."

"What do we do now?"

"Art, I've wondered, thought, fretted, and I am going

home. Maybe a good night's sleep will help. Can you handle this tonight?"

"Easy. There ain't any troublemakers in town."

"We're damn lucky. That mess in Miles City hits here, we'll need a hundred deputies."

"It'll be that bad?"

"Prisoners chained outside. How bad is that?"

"Bad." Art shook his head and rubbed the back of his neck.

"No word from Black Feather?" Herschel stood in the doorway.

"No. He must be having a helluva honeymoon."

They both laughed.

Herschel drove the team home and put them up. He washed up on the back porch as the sun began to sink, and Marsha came out to greet him.

"Is the town in one piece?"

"Quiet. How is that for a change?"

"Fine, I guess. I have some supper. You need some rest. Neither of us slept more than a few hours last night."

He hugged her and kissed her, then looked down in her eyes. "Why did it take so long to find you?"

"You weren't looking hard enough."

"Oh, hell, I wanted a big ranch and then I was going to find a wife."

"Young, pretty, high-class?"

"No, pretty, neat, and practical."

"You were cheated, Herschel Baker."

He pulled her hard to him. "No, I got more than that. I've got three wonderful girls."

"Oh, I spoke to Kate. She was upset about how she acted like it was your fault that Hatch was there and her friends left."

"Hey, I understood. I'll tell her so."

"She thought you could fix anything."

"I did, too."

The next morning, he arrived at the office and Darby stopped him in the outer part and whispered, "You have a guest in your office."

"Who?" Herschel frowned at the man's whispering.

"His name is Thurman is all I know and he's here to see you."

Herschel's heart stopped. "That—that's not his first name?"

Darby turned up his palms and shook his head. He didn't know.

Herschel drew a deep breath, threw his shoulders back, and walked in. "May I help you?"

A mild-faced, clean-shaven man in his fifties rose, stuck out his hand. "It's been a while, Sheriff Baker."

For a long moment, Herschel simply looked at the man and let the memories wash over him. That day when he rode off to San Antonio. When he said, "Take care of your mother for me." His father had been fifteen years younger then, war-thin and wearing a hollow look. That deep voice that had encouraged him as a boy after a small mustang threw him off. "He's tough, but you're tougher," he had said, and tossed Herschel back on the bronc.

Do you hug him or spurn him after that long? What should he do? Herschel dried his hands on the front of his canvas pants and then extended his right hand and shook his father's hand.

"It's been a while," Thurman said. "You have a minute to talk?"

"I've got all day. Take a chair and tell me when you got here."

"Mary and I got here Saturday by stage from Sheridan. Been tough. She had a baby in Cheyenne, so we were traveling in a buggy up here to find you. We took the train and stage from there."

"You have a baby?" Herschel asked, and scooted forward.

Thurman laughed softly. "You want me to start before Cheyenne?"

Herschel smiled. "Yes. I want to hear all of it."

"I'd much rather sit down with your wife and girls who I've heard so much about and tell everyone the whole story. First, I'd like to tell you that your Indian deputy has three prisoners and he should be here sometime today. He has them with a reata around their necks in a row, and they are walking barefooted and their hands are tied behind their back."

"Where in hell's name did you see them?"

"On the road coming up from—Horse Creek, is it? I like that old Indian. He should be here sometime soon. Buster says that girl with him is probably his new wife."

"She probably is. You've been to Horse Creek?"

"Buster told me where your ranch was. I just wanted to see it. I rented a horse to simply go look."

"Well, that's Marsha's home place."

"Hey, I went to look is all. Great water and grass. I guess making hay is part of ranching up here."

Herschel nodded. "A big part."

"Well, after I crossed the bridge, I rode up on that ridge and was looking over the country. I heard something and in my field glasses saw a man driving some cow ponies hooked to a sled and a fresh carcass of beef on it."

Herschel's eyes closed. The anger and fury inside him grew like a tornado, starting out as a small spin and boiling into a great funnel of death and destruction. Thurman told him the whole story, ending with the ferryman's words, and Herschel shook his head.

"They have done that every Sunday morning, you think?" Herschel asked.

"I have no idea, but the ferryman said the dead man did it before Olsen."

"What in the hell do you make of it? My own man stealing my beef. Now I'll tell you what I learned about the other end of this business last week in Miles City." Herschel told him all about the sale of meat there. "I need Thompson 'cause I think he's the main one. Getting Sonny or Olsen won't stop it."

"Exactly. I might ride over there and check the whole thing out and see if I can coax this Thompson out."

"Why do that for me?"

"Maybe I owe you."

"We'll see. Where's your wife and baby?"

"At the Bismarck. Why?"

"Hell, I have a big house, a fine wife, and three girls that might wear the hide off that baby. Besides, Marsha might whip me if I don't take you out there right now."

"What do we do?"

"Get a cab. You and I can walk to the Bismarck. Get your things, and go to the house."

"Mary is a full-blood."

"So?"

"I wanted to warn you."

"That's no problem. When do you think Black Feather is going to get here with the prisoners? Three, you said?"

"Three."

"Go get your things and your wife and baby. I'll have Art cover for me and watch for them. Meet you back here in twenty minutes."

"Fine—Hersch." Thurman stuck out his hand. "Thanks."

"I always heard blood was thick. But we think too much alike not to be kin." Herschel embraced him and clapped him on the back. He couldn't swallow the knot in his throat. Gawdamn, this was more than he could take.

When they broke apart, Thurman held up his index finger. "Two brains are always better than one."

"Yes. See you shortly."

"Yes." What would Marsha think? She'd be tickled pink, Indian or no Indian.

In the outer office, Herschel said to Darby, "Go get Art to take over. Black Feather will be here soon with his three prisoners."

"Three?"

"That's the count I got."

"Who's he?" Darby frowned after Thurman.

Herschel held his finger to his mouth. "Secret for a while."

"Oh, yes, sir."

With Thurman, Mary, and the baby piled in the one-horse cab, along with the saddles and gear, Herschel rode hanging on the outside. When they drew up at the house, he saw Marsha and the girls in the garden, looking up from hand-weeding. He went to whipping his arm at them, and they came on the run.

They unloaded the luggage and saddle on the lawn. Marsha was out of breath and looked at her soiled palms when Herschel introduced Thurman.

"Honey, this is my father."

"Well, I am so dirty—"

Thurman hugged her and told her to never mind, that she was pretty enough for him. The girls surrounded Mary and were appraising the baby.

"Mother, Mother, his name is Cheyenne. And we can hold him."

"My name is Mary." She put the baby in Kate's arms. "There."

"You girls must be easy on him. Babies are fragile," said Marsha.

Then she stuck out her hand and Mary shook it. But the two looked magnetized, and they were soon embracing each other.

"How far did you come from?" Marsha asked.

"The other end of this world," Thurman said, and put his arm around her shoulder. "Maybe even farther than that. But I found her on the way and that was worth the whole trip, besides finding you and the girls."

He broke off from her. "Excuse me. Hersch can't carry all that in. I better help him."

Nina stopped him on the porch as he was carrying his baggage inside. "Sure took you a long time to find us, Grandfather. How far away do you live?"

"Nina," her mother scolded.

He waved her away. "On the other side of the moon, Nina. I've been coming for a long time to get here."

She nodded, satisfied. "That would be a long ways. Even farther than the Soda Springs schoolhouse, I guess. That's a long ways, too, to sit on your butt."

"Young lady—"

"That's what I sat on," she said.

Thurman laughed and agreed. He looked around. This place of theirs was sure a long ways from the dirt-floored hovels of south Texas. Damn.

TWENTY-SIX

E ARLY the next morning at the dining table in the kitchen, Herschel sat drinking coffee. "Where did he go?"

Marsha turned from her cooking on the wood range. "He went to the barn with Kate to help her milk."

Herschel shook his head. "I knew he'd be up before the rest of us. But he didn't go along to milk. I know him better than that. He went to *watch* her milk. I asked him one time why he wasn't cutting firewood, and he said 'cause you need to know how to do it and I don't.'"

"I like him," Marsha said.

"I guess. He did make a big sacrifice to come up here and find me for whatever reason. He has shed some light, too, on that sorry Sonny Pharr."

"What are you going to do about him?"

"Fire him and put him in jail. I trusted him as a man to take care of that ranch. I'm paying him good wages and he's stealing from us. Guess I've been too busy worrying about other business beside my own."

"Now don't go blaming yourself. I could have checked on it."

"You have enough to do here."

She went over and hugged him. "It ain't where we were, it's how we get out of this mess."

"Right. I need to break up this rustling ring and then get Pharr. I move before then, it will telegraph all the others to hide."

"Now that's thinking." She poured him some more coffee and dropped onto the chair beside him.

"Dad said he'd go to Miles City and try to turn up this mysterious Thompson for me. They don't know Dad, and Art and I *are* known over there. I hope that doesn't take too many days. Then maybe we can close in on all of them."

"Good morning," Marsha said as Mary came into the kitchen. "We can finish this later," Marsha said to Herschel.

"I hope I was not intruding," said Mary. "I came to help. I guess all the wonderful smells of food woke me up."

"Let me hold the baby a minute. Oh, he is some boy."

"You didn't interrupt anything," Herschel said to Mary.

Soon, Kate returned with the milk and Thurman. She was busting to tell them about her experience with Grandfather.

Marsha gave Thurman a cup of coffee. Then he checked on Cheyenne, whom Hersch held now. Then he spoke to Mary and found a seat at the table. He shook his head. "You two may not know it, but you are blessed."

"What do you mean?" Marsha asked.

"I have been offered a very generous deal by an old friend in south Texas to take over his large ranch. This is a big ranch. I figured at my age I needed someone to help me run it. So I decided to find my sons. I learned unfortunately we'd lost Travis, and I thought maybe, just maybe, I could coax Herschel and you all to come to south Texas."

He dropped his chin. "I saw a part of your ranch yesterday. Lovely place. A cowman's dream." Then he looked up at them. "This house is a mansion to me, only better. From Kate's fine milk cow to all the love you have under this roof, I wouldn't expect you to leave any of it."

"What will you do?" Marsha asked as the two women served breakfast.

"Go back and take Old Man Hanson up on his offer to sell me the ranch. I have three fine vaqueros that have been close to me. They're good boys. There'll be others, I am certain. But if you and Hersch ever want to go where it never snows, there's a place down there for all of you, too."

Mary nodded, looking pleased.

"You aren't leaving so soon, Grandfather?" Kate asked, taken aback.

"No, your father and I have some business to do first." He looked over at Herschel, who nodded in agreement.

"Tell us about this ranch," Marsha said, at last ready to sit down.

"Well, I'm not certain of the number of sections he does own, but there are lots of them." Thurman began to describe the setup.

An hour later at Pascal's Livery, Thurman and Herschel were looking over the horses that Lem, the owner, had for sale.

"How well broke is that bald-face horse?" Thurman asked.

"Oh, he's not for sale. The sheriff will sell him in a few weeks. He was stolen, we figure," said Lem.

"Those rustlers are on their way to South Platte and trial," said Herschel.

"Is he well broke?"

"Yes."

"Then I'll bid on him."

"What for?" Herschel asked.

"Kate needs a horse of her own. Besides, she's too big for the pony."

"You'll start a war."

"No, I'll find Nina one, too."

Herschel shook his head. "*I* wouldn't want Grandfather to leave either."

"Hmm, saddle up the bay and Hersch can try him," said Thurman.

"There you go again. I don't need any experience riding him."

"Yeah, but you ride better than me."

Herschel shook his head warily and mounted the horse. The bay didn't buck and he reined good. Looked sound. Thurman bought him and after shaking Lem's hand, and hearing more praise of his son, he and Herschel went to the office.

Herschel and Art made Thurman a list of the men they knew were involved in the rustling: Thompson, Hatch, and Olsen as well as four others—Black Fox and those boys with Hatch at the Soda Springs schoolhouse the past Saturday night.

Thurman left for Miles City riding the new bay horse he called Rob. He'd told Mary he needed to get on over there and learn all he could about the rustlers. The sooner they were in jail, the sooner he could get on with his life and so could Herschel.

* * *

It was late in the night when Thurman reached the bustling boomtown of Miles City. Herschel had given him the name of Deputy U.S. Marshal Otter Washington, who could tell Sheriff Harold what Thurman's purpose was being there.

Thurman decided to stay at the stables. He had his bedroll, and the hotels were no doubt bulging from the number of people he observed on the streets riding in. When Rob was put up, grained, and rubbed down, he went to look in the saloons. He had a whiskey in the first one, and couldn't get over the mob. Smoke and lots of bathless souls made all the places reek. Business was so good that the working girls were charging five bucks a trick and getting all the business they could handle. In fact, most of them had lines of customers waiting. The faro and roulette wheels were churning with men waving money to get in. Looked like a gambler's paradise—he found all of the places were busy.

He realized that it would be hard to find any information in this mass of people. At last, he decided to get some sleep and try the next morning, when things were calmer, to find someone who knew something.

In the hay, he slept with his six-gun handy. It wasn't a sleep that ever reached a deep level. Drunks arguing in the barn woke him. He held the .44 in his fist until their anger melted or they went away. In the predawn, he woke and found a diner that served him a tasteless breakfast.

Later, he learned from a bartender that Hatch had a place north of town, and was seeing some gal named Ruby who worked in the Liberty Saloon. Hatch's place interested Thurman more than anything else. It was on Swan Creek north of town. He didn't press the man for a whole lot more, and paid him a couple of dollars. That was too generous, but he hoped he was buying loyalty and the man wouldn't report him to Hatch as asking a bunch of questions about him. It was enough of a lead to check out.

He rode Rob out the road that the livery man told him would take him up there. At a crossroads store, he bought two cans of peaches and some jerky. He was spearing out halves from a can when the man who owned the place came out and took a chair beside him.

"You're new up here, ain't'cha?" the thin man in the soiled apron asked.

"Yeah, Roscoe lives up here someplace."

"You mean Roscoe Hatch?"

"Yeah."

"About a mile up there. But he ain't home. Wednesday, he delivers in town."

"Guess he has a route?"

"Damned if I know. He just delivers."

"He got a nice place up here?"

"Naw, it's the old Granberry place. He was some old worthless lazy guy from Missouri. Was going to lose it to the bank. Hatch bought it for a song.

"You can't miss it. There's old running gear for a wagon that Granberry abandoned right by the lane goes in there."

"Thanks."

Keeping an eye out, he rode up the road, turned in seeing the fresh tracks of the big horses going toward town. He must have missed them on the way out. The house looked fallen in and unlived in. The stout-looking barn had obviously been built by someone else. The recent work on the fences showed someone had repaired them—patched would be a better word. He dismounted behind the barn and hitched Rob there in case someone showed up.

He eased his way inside the barn, which smelled of hay for the horses and also had a copper smell of butchering. In the center of the barn was a windlass to hoist the carcasses up. In the dim light, he saw the long table with knives, a saw, and axes to break down carcasses. Then he noticed a stack of salted dry hides. He went over and checked them. Even in the dim light, he could see they all bore different brands—the butchers weren't wasting a thing. Something like that would get them arrested.

They got the meat on Sunday. Then, by Monday, they brought it here. Tuesday, they processed the carcass. Early Wednesday, they delivered it.

How could he find this Thompson? Maybe next he needed to become a cattle buyer. They rubbed elbows with the big cattlemen. Thompson was not one of the common folks from all he knew about him. Shame that Hersch wasn't here. He would have enjoyed discovering this place and the orderly operation.

He rode Rob back toward town. In a long trot, he crossed the open rolling grassland. He needed to speak to this deputy U. S. marshal when he got back to town. Suddenly, there was the report of a rifle and Rob stumbled.

Thurman kicked loose of the stirrups and spilled on the ground as the horse collapsed and bullets buzzed over him like mad hornets. On the ground, he scrambled around to use the grunting horse in life's last throes as a shield. Two more bullets struck the animal. It sounded like hitting a ripe watermelon.

The .44 in his hand, he wished for the rifle instead. If the fall hadn't cracked the stock, it was pinned under the horse. Where was the shooter? No way that Hatch had discovered Thurman's intentions. Those damn pistoleros.

He closed his eyes and reached in his shirt to look at the good-luck charm Mary had given him the first night. Maybe it had saved him. This went back to the night he had taken the pistoleros' boots and horses. He should have killed them then and there. It wasn't his way, but in the end, it might cost him his life. They must be somewhere around those box elders in the draw.

He took his hat off and set it aside. It would be hours until dark. Let them think they'd got him. It was the only plan. Or if someone came by, that might scare them off. He needed patience. Let them do the impulsive thing.

TWENTY-SEVEN

Art burst into the office. "Black Feather is coming up Main Street."

Herschel frowned at his deputy. "What took him so damn long? Dad saw him on the road down there Sunday."

"I guess he was still on his honeymoon."

Herschel shook his head and hurried down the stairs. He and Art stood on the street corner, and could see the black hat on the rider aboard a big black piebald. Folks on the boardwalk were clapping their hands, and the prisoners, wearing the ropes for collars, looked haggard.

Herschel saw that one of the prisoners was Anton. He should have left the county.

"Oh, thank God," the first prisoner said, looking at Herschel. "Why in hell's name didn't you come up there and get us? We'd give up, I swear."

"Maybe you learned a lesson," Herschel said, nodding at Black Feather. "You did well."

"I come back to get my money." He tossed the end of the reata at Herschel.

"You did very well."

"You need me, you know where I live." He and the young woman leading the packhorses went off at a trot for the river.

Art and Herschel herded the footsore prisoners toward the courthouse. In a short while, they were in cells.

"I better go collect Black Feather's reward," Herschel said. "He'll be needing it to feed his women."

Phil was back from the land office upstairs. "That land where that dugout full of ice is belongs to a W. C. Thompson."

"You talk to those Danes—Olsen's a Dane, isn't he? There's several of them that cut river ice. No, I mean the one that's involved with Hatch. He's the one drives the big horses now that Hamby is dead."

"He's the one that also warned Hatch you were up there, too," Art said.

"I know. I've been thinking about him. It was why he wasn't at the dance this past Saturday. He was waiting for the beef delivery at the dugout."

"Wasn't he the one you told us had cut out some heifers?" Phil asked.

"Yes, he was. We need to go find him and bring him in. He might tell us all we need to know."

"He ain't up at the dugout. But it's half full of ice," Phil said.

"You know, Thompson planned this for some time. That ice was cut last winter and put in there." Herschel felt certain that Olsen might have arranged for the ice to be stored up there.

"Olsen sure could have handled getting that done," said Phil.

"Where do we find him?" Herschel asked them.

"Miles City?" Art suggested.

"That's too wild a place right now. Anyone know if Hatch's ranch is in this county?"

"I can go check on the records," Phil said. "It would be east of Soda Springs school?"

"Yes. Roscoe Hatch."

"What'll that do?" Art asked.

"We'll get a search warrant if he's got a place in our jurisdiction. Maybe we can find some evidence."

"Won't that warn the others?" Art asked.

"Once we start, we'll keep on going. Jurisdiction or none."

"What about your father?"

"It won't take him long. I expect a report anytime."

"What else do we need to do?" Phil asked.

Herschel went to the window and looked down at the street. "Let's start a list of men to ask to go with us. Men we want for posse members. That way, when we move they'll be ready. Art, we'll need two men to marshal the town in our absence. Darby, the new man, can man the desk and keep things going here on a temporary basis. I want this sweep made in three days, not over four.

"Every man needs a bedroll and a stout horse. We'll need camp gear and food. Two packhorses, and not plugs, they've got to move. Two men can go down and arrest Sonny Pharr and Olsen if he's up here. Then the rest will raid Hatch's, and by then I hope we know where Thompson's at. When we're done, I want them all behind bars with cases that will stick.

"It's time we ended this rustling and bullying."

His men went off to get to work. Herschel went to talk to Lem Pascal about joining the posse.

"I was wondering when you'd have enough of Hatch,"

Lem said as they sat in his office, which reeked of neat's-foot oil and grain.

"Law's funny. You need evidence or a confession. I have two sworn confessions tying Thompson to the stolen horses. But with a smart lawyer, you might not get two feet in court with 'em. I want them all looking out of bars."

"You think you have enough now?"

"Yes, and when they start talking, it will take a dam to hold them back."

"I'll be packed and ready."

"I'll be looking for a telegram and then we can go."

They shook hands and Herschel went back to his office. Nothing from his father.

Phil found three sections in the east that were listed as Roscoe Hatch's. That was enough to encourage Herschel. He felt things soon would be under way.

TWENTY-EIGHT

T HURMAN was sitting near his dead horse when out of the north two cowboys came rattling up in a large farm wagon pulled by two black draft horses.

"What happened to your horse, mister?" the driver asked, reining up his team.

"Someone didn't like him," Thurman said. "I'd sure appreciate a ride into town."

"Throw your kack on. Is the guy that shot it gone?" The driver and his sidekick were looking all around.

"Yeah, they quit me about an hour ago," Thurman said.

"They want you or the horse?"

"I think they wanted me, but they were up in those bushes and that's too far for their rifle."

"I see what you mean. I take it they didn't want to get close to you."

"I guess." He tossed his gear on the wagon and climbed in the back. These two must be going for supplies. He found a seat on the floor and took the rocking on the springless wagon as the team trotted southward.

"Guess you're going to Miles City?" the driver shouted back.

"That's fine."

When the wagon stopped on top of a hill to give the horses a breather, Thurman and the cowboys climbed down to get the kinks out. Shaking his stiff legs and stretching, the driver asked, "You the law?"

"Just a cow buyer," Thurman said.

"I never knowed anyone get mad enough to shoot one of you fellars."

"We all have our enemies."

"Where did they go?"

"Lost their nerve, I guess. And rode on. Or they figured I was dead and left."

"So that I don't ever insult them shooters, what's their names."

Thurman shook his head. "It don't matter."

"Could I ask what you're going to do about it?"

"Send 'em to Hell."

"Yes, sir. Good place for them. Let's load up. I need a drink—bad."

So did Thurman. In fact, his teeth were about to float away for one.

It was past dark when Thurman sent Herschel a telegram.

FOUND HIDES STOP NOT FOUND T STOP THURMAN

He went back to the livery and slept a few hours in the hay. Then, brushing out his clothing, he went in the pre-dawn for breakfast. Nothing defined a man as dirt poor as looking like he'd slept in a haystack the night before. He had early breakfast at a café filled with construction men, and he shared a table with two railroaders, a conductor and a brakeman.

"Railroad's coming along?" he asked.

"Slow. The demand for new rails everywhere has them in short supply."

"Hard to get, huh?"

"Yeah, we're weeks behind, and you can't build railroads in deep snow."

Thurman nodded. He paid for his breakfast and walked outside picking his teeth. A bullet crashed in the front glass of the café and shattered it. He dove at the hooves of the horses tied at the hitch rack, and on the ground drew his gun. If they shot anything, it would be the horses.

On hands and knees, he tried to locate the pair, but the upset horses were milling around until a walleyed one broke his reins and jerked loose. When the cow pony tore out into the street, it left a small opening and Thurman shot through it. His bullet cut down one of the gunman standing on the porch across the street. The other gunman hightailed it around the corner.

"Who in the hell are they?" an irate man who stormed outside demanded to know.

"Pistoleros." Thurman ran across the street and then between the buildings into the alley. He could hear someone running over a stack of bottles. Where was he?

Thurman sprinted down the alley and saw the pistolero round a corner. The gunman stopped and swung around to use his pistol. Thurman's two shots took him out and he crumpled in a pile.

Thurman walked over and found money in the man's pocket. From the roll of bills, he took seventy-five dollars and when the out-of-breath marshal arrived, he handed him the rest of it. "That should fix the damages they caused."

"Who in the hell are you?"

"My name's Thurman. His name is Petrillo. He's a hired gun from Mexico. He and Sanchez, the one around there on the porch, hail from the same village. They have been trying to kill me for two days. They shot my horse out from under me yesterday morning. I took out money for for the horse that they shot, and the rest is yours. Now I'm going to go have a glass of whiskey."

"Stick around town. Sheriff may want a hearing on this."

"He knows who I am."

"You heard me."

One of the onlookers that Thurman passed used his finger for a gun. "Bang. Bang. You dead." Then he laughed. Thurman smiled. One less obstacle in his way to having a sane life again.

In the Liberty Saloon, he bought a bottle of whiskey and went to a back table with two glasses. He sipped his first splash in the tumbler.

A large man came in the batwing doors and looked around. The bartender nodded toward Thurman. The man walked up to the table. "You must be his old man."

"You must be the sheriff."

Sheriff Harold dropped in the opposite chair, and nodded when Thurman went to pour him some whiskey in the other glass.

"Rich Mexicans. Had over four hundred bucks on them," the lawman said.

"I took seventy-five to buy a new horse. They shot mine."

"Hell—" Harold lowered his voice. "I thought you were up here on the rustling deal."

"I am. This was leftover baggage. Sorry it happened here."

"What did you learn? Anything new?"

"They break down the beef at a place Hatch owns up the road. There's enough hides up there with brands on them to send everyone away. But Herschel wants Thompson. What can you tell me about him?"

"Big man. He runs a large corporate ranch up north on the Milk River. He'll be hard to attach to the rustlers."

"Means he can hire sharp lawyers that will tie things up in court, right?"

Harold nodded. "Talk rings around these county prosecutors."

"Then we better get things right. I'm going to wire Herschel to get ready to start out and hope we can get enough of them to testify against Thompson. When does the stage go back to Billings?"

"Sometime this morning."

"I better be on it. What about those two?"

"Foreigners. I don't know what they were doing here anyway. Self-defense." He raised his glass. "Tell him good luck." He grinned at Thurman. "I damn sure see what tree Herschel came from."

"I'll tell him."

"Oh, and Thurman, you ever need work, you come look me up."

"I'll do that."

Thurman hurried to get his saddle and bought a stage ticket for Billings.

It was close to ten o'clock that night when the stage arrived in Billings and Thurman climbed down. The cab was there, and the man who drove it nodded to him. "I'm here to take you home, sir."

Thurman put his saddle in the back and climbed in. "How are you doing tonight?"

"Fine, sir. Very fine."

"So am I. So am I."

When they arrived at Herschel's house, Mary rushed out to hug him, and he swung her around in the starlight.

"I'm so glad you are all right. I had a bad dream that they shot your horse."

He set her down and looked hard into her face. "They did."

TWENTY-NINE

HERSCHEL checked the packhorses and the diamond hitches with a lantern. He had one of the rustled horses, a big dun, saddled for Thurman. At the sound of other horses coming up the street in the dark, Herschel nodded at his father. "These men are all real posse men. They'll back us in whatever we get into. I believe in them.

"Art and Lem Pascal are going down to arrest the man on my place, Sonny Pharr. And try to find a man called Olsen, if he's around up here.

"Meanwhile, the rest of us're going to arrest Roscoe Hatch and anyone with him. Once we secure him, we're going to ride up to this place where Thompson is at and arrest him."

"What for?" Thurman asked.

"Offering to buy stolen horses brought over a state line. It's a federal law. My deputy U.S. marshal badge will be good anywhere."

"I guess we're headed for Hatch's place first?"

"Yes. Black Feather and his bride are coming, too. He's our tracker if we need him."

"You ever been to Hatch's place?"

"No, but I have a man's been there, Bailey. He's meeting us at Soda Springs."

Thurman nodded and reached back to hug Kate, who was there with her bucket and lamp to milk the cow. "Don't let old Sukky kick you milking her."

"I won't, Grandfather. You two be careful."

"We will," Herschel assured her.

They mounted up and rode out. Art and Lem went south. Herschel led the way north for the others.

"Shultz, meet my dad," Herschel said as they rode by dark houses and past a few with lights on in their sheds.

"That's John Frank over there, Shultz, and Curly Manning. Bailey said he'd join us at the schoolhouse site."

At mid-morning, they reached the burned-out school. There were half a dozen men, black-faced with soot, using wheelbarrows and scoop shovels to clean it all up. Herschel nodded at them in approval.

"We're going to have her ready by Saturday to start back up. Lumber's coming."

"Keep it up, boys. I'll try to be back by then. We're going to arrest a few lawbreakers."

"Reckon we could ask who?"

"Hatch and his whole gang. You know any more in his bunch, let me know."

"Aw, Sheriff, we'll work twice as hard now."

He smiled and waved at them. Bailey came short-loping in on a good-looking bay horse to join them.

"Follow me," he said, and took the lead.

They crossed the rolling grass country, the ridgetops bristled with pines. It was a vast land supporting lots of cattle that were shedding winter's long hair and licking their sides.

Late afternoon, Bailey drew them down. "Hatch's spread is over this next rise. There's several pens, sheds for them to hide in. The main house faces the south. We'll have the sun to our back riding in."

"I don't know how many are here," Herschel said. "Those three kids we saw last weekend at the dance, they say, do the work around the place. They won't fight. But they say Black Fox is up here. He's a son of Crazy Horse. You know him, Black Feather?"

The Crow shook his head.

"Tell your woman to stay here with the packhorses," Herschel said to Black Feather. "The rest of you spread out at least fifteen feet or so apart. We'll go in together like that. First one of them offers any resistance—open fire." Herschel turned to his father. "What else? You're the veteran."

"I like the plan. Daylight's burning."

In position, Herschel waved them on. They went over the rise in formation, and soon looked down on the place. Halfway off the hill, Herschel saw someone shade his eyes against the slanting sun to look at them. Then he took off screaming and running for the house.

"They've done seen us," Curly said on Thurman's right.

Three of the outlaws rushed out of the house armed with rifles.

Herschel held his men up. "I'm the law," he called. "Put down those weapons and get your hands in the air. One deputy dies and you'll all hang."

"Someone's leaving," Bailey pointed out.

"We'll get him. You've got till three to die. One—"

The three obeyed, setting down their rifles.

Thurman said, "Bailey and I want to go after the one that ran off."

Herschel nodded. "Watch him. It may be Hatch or that gunman Black Fox."

They swung wide of the ranch, and Bailey's dun really turned on the power. On the next high point, they caught sight of the one who'd run off, but his horse was slowing and the man had to beat him to make him gallop.

Bailey grinned. "He ain't getting away."

He set his spurs to the dun and charged off again. He was three or four lengths ahead of Thurman when Bailey jerked out the rifle and stood in the stirrups to take aim. When he shot, the rider's horse broke in two and went to bucking. He threw the rider off, and Thurman and Bailey raced up.

Thurman pointed his pistol at the hatless 'breed holding his hands up. "Just stand there. I'm checking you for weapons."

"Where's Hatch at?" Bailey asked the gunman.

"How should I know?"

Thurman took two knives and a pearl-handled six-gun off the man. He put them in his saddlebags. Bailey rounded up the man's horse and brought him back.

There were soon four rustlers in irons, and Curly found the hide pile in a shed. He stuck his head out the door. "Hell, boys, they've got brands from everywhere in here."

"None of them knows where Hatch is at," Herschel said.

"Maybe they don't know," Thurman said. "I sure don't. You already said they were his dumb help, and that slant-eyed buck ain't going to tell you shit."

"When they realize they are not only facing rustling charges, but murder, they may talk."

"We can check that place over by Miles City. It's got lots of cowhides, too. But I don't think he stays there."

"You think he may be up there at the ranch that Thompson runs?"

"You're headed that way, aren't you? Thompson's?"

"That was going to be my next stop. I'm sending two men, John Frank and Curly, back with the prisoners using a wagon and a team they have here. We'll need to load those hides as evidence."

"Sounds good," Thurman said, then lowered his voice. "But you better chain that 'breed up good. He's the cagy one."

"I think so, too. The rest of us will ride north in the morning."

"I took a fancy Smith and Weston pistol off Black Fox. I was going to say for you to give it to Bailey to keep. He's the one that got Black Fox."

Herschel blinked. "What caliber?"

"Damned if I know." They walked over to his horse and took the revolver out.

".38-caliber Smith and Wesson." Herschel spun on his boot heel and walked over to Black Fox.

Herschel shoved the gun in his face. "This is the pistol that shot Wally Hamby."

"I wasn't here then."

"Can you prove it?"

"I was in Cuttbank in jail."

"I can check on that."

Black Fox shrugged.

"Put them all in leg irons, too." Herschel scowled at them. "I want the judge to hang 'em all."

One of the younger ones paled and looked ready to faint. Herschel stepped over and jerked him up by the shirt. "Did you kill Hamby?"

"No. No. I wasn't even there. I swear to God. Oh, mister, I never done no killing, I swear."

Herschel lifted him on his toes. "Then who killed him?"

"Hatch, Olsen, they were there. But I swear to God, none of us were there."

"Was Thompson there?"

"I don't know him."

Herschel let him go and shook his head in disgust. "Load them in the wagon. In the morning, you can take them into jail."

Thurman caught him by the sleeve. "Who's cooking supper?"

Herschel clapped him on the shoulder. "I know you don't need any practice at it."

They both laughed.

They all pitched in and made a meal. It was past sundown when they finally sat down cross-legged on the ground, eating off tin plates in the fire's glow. Herschel told Thurman and the others his plans.

"John Frank and Curly are taking the prisoners back to jail in the morning. The rest of us are riding for this ranch that Thompson runs. That'll cut us to five men. He might have an army on that payroll. Anyone wants out, speak up now."

No one said a word. He continued. "I'm arresting Thompson as a deputy U.S. marshal for being an accessory to rustling horses from Nebraska. I figure he has a bunch of tough lawyers that are going to fight it. But I hope to implicate him in Hamby's murder at the same time."

"Can we get up there in a day?" Thurman asked.

"We're going to try."

Hard as they pushed, it took them two days. They arrived in late afternoon and with their rifles across their laps, they rode double file up the lane between the pole-rail fencing. The main house loomed larger than most hotels. Herschel had been seeing men running around as they approached.

"Keep your wits about you, men. They may plan to resist us."

Thurman agreed, and looked over at the short cattle buyer riding beside him. "You do much of this kind of work?"

"Only when he needs me." Then Shultz shook his head like he'd been in better deals than this one.

"Spread out," Herschel said. And when they reached the yard, each posse member moved aside until they were stationed fifteen feet apart.

A man in a starched white shirt came out on the high porch and looked them over. "What can I do for you gentlemen?"

"W. C. Thompson?" Herschel asked.

Herschel noted there were now several ranch hands at the front of the house. Some were armed. They all looked hard at his posse.

"I'm Deputy U.S. Marshal Herschel Baker and I have a warrant for your arrest."

Thompson showed no emotion. "Oh, I know your boss, Chief Marshal Earl Martin, very well. I talked to him in Butte just a week or so ago. He never mentioned any charges being brought against me."

"Mr. Thompson. I'm here to arrest you, sir. Any resistance on your or your men's part will be met with force by my posse."

"Come now, my good man. I'll post a bond and be at the hearings whenever they are scheduled. I run a large operation here and my presence is very important to its economic soundness. I am certain you have not discussed this matter with your superiors. A twenty-thousand-dollar bond should be sufficient. I'll—"

"Thompson, you make one step to move and you'll be dead."

"There's no need for this show of force. I have several men you can see that could, on one word from me, shoot all of you."

"You wouldn't live to talk about it."

"I suppose you intend to take me in irons to your jail?"

"Yes, sir, we do." Herschel stuck his rifle in his scabbard and dismounted. He took a pair of handcuffs out of his saddlebags and started for the steps. He never looked aside at any of the ranch's men on either side of the house. His full attention was on Thompson.

When he reached the man, he took Thompson's right hand and locked the bracelet on that wrist, then his left one.

"I'll have your badge for this," Thompson snarled.

Herschel ignored his threat. "If you want a jacket and a hat, say so now."

"I do."

"Tell someone to saddle you a horse, or you can ride belly down over a packhorse."

"You'll never hear the end of this."

"One of you go saddle him a horse and bring it around," Herschel said toward the ranch crew.

An older man nodded and sent two others to do it.

Herschel stepped aside, and then he went inside the door. From a wall rack, he took a fancy-tooled gun belt and holster with a pearl-handle Smith and Wesson pistol in it.

"What are you doing? That's my personal property," said Thompson.

Herschel removed the revolver and looked it over. "A .38, huh?"

"You have no authority to take that."

"Why, Thompson, this gun will be evidence, sir." Herschel patted his palm with the barrel. "Yes, you shot Wally Hamby with this very gun."

"You're crazy. Mad. Why, I'll have you incarcerated in the state mental hospital when this is over."

A butler brought Thompson's suit coat and hat. He handed them to Herschel.

"Wire my lawyer and tell him to meet me in Miles City," Thompson said to the butler. "Tell him I have been arrested by a madman who is beyond reason. Wire the governor, too."

"What shall I tell him, sir?"

"For him to order my immediate release from custody. What is your name again?"

"Deputy Marshal Herschel Baker."

"You heard him!"

Herschel guided Thompson down the steps. At the base, he stuck the hat on Thompson's head and laid the coat over his arm. "You can put that on later." He took the bridle from the cowboy who delivered the horse. "Get on."

When his prisoner was in the saddle, Herschel led him over and put a lariat around the horse's neck, then mounted up. With a sharp farewell nod at the ranch hands, Herschel turned to leave. When Cob made his first step for the driveway, the skin under Herschel's shirt collar crawled. Soon, he had Cob trotting and one by one, his posse filed out after him.

Thurman rode up on the opposite side of Herschel from the sour-looking Thompson as they left the drive and turned south. He reached down in his saddlebag and produced a pint of whiskey. He cut the seal and took the cork out with his teeth as they rode.

"Here, have some," Thurman said, handing Herschel the pint and then letting out a deep breath. "That was the toughest deal I think I've ever been through to come out unscathed."

Herschel nodded, took a pull, and handed the bottle back. "It ain't over yet."

Thurman tried a snort of it, then reined the dun in beside Shultz and handed him the bottle. After Shultz gave it back, Thurman rode in beside Bailey and handed him the bottle. "After you get some, give it to Black Feather. He needs some, too."

Last time Thurman saw his pint, Black Feather's woman was emptying it. She tossed it aside and never missed a beat, leading the packhorses in a short lope.

That evening when they made camp, Hershel talked to them about not finding Hatch. "I hate that he wasn't there."

"We never checked around there very good for him either," Thurman said.

Shultz laughed out loud. "I was about to crap in my pants anyway. I'm glad you didn't send me to look for him."

"I'm glad, too. That whole deal at Thompson's was damn spooky for me, too," Bailey said.

"He wasn't there." Thurman shook his head.

"I wonder where he went." Herschel got up and walked over to where Thompson sat on the ground. "Where's Roscoe at?"

"Roscoe who?"

"My star witness against you."

"I don't know any Roscoe."

"You will in a short while."

"He don't know him, my ass," Shultz said under his breath.

Thurman agreed.

Sunday morning, Herschel and his posse arrived in time for church services at Soda Springs. The new structure was framed in fresh lumber and looked commanding. The folks left the new schoolhouse, and several came over to congratulate Herschel. Others stood back and talked behind their hands about his prisoner.

"Who are you looking for?" a man asked.

"Hatch." A quiet wave went over the crowd. Even the children fell silent.

"His days are numbered," Herschel said. "We'd stop and share your services, but our horses are jaded and we've not been home in five days."

"Then, Sheriff," Preacher Green said, "let us thank God for handing over these criminals to you so we may again live in peace."

They all removed their hats. Shultz booted his horse over and jerked off Thompson's hat.

"Our Dear Heavenly Father, we thank—" The prayer was lengthy, and Green even prayed for the outlaws' souls.

Herschel thanked them, told them the schoolhouse framing looked great. He and the posse had ridden out of the schoolyard and come off the long hill to cross the creek when he noticed what he thought was a man swinging in the breeze by his neck from a tall cottonwood.

Thurman rode in close beside where Herschel had stopped in the road and said, "Thou shall not ever burn down a schoolhouse."

Herschel shook his head in disapproval.

Shultz checked his horse and twisted in the saddle to look back before he said, "And the meek shall inherit this earth."

"Damnit to hell, I still don't like it." Herschel rode over and cut him down.

They wrapped his corpse in a blanket, and it required Herschel, Thurman, and Shultz to load his heavy body over a packhorse.

Hanging a man even as bad as Hatch was not the way to make Montana a place to raise your family. They had laws to handle his kind. They had courts and prisons. Herschel slapped his leg hard with his reins. They had lawmen to enforce those laws. He was one of them.

THIRTY

MARY carried little Cheyenne in her left arm, and smiled at the sight of the mule Ira when the livery-man brought him out to hitch him to the buggy. Blacky was making excited circles around them.

"Mrs. Baker," Thurman said to her. "We can still sell Ira's worthless hide and take the train back to Texas."

She wrinkled her nose at him. "This is fine. I want to go home on my honeymoon like we came."

He took off his hat and scratched his head. "Why are you so damn stubborn?"

"I enjoyed the ride up here with you. I want to enjoy it going back."

"Fine, fine, just don't complain about the buffalo-chip fires."

"Oh, my man will find lots of wood for me."

"Maybe he will."

She hugged his arm. "I am lucky to have you. Those

girls about stole you from me. Especially over that bald-face horse you gave Kate, and the Welsh pony for Nina."

He laughed. "That's what grandfathers are for—spoiling them."

"Do you think that Herschel and his family will ever come to Texas and help you run the ranch?"

"I don't know. Montana is a great place. He's such a dedicated lawman now, it would be hard for him to ever leave both the county and the job."

"Who else do we need to find?"

"My daughter Rosie."

"I figured that. What do we do first?"

"Go find my boys and take over that ranch."

With her on the buggy seat, he paused to look off at the hills north of Cheyenne and the wide azure sky as he hitched the dun and the bay horse on behind. He'd sure never regret this trip—coming or going.

They had a long ways to go. Hell, he'd better stop thinking about all that sentimental stuff and go back to chasing sundowns.